Annabelle's Joy

Betty Thomason Owens

Write Integrity Press
Annabelle's Joy
© 2019 Betty Thomason Owens
ISBN-13: **978-1-944120-87-0**

This book is a work of fiction. Names, characters, places, and incidents are either products of the author's imagination or used fictitiously. Any similarity to actual people and/or events is purely coincidental.

All quoted Scripture passages are taken from the KING JAMES VERSION (KJV): KING JAMES VERSION, public domain.

Published by Write Integrity Press, PO Box 702852, Dallas, TX 75370
Find out more about the author, Betty Thomason Owens, at her website: BettyThomasonOwens.com
www.WriteIntegrity.com
Printed in the United States of America.

What readers are saying about
The Kinsman-Redeemer series...

This beautiful retelling of the story of Ruth held my attention from start to end. Though I knew the biblical account, Owens provided a fresh spin on the kinsman-redeemer story by setting it in Tennessee during the racially charged 1950s. I appreciated her attention to historical detail in the book and highly recommend it!
~Kristen Hogrefe Parnell
Author of The Rogue series

Owens gently weaves a picture of the South with all its charm and bigotry. Through Connie's eyes, we feel the pain when asked to leave a store because of color. We understand her remorse when friends are not treated like other folks. And we empathize with her when she and Alton are kept apart by family members. The second installment in the Kinsman Redeemer series is a crawl-into-your-favorite-chair-and-sit-awhile kind of book. Anyone who enjoys family, history, and the South, will enjoy Sutter's Landing.
~Gail Johnson

The author's depiction of life in the segregated south of the 1950s is both realistic and insightful. She paints an accurate picture of how hard the people in this cotton-centric community worked just to live day by day, and she does it with respect, humility, honesty, and without the Hollywood sensationalism or stereotyping. She also shows their faith with gentle, non-threatening assurance. Sutter's Landing is a sweet, inspirational, and very well written story where the characters come alive on the pages. Their dialogue is so realistic you find yourself right there with them, wanting to join in on the conversations.

~*Elizabeth Noyes*
Author of The Imperfect Series

Dedication

For Patti Thornton Coleman
and Linda Herrick Hillenbrand,
whose true-life stories
inspired me
to write this final chapter.

Thou wilt shew me the path of life:
in thy presence is fulness of joy;
at thy right hand there are pleasures
forevermore.

Psalm 16:11

Chapter One

February 12, 1957
Trenton, Tennessee

Annabelle Cross stepped onto the back porch into spring-like warmth. It was too early for spring, but she looked forward to a warmer day, however fleeting it may prove. Her white-washed clapboard house sat on a slight rise in the middle of forty acres or so of furrowed fields. An old split-rail fence separated the lawn from the garden and the hen house.

Humming "I'll Fly Away," she set off across the yard to the chicken coop, where hens clucked contentedly. Before unlatching the gate, she filled a scoop with dried corn.

"You like the warm sunshine too, don't you?" After scattering the corn, she checked the nest boxes. "Only two eggs today?" With a sigh, she deposited them in an apron pocket. Outside the gate, her gaze rose to the fallow fields between her small house and the larger farmhouse across the creek half a mile away. Sutter's Landing. As she watched, a woman walked up the long drive and entered the back door. Regina, their cook and housekeeper, only had Lillian to look after these days.

Lillian was one of Annabelle's dearest friends. She was also family, since Lillian's son, Alton, married Annabelle's daughter-in-law, Connie. Annabelle's shoulders drooped as she drew a breath and eased it out. Connie, Alton, and their son, Joseph, were in Hawaii by now, visiting Connie's family.

Thinking about Little Joseph brought a smile to Annabelle's face. At almost two, the boy reminded her so much of her late son—the boy's natural father.

The air cooled as a cloud crossed over the sun. Her eldest son, Joseph, and his younger brother David, along with Annabelle's husband, Ray had drowned in a tragic accident during a weekend fishing excursion. She pressed a palm to her forehead, hoping to relieve the painful memory.

A rooster's crow in the distance jerked Annabelle back to the present. "No use in idling the day away in remorse." She began to hum again as she retraced her steps to the back porch. By the time she entered the kitchen, a full-blown song of praise filled the air. Music always lifted her low spirits and calmed her anxieties.

While frying an egg, she couldn't keep her gaze from drifting to the house next door, prompting a whole new set of emotions. Tom Franklin's house. It had taken shape over the last year, as he and Annabelle's cousin-in-law, Riley Franklin, put in hours of laborious building. Besides being first cousins, Tom and Riley shared a lifelong friendship. They'd spent every spare hour out there, till darkness stopped them. She worried, lest one of them fall in the dim light and be hurt.

Many times, she'd walked over under the guise of carrying food or beverage, just to get a look at what they were doing. Though she said nothing, she marveled at their abilities. How had they learned to do so much? It wasn't like they built houses for a living.

This morning it was quiet, as both men worked their day jobs. Riley had two, a cotton gin in season, the feed mill the rest of the year. Tom was a pharmacist. He owned the only drug store in their small town.

Using the skirt of her apron as a potholder, Annabelle picked up the skillet and moved away from the window, to drop the egg onto her waiting plate. She poured her coffee and then sank into a chair. Two framed photographs sat on the table across from her. Connie, Alton, and baby Joseph smiled from one of them, Joseph, David, and Ray from the other. She kissed her fingertips and touched each photograph before she bowed her head and asked a blessing over her food.

This was her every day now. A lonely meal, two or three times a day.

But she wouldn't let sorrow weigh her down. She kept busy. Today, the sunshine encouraged her to start spring-cleaning, get a head-start on her chores. She had just the project in mind. That big shipping crate in her bedroom she'd used as a catch-all for extra quilts, pillows, and such. Now that her young cousin Judith had gone back to college in Jackson, Annabelle had storage space in the spare bedroom.

After washing up the breakfast dishes, she stowed the quilts and whatnot in the spare dresser. On the way back to her room, she stopped to prop open the backdoor screen so she could move the crate out on the porch. She took a moment to survey the spot where the crate would sit. It would make a fine storage box for all her garden tools.

A distant "halloo" reached her ears. She shielded her eyes to peer out across the fields where a neighbor, Miss Lucy, walked with one of her grandchildren. Lucy was the daughter of slaves, second-generation freed, well-loved in the neighborhood, a cherished friend to Connie and Annabelle. The local midwife, Miss Lucy had attended little Joseph's birth.

Annabelle returned the greeting with a wave before heading back into the house and the crate. She gave the box a tug, but it didn't budge. "Hmm, must be stuck to the linoleum flooring."

Ginger, her red tabby cat, hopped in through the open door. She wound around Annabelle's ankles. Annabelle leaned down to give the cat a rub behind the ears, then a gentle shove. "Get out of the way, now. I've got work to do."

The cat jumped up on the bed and lay down.

Annabelle pressed a foot against the stubborn crate and pushed. After a soft, crackling sound, it moved a fraction of an inch. The thing was heavier than she remembered, but she'd had Connie's help when they first stowed it here. Sweat broke out on her forehead as she dragged it across the linoleum.

The cat gave a loud meow.

Annabelle shook her head. "I know what I'm doing." After she stepped out the door, she grabbed the edge of the crate, intending to pull it forward, through the doorway.

Ginger jumped on top of the crate. Startled, Annabelle straightened. "Scat!"

Ears back, the offended cat jumped off the box into the bedroom, plopped down again, and glared at

Annabelle.

Why was the creature acting so weird? Annabelle rubbed her hands together, then gripped the crate again and tugged. It moved, but only a little. Undaunted, she tugged again and again, until it was nearly halfway through the door, teetering forward over the threshold.

One more tug ought to do it. She gave it all she had. The crate fairly flew through the opening, catching Annabelle by surprise. She fell to the porch floor onto her backside with a loud cry as pain shot from her ankle upwards. The pain came from her shin, where the crate had carved a large valley quickly flooding with blood.

It flowed faster than Annabelle could staunch it with her hands. She grabbed at her apron strings and fumbled them free. Then she folded it over and wrapped it around her leg, tying it tight with the strings. Within seconds, it was soaked through.

She was going to die right here on the back porch, all alone. "Oh, Lord!"

"Miss Annabelle, you all right?"

Annabelle's head swam as she turned to see Miss Lucy climbing the steps. "Thank you, Jesus!"

"I heared you cry out. Me and Sis come-a-running." Miss Lucy knelt beside Annabelle and touched her leg. "Oh, my. You sit still. We need to raise this up."

With her granddaughter's help, Miss Lucy lifted the crate off Annabelle's leg, then she instructed the child. "You run fast as you can over to Sutter's. Tell Miss Lillian we need help."

The little girl slipped past them, ran down the steps, and across the yard.

Annabelle's stomach lurched. "I might be sick."

"You just sit still and breathe, Miss Annabelle. Take deep breaths. Try to stay awake."

Try to stay awake. Annabelle watched as Lucy propped the leg on her lap and fingered the apron strings. It seemed unreal. Like somebody else's leg, not hers.

Miss Lucy replaced the apron and put pressure on the wound with her gnarled fingers. "This here's a bad gash. It's got wood splinters in it. You gonna need stitches."

A doctor. But how would she get to town? Alton was gone away. Lillian was all alone at Sutter's. What were they going to do?

Annabelle braced herself in the back seat as Lillian barreled down the highway, headed for Trenton. When Lillian topped a hill and took the curve a bit too fast,

Annabelle had to speak up. "Slow down, I'm not going to bleed to death." The woman had to be doing at least forty-five.

Lillian didn't let up on the gas pedal. Both hands gripped the wheel as she approached town. "Miss Lucy said to hurry. So that's what I'm doing."

Annabelle sucked in a breath as they whizzed past the 31-miles-per-hour speed limit sign, a sight seen only in Trenton, Tennessee.

Another car approached a main intersection. Lillian never touched the brakes, just the horn, several times.

"I thank you kindly, but I hope to get there in one piece." Annabelle had never ridden anywhere with Lillian at the wheel. The woman seldom drove.

When Lillian pulled into a parking spot on the street in front of the doctor's house, she hit the curb a bit too hard.

Annabelle gasped as pain shot through her injured leg. She bit her lip and tried not to whine.

Lillian opened the door and got out. "Sorry about that, Annabelle. Now, you sit tight while I go find someone to help us."

Sit tight. Where could she go? Leaning back, she tried to relax as waves of pain rolled over her. Why had she thought to move that old crate on her own? The day had started out so well. Now she'd be laid up for who knew how long.

Lillian's voice brought Annabelle's attention to the front of the once-elegant residence that now housed the doctor's office. Lillian held the door open for another woman dressed in a nurses' uniform and cap. The nurse pushed a wheelchair out and down a short ramp to the walk. Annabelle didn't recall the nurse's name, though she had talked to her on the phone once or twice. The nurse was followed closely by a young man with his sleeves rolled up past the elbows.

Lillian opened the door nearest Annabelle's feet, allowing the nurse to address Annabelle. "Careful now, hon. I'm going to get in so I can lift that injured leg for you."

The young man opened the other door, holding out his hand to keep Annabelle from falling out. He then slid his arms under hers and lifted her into the wheelchair. She nearly bit through her lower lip, holding back the cry of anguish as tears flowed down her cheeks.

When the nurse leaned forward to unlock the wheels of the chair, Annabelle got a close-up look at her dark, brown hair tucked beneath her cap. Bobby pins held the cap in place. She smelled of rubbing alcohol, soap, and antiseptic.

Once they had her in the chair, Annabelle tried to focus on the deep green foliage of a holly tree in the front yard as the pain in her leg almost overwhelmed her. Bumping along in the ancient wheelchair made it worse.

Doc met them at the door. "Heard you had a scuffle with a wooden crate, Miss Annabelle. Come on in, we'll take a look."

Lillian stayed with her as the young man and the nurse lifted Annabelle onto an examining table. She patted Annabelle's hand. "I'll be right here."

The young man pushed the wheelchair out, closing the door behind him.

"How are those children doing?" Doc asked. "Over in Hawaii, is it?"

Annabelle grimaced in pain as he removed her ruined apron. "Maui."

"I always wanted to go to the Islands. Sounds like paradise."

Lillian kept her hand planted on Annabelle's shoulder. "We each got a postcard yesterday."

Doc frowned over the wound. "Hmm, looks pretty deep, Miss Annabelle. There's some splinters in here. You're going to need stitches once I get it cleaned out." He glanced at Lillian. "You can go if you need to."

"Not going anywhere."

Annabelle relaxed. "Thank you, Lillian."

"I ought to be thanking you, I reckon. I haven't driven a car in a couple of years. I got to where I was almost afraid to get behind the wheel. Now, I know I can do it." She angled a glance at Annabelle. "Though you might not agree."

"You did fine. A little too fast for my liking, but fine."

Lillian giggled. "I was trying to keep your mind focused on something other than your pain."

"You sure enough did that—ouch!"

Doc straightened. "Sorry, Miss Annabelle. That was the local anesthetic going in. In a minute, you won't feel anything." He grinned as he handed the syringe to the nurse.

Emily. The nurse's name popped into Annabelle's mind as the woman arranged instruments on a tray. She looked up, met Annabelle's gaze, and smiled. "Are you all right, hon?"

"I reckon I will be."

Lillian patted her shoulder. "Wonder how little Joseph is taking to the sea?"

Little Joseph. Annabelle smiled at the memory of her sweet grandson's chubby face. A happy baby, he took delight in the smallest of things. "I reckon he's having the time of his life."

After Ray and her sons drowned, her daughter-in-law Connie had stayed by her, even though it meant moving three thousand miles away from their home in San Diego, California. She'd become a daughter to Annabelle. She'd married Lillian's younger son Alton. Now, Annabelle had a family again. A family, a home, and so many wonderful friends. God had been good to her.

"Nineteen stitches."

Annabelle looked at Lillian. What was she talking about?

"Doc said it took nineteen stitches."

She seemed right impressed, but Annabelle's stomach lurched. What kind of scar was that gonna leave?

"Closed it up nice and neat to keep it from scarring so badly." The doctor washed his hands at a nearby sink. "Looks like you lost a lot of blood, Miss Annabelle. Some bleeding's good. It cleanses the wound naturally. But you lost a bit too much. You're going to have to take it easy a few days. Keep that leg elevated." He shifted his attention to Lillian. "Does she have someone to be with her?"

Lillian gave a nod. "She'll stay at Sutter's until she can get around on her own."

Annabelle shook her head. "I can't leave my house

unattended. Who'll take care of the chickens?"

"Miss Lucy said she'd take care of everything. You know she will."

"She's got her own to look after."

Lillian bent to make eye contact. "She'll send one of her young-uns over. In the meantime, you're staying at Sutter's where I can take care of you myself."

Annabelle clamped her mouth shut on all the objections forming in her mind. Sure, there was plenty of room at Sutter's, but the beds were all upstairs. How would she get up there? Her leg throbbed at the thought of climbing all those steps.

"You'll need to stop by the pharmacy on the way out of town," Doctor said, as he and Emily helped Annabelle into the wheelchair. "I'll call in a prescription. Don't want you to get an infection."

Land sakes. Annabelle blew out a breath. Now Tom would have to know. She'd never hear the end of it.

Chapter Two

February 12, 1957

Annabelle, hurt?

When Tom Franklin hung up the phone, his thoughts raced ahead. Doctor said she'd lost a significant amount of blood and would need to be on bed rest for a few days. What if she'd bled to death? The thought sent a pang of regret straight to his heart as he stepped toward the pharmacy shelves to fill the order.

If she'd had a phone, she could've gotten help sooner. Stubborn woman! Both he and Alton had tried to talk her into getting a telephone installed. Though she'd kept him at arm's length for over a year now, he loved her still. She might be a little mulish, but that could be a good thing, right? Once you had Annabelle Cross in your corner, she was there for life.

The door opened and shut. He recognized Lillian

Wade's white hair before she stepped to the counter.

"Almost ready, Miss Lillian. Do y'all need anything else? You got plenty of fixin's for the bandage change?"

"I believe so, Tom. We stocked up when my grandson stayed at the farm last summer." She scrutinized his face. "How are you doing?"

"I'm fine. How's Annabelle?"

Miss Lillian shook her head. "In a deal of pain at the moment, bless her heart."

"I hope you're taking her home with you." He added up the ticket and handed it over.

Miss Lillian applied her signature. "Yes sir, I am." She gave him a sideways glance. "You're welcome to visit, of course."

"Thank you, Miss Lillian. But I don't know if she'd welcome it."

Her smile warmed his heart. "Don't you give up, Tom Franklin. She'll come around."

He turned away to hide the rising warmth in his face, stepped around the counter, to open the door for Miss Lillian. Outside, he lifted his hand to greet Annabelle. He wouldn't trouble her to roll down the window since Miss Lillian said she was in pain. Most likely, she wouldn't want to speak to anyone right now. He watched till they'd driven out of sight. Only then did he realize Miss Lillian was driving. When had he last seen that? He opened the pharmacy door and stepped through, wondering whether he'd ever seen it.

Back at his desk, he picked up the phone, then cradled it again. He'd been about to call his cousin-in-law, Thelma. As Annabelle's first cousin and lifelong friend, she'd want to know about the accident. But Thelma didn't have a phone. He still went to call her whenever something happened.

Phones had become so much a part of his life, it was difficult to do without. But he had, for nigh on two years as he worked to complete his new house. After his childhood home washed away in the fifty-five flood, he'd moved in with Thelma and Riley. He gave a soft chuckle. Their friendship had survived living together for nearly two years. He was gone most of the time anyway, which was probably why they were still getting along so well.

Tonight would be soon enough for Thelma to hear the news. That way, she wouldn't want to dash out there and get in Miss Lillian's way.

Annabelle reckoned she had enough regrets to fill a hundred-pound cotton sack. Her leg hurt like the dickens, but this was a setback, nothing more. Far less serious than losing everything you had in the world. Well, practically everything.

She picked up the latest postcard signed by Alton. One of those real pretty flower necklaces graced the front, along with the word "Aloha", a word that apparently meant both hello and goodbye. How confusing would that be?

When Regina appeared in the doorway, Annabelle lay the card aside. "Is it time?"

Regina set a dark blue enamel pan on the bedside table. Her black eyes held sympathy as she answered, "Yes'm, it is."

Annabelle bit her lip as the woman bathed and redressed the wound.

"It's a mite inflamed still but looks like it'll heal up fine." Regina practically lived at Sutter's, doing most of the cooking and heavy cleaning. Lillian "kept house" and warmed up leftovers. By her own confession, she'd never been much of a cook.

From the doorway, Lillian gave a stiff nod. "I should probably call Doc and let him know."

"Stayin' off it is the thing. We don't want no blood-poisonin'."

Annabelle grimaced and sucked in a breath as Regina stuffed a rolled-up feather pillow under the wounded limb. "I thought that was why you had me drink that terrible tea concoction—so I wouldn't get an infection."

Regina picked up the cast-off bandages on the way out the door. "It ain't a miracle cure."

Lillian's voice echoed from the hallway. "That'll be fine, Doc." A moment later, she stepped back through the door. "Doc's going to stop by on his way home and take a look at it. Barring any emergencies, he'll be here around five-thirty."

Misery swirled in Annabelle's chest. How she hated being bedridden, dependent on others.

Lillian's eyes reflected understanding. "At least you're warm, Annabelle. If you were home, you'd have a time stoking that old wood stove."

"You're right. I'd still be beholding to somebody." She gazed at the ceiling. It would probably be Tom. She looked at Lillian again. "You know I appreciate all you've done."

"I've done no more than you'd do in my place. Except for driving you to town." She grinned. "I don't reckon you ever did learn to drive a car. Will you be all right for a bit? I'll go help Regina get supper finished. Weather's taking a turn. I want to send her home early."

Before Annabelle could respond, a knock sounded at the back door.

Lillian turned to head that way. "Who could that be?"

Annabelle hoped it might be Miss Lucy. She hadn't heard from the woman since the accident. Thelma and Riley had already paid a visit, and Brother Nathan, pastor of the First Baptist Church, came soon after. Surely, it was Miss Lucy or one of her bunch. But the voice she heard was masculine. Her heart beat faster as she recognized it. Tom Franklin.

Tom lowered his six-foot frame onto the cane-bottomed chair near the foot of Annabelle's bed. "You're looking well, Miss Annabelle."

"You don't have to lie, Tom. I know I look a fright." Had she even combed her hair this morning? She resisted the urge to touch it and find out.

He grinned, deepening the crinkles around his eyes. "You always look fine to me."

Thank goodness Lillian showed up in the doorway. She held a lovely bouquet of pink roses and baby's breath, arranged in a white hobnail vase. "Look what Tom brought you. Aren't they beautiful?" She set the vase on a table near the door. "Mighty thoughtful of him."

Tom cleared his throat.

Annabelle didn't miss the slight rise of color in his cheeks. While his attention was drawn away to Lillian, Annabelle touched her hair. Maybe she had combed it.

"They're lovely."

Lillian excused herself.

The old chair creaked as Tom turned back to Annabelle. "I can't stay long. Riley's already over at the house."

"How's it coming?"

"Wallboard's up. Won't be long now, we can paint."

"That's good." Soon after that, he'd be living next door.

"I was hoping you might help me pick out some colors."

He had her full attention. "Me?"

His shoulders rose and fell. "Yes'm. I'm not talented that way. I figured maybe you, being a woman and all, might give me some suggestions. When you're able, of course."

Typical man, uneasy with decorating choices. She watched him squirm. Ray never cared about decorating either. Left it all for Annabelle, along with cooking, cleaning, and childcare.

Tom interrupted her thoughts. "If it was up to me,

they'd all be white. The rooms, I mean. I guess that'd be dull."

She gave a soft chuckle. "It would. A room needs a bit of color to break up the monotony."

"So, you'll help me out?"

Maybe this could be another something to look forward to, like the day Connie, Alton and Little Joseph returned home. Another date for her calendar. She brought her gaze to his expectant face. Warmth flooded her cheeks. "I reckon I could do that."

"Good." He leaned forward. "Well, I just wanted to stop in and see how you're doing. I'd better get."

She allowed herself the luxury of observing his face as he rose to go. The light in his eyes spoke volumes. She'd made him happy. Given him hope. Maybe more than she'd meant to, but right now, it didn't seem to matter. "Thank you again, for the flowers. And for the visit."

Lillian stopped in the doorway. "Won't you stay to dinner, Tom?"

"I reckon not, Miss Lillian. Riley's waiting for me."

"Well, come again when you get the chance."

After he'd gone, Lillian returned to the kitchen.

Annabelle expelled a breath. Whew! She grabbed the postcard and fanned herself. The visit was inevitable, but not too terrible. That man sure could set her heart racing, more than Ray ever did. Something about that didn't seem right.

Tom's brain perked away as he drove the short distance between Sutter's and the old Sterling place where Annabelle lived. His new house sat on a rise above her house a little farther back from the road. As a new widow, she'd needed the money from the sale of the land. He'd been happy to supply it. After most of his life living in a flood plain, building on a hill—small as it was—pleased him.

This past year had tried him in more ways than one. Yes, he knew full well why Annabelle kept a distance. It wasn't only that her widowhood lay so near her heart. She'd told him straight out. She couldn't see him if he didn't attend church. He'd been a churchgoer at one time. Most of his life, really. Until the day Jensen Wade sullied Tom's uncle's good name and completely offended the entire Franklin family.

Tom had forgiven the man but going back to church had proved more difficult. After Annabelle's pronouncement, that she wouldn't marry a non-churchgoer, Tom had taken time to think. He'd even sought counseling with his good friend, Rev. Nathan, pastor of the First Baptist Church. He'd gone to church once. Late last summer, he'd slipped in during the song service and sat on the back row. He left before Pastor ended his final prayer. Only a few folks saw him. Annabelle never knew. That's how he'd wanted it.

Then he'd gotten busy building the house. The home he hoped Annabelle would share with him someday. When the majority of the work was done, he planned to put church back on his calendar. Not just for Annabelle, but because he knew it was time. He needed to get right with God.

He pulled into the dirt drive that led to his new house. Riley's car sat in front of the garage. No doubt, he was already working, wondering where Tom had gotten himself off to.

"'Bout time you showed up." Riley stood on a ladder, spreading drywall mud.

Tom changed out of his dress shirt, into a flannel work shirt. "How long have you been at it?"

"Not long. It took a while to mix it just right." He frowned at the work surface. "How's Annabelle?"

"A little better. Miss Lillian said it rankles her some, to be waited on."

Riley cackled. "Wouldn't rankle me none."

"No, I reckon not. You'd love every minute of it."

Tom picked up a wallboard tool and scooped out some mud. "Especially after me working you to the bone building this house."

"It's been my pleasure, Tom. It'll be good for you to have your own place again."

"You'll be glad to get rid of me." He spread a thin layer of mud on the wall.

Riley climbed down the ladder, repositioned it, then went back to work. "I'm going to miss you, my friend. You've helped keep me sane through all the craziness at home. What with having that first grandchild, then Judith heading off to college. If I hadn't been out here helping you, Thelma would've kept me busy morning till night with chores. Ain't nothing I hate worse than a list of jobs greeting me when I get home from a hard day's work."

Tom shook his head. "So, you're over here, working every night and most weekends, to keep from working at home?"

Riley turned to look at Tom. "One day, you'll understand. If you ever manage to talk Annabelle into wedded bliss, you'll find out for yourself. Right quick."

Tom chuckled, but he couldn't agree with Riley. If Annabelle ever accepted his hand in marriage, he would happily do whatever chore she asked of him. Within reason, of course.

Riley moved the ladder again, making good progress. "You met those new folks, yet?"

Tom eyed him. "What new folks?"

"The McCoys, a brother and sister. Thelma met the sister in the grocery store. She said her brother has come to town to build a warehouse over on 10th. They'll probably be in the drug store sometime or other. I reckon you'll meet 'em before I do." He moved the ladder again.

"Warehouse for what?"

"Don't know. Thelma didn't think to ask about it." He chuckled. "They got to talkin' church and that was that."

"Right." Tom knew Thelma well enough. She'd invited the woman to church, told her all about everybody in the congregation, then asked if Miss McCoy could sing and play piano. That was Thelma.

"Yeah, I reckon we'll find out soon enough." Riley climbed down and stepped over to scoop up more mud.

After a short break to wolf down the sandwiches Tom brought, he and Riley worked till dark, then cleaned up the mess. After Riley drove away, Tom took a walk. He inspected Annabelle's house and grounds. The chickens had already gone to roost. One of Miss Lucy's family was looking after them. He checked to make sure the coop was secured well enough to suit

Annabelle. Satisfied, he headed to his truck.

Stars twinkled overhead as Tom pulled onto the road. One day soon, he'd be home out here, sitting on his porch, whiling away the evening. In his imagination, Annabelle sat beside him, holding his hand. An ache in his heart sent his imaginings elsewhere. Only a fool would set all his hopes on one destination. A fool, or a man convinced he was on the right path. Which one was he?

"You're no fool."

An old memory unfurled like an oak leaf in spring. The kids at school used to call him Tomfool. But Annabelle took up for him. "Don't you believe it, Tom. You're no fool. You're the smartest boy in class."

A broad smile split Tom's face as he pulled out on the highway, headed for Riley's. Good thing it was dark, and he was alone. Folks would think he was feeble-minded.

Chapter Three

March 3, 1957

Annabelle's church friends greeted her as if she'd been away for a year, rather than a couple of weeks. After Sunday school, she limped into the sanctuary and took her usual seat next to Lillian. As the church filled, it seemed everyone filed past to greet her. Even Lillian's eldest son Jensen.

"Miss Annabelle, I'm glad to see you out and about."

"Thank you, Jensen. I'm happy to be here."

He didn't waste any time but quickly moved toward the pew where his wife, Marla, and younger son, Landers, sat waiting.

Lillian patted Annabelle's wrist. "You're a very important person this morning."

Annabelle giggled. "Don't make fun of my moment in the limelight."

"I wouldn't dream of it." Lillian glanced over her shoulder. "You've been out, so you haven't met the new folks yet."

Annabelle followed Lillian's gaze to the other side of the aisle, back a few rows, where a man stood next to a much shorter woman, in whispered conversation with those around them.

When the organ sounded the opening hymn, Annabelle and Lillian faced the front. Annabelle frowned at the words in her hymnal. Who were those two? More importantly, why had they come to Trenton? There weren't many job opportunities in the area. Perhaps they'd come home to family, as Annabelle had done. She dismissed the thought as Pastor took his place behind the pulpit.

Pastor Nathan preached a good sermon on righteousness. Annabelle drank it in. She'd missed being in the service. She'd tried to keep up by reading her Sunday school lessons, and daily scriptures, but it wasn't the same. How did folks do without church?

All too soon, the service ended. Everyone rose for dismissal. As she and Lillian walked out, Pastor Nathan introduced Annabelle to the newcomers, Mr. McCoy, and his sister, Miss Rosella McCoy. The short woman wore her blond hair in a puffy bun, with waves covering each ear. A cornflower pillbox hat crowned her head, reminding Annabelle of a pixie.

The woman laid her hand on Annabelle's forearm, smiled and began to speak so fast, Annabelle could barely keep up. "I'm so glad to finally meet you, Mrs. Cross. I've heard so much about you and your family. What a tragedy you've endured, but how blessed of God you are now, with such great connections. I've met Mr. Jensen, of course, and his lovely wife, Marla. I can't wait to meet Mr. Alton and your daughter and grandson. When are they due back? Next week? I think that's what I was told." She finally paused to take a breath.

Annabelle spoke quickly. "Yes, next week. I thank you most kindly, Miss Rosella. But I do need to get to the car. My leg still hurts when I'm up too much." It was not untrue; her leg did throb a bit.

The woman would not be put off. "My name is actually Rose Ella, but everyone calls me Rosella. Kind of like Annabelle, I guess. Are you Anna Belle?"

Annabelle shook her head. "No ma'am, I'm Annabelle. All one word."

Lillian stepped forward. Mischief sparked in her blue eyes. "Annabelle Frances, we need to get you out of here. Excuse us, Miss McCoy."

Miss Rose Ella McCoy smiled. "Good day to you, Mrs. Wade. I hope to see you soon."

Lillian linked her arm in Annabelle's and tugged. Once they were on their way to the car, she groaned. "I hope not too soon. My goodness, that woman can dominate a conversation."

Annabelle chuckled. "I noticed that."

These days, Lillian drove in a more normal fashion. Even so, Annabelle longed for Alton's return. She felt safer when a man was in charge.

Lillian interrupted her thoughts. "I hope you're planning to eat dinner with me today."

"I hoped you'd ask. I'm still a bit lazy."

"Ha! You, lazy? I don't believe that, not for a minute. You know you don't have to be asked. You're welcome at Sutter's anytime."

They passed the rest of the drive in peace, which puzzled Annabelle a bit until they arrived. There sat Tom's truck.

Lillian shut off the engine. "Oh, I've invited Tom to dinner, too."

Tom Franklin sat in the swing on the front porch, enduring the affections of a blue-tick coonhound until he darted down the steps and out to the road. Moments later, Miss Lillian pulled into the drive.

Tom stood and brushed dog hairs from the front of his freshly pressed slacks before descending the steps to open Annabelle's door. He looked up as Miss Lillian got out of the car. "I still cannot get used to seeing you behind the wheel, Miss Lillian, but I have to admire your spunk." For years, Riley's dad had served as the Wade's chauffeur. Miss Lillian had never driven herself anywhere.

Miss Lillian cackled. "Why, Tom, you're more than welcome to come drive us about the countryside."

He met Annabelle's gaze before glancing away. He could guess her thoughts. He half expected a comment, but she said nothing. That might not be a good thing. Maybe she was tired of waiting for him to show up at church of a Sunday.

He followed along as the two women entered the house.

Miss Lillian removed her hat and hung it on a coat rack near the door. "Make yourself to home, Tom, while we get dinner on the table."

"Anything I can do to help?" He knew the answer, but good manners compelled him to ask anyway. After he'd received a negative reply, Tom entertained himself by looking at the many photos on the parlor wall. Some were definitely of the last century. A few wore civil war uniforms. Two men Tom recognized as

John Wade, Annabelle's father, and Lew Sutter, wore infantry uniforms, circa 1912. Neither man had returned from WWI.

A fine aroma wafted in from the kitchen. He'd skipped breakfast this morning to catch up on work at the drug store, so he was hungry.

Annabelle appeared in the doorway. "Dinner's on the table."

Her flushed cheeks, followed by a quick exit, led him to believe she may not welcome his company. Or perhaps she hadn't expected him here today. He grinned at the thought. That was more like it. Miss Lillian was trying to play matchmaker. He hoped her efforts proved successful.

Annabelle sat across from Lillian. Tom sat in Alton's chair at the head of the table. After he'd blessed the food, Lillian passed the ham, already neatly sliced. Everything on the table had been prepared by Regina on Saturday. This included a spice cake on the kitchen counter, the sight of which had set Annabelle's mouth to watering.

Lillian glanced at Annabelle before addressing Tom. "How's business these days, Tom?"

"Very well, thank you. I'm hoping to hire an assistant this summer, soon as school lets out."

"That sounds like business is booming. Not sure that's a good thing since it involves pharmaceuticals. Lots of sick folks."

He sipped his tea. "Well, you could look at it that way, I guess. Though, a lot of my customers buy more than drugs. Annabelle, may I trouble you for the biscuits?"

Annabelle passed the bread plate. "Last time I was there, I noticed you'd added some doodads and knickknacks. Are folks buying those?"

He nodded. "They are. The magazines and newspapers, too. Of course, we keep a steady business at the snack bar."

"Your ham sandwiches are legendary in these parts," Lillian said. "I hope you continue to do well."

Annabelle hoped so, too, but she kept her mind from seeking the reason for her hopes. He was much too close for her to contemplate it. Instead, she sought to change the subject. "Do you intend to hire an intern?"

"I do. It's common practice. Good for both parties. The intern gets a good deal of practical experience. It's how I started out."

Lillian rose to freshen the tea glasses. "You'll be a

good teacher."

Annabelle thought so too. She'd never known anyone as patient, and he certainly was knowledgeable.

Tom finished off the last of his green beans and sat back. "I hope so. I've been blessed through the years. That's something to be thankful for. The best way to show that is to pass it on."

As he spoke, his gaze found its way to Annabelle. It took great concentration to keep the color from rising to her cheeks again. Would this meal never end? She half wanted the time to pass slowly but couldn't seem to keep still. After what seemed an eternity, though she figured it was more like ten minutes, Lillian stood and began to clear the table. This time, they could not keep Tom from pitching in.

After they'd piled up the sink and put away the food, Lillian brushed her hands together. "The weather's so fine, I thought we could sit a spell on the front porch, then have some of that spice cake with our after-dinner coffee."

Tom led the way to the porch, where he took a seat in a rocker, leaving the double swing for the ladies. "Are Connie and Alton coming home next week, or the week after?"

Annabelle gave the swing a push. "The week after, on the sixteenth. They'll arrive in Memphis early

Saturday evening." She looked at Lillian. "Did he say three, or four?"

"He said three, but thought it'd probably be closer to four."

Tom's eyes widened. "That's coming up fast."

Lillian agreed. "It is. Too fast for them, I reckon, but not fast enough for me. We sure have missed them."

Tom smiled. "I'll bet that boy has grown an inch or two."

Annabelle could easily imagine it. He was going to be tall, like his daddy. "I can't wait to find out."

"Who's going to pick them up?" Tom propped his elbows on his knees and leaned forward, his gaze flitting between Annabelle and Lillian, probably wondering who would answer first.

Lillian spoke up. "Alton said they'd take the bus to Jackson, but I'm hoping to find someone who can meet them. I haven't the confidence to drive all the way to Memphis."

Tom lifted his head and sat back.

Annabelle ventured a glance at him. What was he thinking about?

A mockingbird warbled its varied song into the peaceful afternoon.

"Y'all about ready for coffee and cake?" Lillian stopped the swing. "If so, I'll put the coffee on."

"Sounds good," Tom said.

Before she left, Lillian looked at Annabelle. "You keep Tom company."

Tom had been quiet so long, Annabelle thought he might be tired. Sometimes keeping company was just that. Sharing the same space. Not talking. Tom was not one to waste words. If he had nothing to say, he kept his mouth shut. Unlike Ray, whose mouth stayed in perpetual motion as though he loved the sound of his voice. But at least, he'd usually been interesting, or funny.

A snuffling noise preceded the dog's approach. Samson climbed the steps, greeted Tom, then Annabelle. Afterward, he plopped down near the edge of the porch with a loud sigh.

Tom chuckled. "I reckon he misses his master."

"His mistress, too." Annabelle smoothed a lock of hair, tucking it behind her ear. When she raised her eyes to Tom's he was watching her. He looked as though he meant to say something, but Lillian's steps in the foyer sent him into action. He rose to open the door.

"Thank you, Tom." She set a tray on a small, round table. "Here's the cake. I'll be right back with the coffee."

Once they all had coffee and cake, Tom looked at Lillian. "What if I drive your big, fancy car to

Memphis? There'd be room for all of us. I know you'd like to be there when the train arrives."

Annabelle sucked in a breath. She had wished for this. Tom intended to make it happen. She watched Lillian's face light up as a smile transformed her expression.

Lillian set her cup down and clapped her hands. "Oh, Tom! Could you? Could you be away from the store in time?"

"I usually close at noon of a Saturday. I could be out here about half-past twelve. That ought to be time enough."

"Glory!" Lillian leaned toward Tom. "You've made two lonely widows very happy, Tom." She glanced at Annabelle. "Very happy."

Tom beamed.

If they'd been alone, Annabelle would be tempted to give him a kiss on the cheek. Maybe even a hug. She hadn't been this happy since … well, she couldn't say when.

Though Lillian tried to keep him longer, Tom rose to go. But she wouldn't let him leave without taking a couple more pieces of that cake. "One for you, and one for Riley. I know you're headed over to your house."

"Thank you kindly, Miss Lillian."

Even though Tom would pass right by her house, Annabelle remained at Sutter's. She told him she needed a walk. That was true. She also wanted to help with the dishes.

Lillian handed her a dishtowel. "Regina told me to leave them until morning, but I didn't want to do that. She works hard enough as it is. We'll have a busy time getting ready for Connie and Alton's return." She passed a washed plate to Annabelle.

"I bet they'll have some wonderful stories to tell."

"And movies. Alton took his new movie camera. Won't that be fun?"

"I'd forgotten about that. It'll be like we were right there."

Several quiet minutes passed as they finished the work. Lillian put away the dried dishes and then hung the dishtowels on a hook. "I'll walk you part way home."

Samson joined them, his tail high, his ears perked.

As they crossed a bridge over the creek, Lillian spoke, "How long are you going to hold that poor man at a distance?"

Annabelle drew a breath then eased it out. "I don't think I'm holding him off."

Lillian gave her a sideways look then paused her steps.

Shaking her head, Annabelle laughed. "I can't go back on my word. I told him I want someone who attends church. He's still not doing that."

"I understand, but you know he'd be there if he could. He's determined to finish his house." She touched Annabelle's chin. "And why do you think he's so bent on doing that? Could be he hopes you'll live in it with him."

Annabelle turned away, only to have her gaze light on the object of Lillian's discussion. The low, red-brick house still startled her at times. Tom's truck and Riley's car sat in the driveway. It was true, they were working day and night to finish the thing. But she'd assumed it was because Tom wanted out of Riley's house. "A man needs a house of his own," he'd told her once. Then he'd changed it. "A home, I mean." His eyes had held onto hers for a long moment. Yes, it was true. He was building it for her. But he'd never repeated the question he'd asked last year, about a year too soon.

"Annabelle? Are you still with me?"

Annabelle turned back to Lillian. "I guess my mind went wandering."

Lillian cast her gaze toward the red house. "I can guess where it wandered." She set off walking again.

"I'm saying you need to search your heart. Let the man know how you feel about him. Encourage him. He'll come around. You'll see."

Chapter Four

March 12, 1957

Annabelle lit a fire in the potbellied stove. An overnight cold snap left a definite chill in the air. She wrapped her arms around herself and peered out the window at the overcast sky. Spring could be petulant at times. In the distance, redbud blooms showed pink among the gray branches of trees in the woods. She'd hoped for an early spring, had even been sorting through her seeds, but frost this morning delayed those plans.

In the kitchen, she spooned coffee grounds into the percolator basket. After plugging it in, she bundled up for the trip outside to see to the chickens. Two of the hens were broody. She figured they'd be nesting soon. After feeding and checking for eggs, she started back to the house picking up speed as the rain started. How she loved the sound of those loud plops hitting the tin roof. But the rain would keep her inside. She'd already scrubbed the floors, dusted, and tidied up, how would she while away the hours?

She could sort through her clothes, decide what to keep and what to turn into a quilt top. But looking at the pile of folded castoffs spurred too many memories. This sent her thoughts back to Lillian's caution. Maybe it was time.

Back in the kitchen, she picked up the frame containing the old family photo. She didn't look at it but headed to the parlor, where she gathered three more. She only left one on top of the bureau in the spare bedroom. The others she placed in the bottom drawer where she kept her photo albums.

"For a while," she told herself, "until I get my bearings. Until I can make it through the day without thoughts of them." Too often, sad thoughts weighed her down and kept her from moving forward with her life.

Tom's handsome face filled her thoughts, followed closely by guilt. She closed the drawer that contained the photos. With a sigh, she sat back on her heels, her hands clasped in prayer.

"Lord, I'm not pretending to know the future. That belongs to You. But I'm leaving it in Your hands. Help me. Give me the strength to face whatever it holds."

Afterward, she turned on the radio Alton had given

her for Christmas. But the reception was bad, probably because of the rain. It emitted only bits and pieces of music and news, so she switched it off again.

"Looks like it's going to be another long day." Saturday afternoon couldn't come soon enough. She laid her hand on the door frame leading into the kitchen, where nicks and dents told stories of moving furniture in and out over the years. Maybe a juvenile sword fight or two, way back in the early days, when her Granny and Grandpa raised their children. Lifting her eyes to the window, the dark silhouette of Tom's house pricked her heart. Though she loved this house, along with its history and memories of Granny Sterling, the time had come for her to look to the future.

Even if she didn't marry Tom, move into his new house, she'd need to give up this one. She needed a tenant farmer to move in. Someone to raise cotton on her acres. It was the right thing to do.

But if she didn't marry Tom, where would she go?

"Don't borrow trouble," Ma used to say.

"Sufficient unto the day is the evil thereof." Annabelle spoke the words aloud to fortify herself, still the anxiety that managed to creep in unexpected and unwelcome.

A loud rap on the door nearly stopped her heart. Who could be out in this weather?

An old friend, Billy Nichols, stood on her front porch.

Annabelle greeted him. "Well, hello, Billy, won't you come in?"

He removed his hat, then smiled and shook his head. "No thank you, ma'am. Tom told me you'd be happy to let me in over at his house. I've come out to install the furnace."

Annabelle nodded. "Of course. Let me get the key."

He lifted his hand. "I'll meet you over there." Without waiting for her reply, he turned and headed down the steps.

She lifted an eyebrow. Land sakes. She would've given him the key. Why'd she need to go over with him? Oh, well. At least this would give her something to do for a bit. She pulled on her galoshes, slipped into her raincoat and hat. She lifted the keys from a hook behind the kitchen door.

Most folks out this way didn't bother to lock their doors, but Tom worried lest someone decided to help themselves to his building materials. She guessed that was good reasoning. Best not to leave the door open to temptation.

Billy had backed his truck into the gravel drive in front of the new house. He got out as Annabelle let herself through the wooden gate that divided her yard from Tom's. At least the rain had slowed. A patch of blue overhead hinted that it may let up entirely.

Billy's son, Jake hopped out of the truck to help his dad uncover the furnace.

Billy paused as Annabelle approached. "It's going in the garage. Tom said he'd cleared out space for it."

Annabelle found the key labeled "garage" and bent to unlock the door.

Jake strode over and tugged on the handle. The door rolled back on its overhead tracks, revealing a garage filled with building materials and supplies. A wide path through the middle led to a spot near the kitchen door. Annabelle supposed that was where the thing was meant to go.

"We'll need the inside door open too," Billy said, "So's we can install the thermostat and make sure everything's working properly." He grunted as the two pushed the furnace onto a ramp, then slid it down to a dolly.

Annabelle figured the inside door was unlocked since the garage door had been bolted. She was right. She stepped inside the kitchen to flip the light switch, then stood still a moment as she surveyed the scene.

Brown paper crackled beneath her feet, protection for the wood flooring, not yet stained, or sealed. The cabinets were installed, along with a sink, but the plumbing was still incomplete. She crossed to the sink and looked out the window. She could see the lake over behind Sutter's, the barn, and the fields beyond. Tom's backyard was mostly mud, but he'd told her he planned a large garden there.

"Miss Annabelle?"

She turned to find Billy peering at her from the garage door. "We'll be a while if you want to wait at home. I'll shut the garage door when I leave. Tom said Riley would be here around four-thirty."

Annabelle answered with a nod. After one last look around, she headed for the door. Her hand on the doorknob, she hesitated long enough to draw a breath. This could be her house someday. Her gaze found the picture window, set in the back of the house instead of the front, to take in the view. Tom had boasted about that decision. She had to agree. Better to look at woods and pastures, rather than a dusty road. She stirred herself. Time to go, Annabelle.

With every homeward step, she wondered if what Lillian said was true. *Is Tom really rushing to finish the house for me?* He still loved her, that was plain to see.

Back at the little white clapboard house where she'd grown up, a tendril of smoke curled into the moist air. Ginger huddled near the door, waiting to enter.

Warmth enveloped Annabelle, even before she stepped inside.

Words rolled off her tongue as she turned to close the door. "Your will be done, Lord. My life is in Your hands. You lead, I'll follow." She stood still a moment. Even if Tom never set foot in church? Could she do that again?

He had real faith. She'd seen that. He had not abandoned his love for the Lord. But, was it enough? She'd dreamed of him sitting beside her on the pew … holding her hand. Was it a dream that would never become reality?

Heaving a sigh, she lowered herself into her favorite chair and removed her galoshes. When you turned a thing over to the Lord, it wasn't yours to worry with anymore. "All right, Lord. I'm listening."

From behind the rack of postcards, Tom eyed the newcomer. This must be the woman Riley had told him about. Didn't look to be much over four-foot-ten, blond hair tucked up under a sky-blue hat, which did little to hide an odd neck. She reminded him of a baby bird, stretching over the side of the nest. Or maybe a pixie. He gave a little half-laugh, followed by a cough to cover it up.

After picking through everything on the knickknack shelf, she quick-stepped over to the counter and picked up a menu. When she cocked her head his way, he ducked behind the dry goods shelf. Had she seen him eying her? He didn't want her to get the wrong idea, her being single and all. Spinster ladies could be difficult to shake.

Which compounded his need to get a positive answer from Annabelle. The sooner he got a ring on her finger, the better. Surely by now, it had been long enough. Maybe he'd know something more on Saturday when they spent the afternoon driving to Memphis and back.

After what he considered to be a decent amount of time behind the shelf, he squared his shoulders before making his way to the prescription counter. The woman was talking to Arnie full throttle. Tom had never heard a Southern woman talk so fast.

Arnie took it in stride. "The malted's my favorite, but you may prefer the vanilla shake."

"I would, thank you, sir. And don't forget the whipped cream and a cherry."

"Oh, I wouldn't dare forget that." Arnie turned away to prepare the treat.

The woman set her purse on the counter before

making a major ordeal of climbing onto a stool.

Tom choked back laughter. He was fixing to ask if she needed a stepstool when she raised her voice in his direction.

"Being petite has its drawbacks. Tall as you are, I'm sure you don't realize the need for a couple of shorter stools at the bar, how handy that would be."

Right about that time, Arnie flipped the switch on the milkshake machine. Tom had no need of a quick answer, but as a business owner, he did need to reply. When the soda jerk shut off the machine, Tom spoke. "That may prove problematic. We'd also have to lower the counter."

This brought a trill of laughter from the woman. "Oh, my, what a quick wit you have, sir. I know we've not been introduced, but may I assume you're the owner, Mr. Tom Franklin?"

He nodded. "Yes, ma'am, I am." For some odd reason he couldn't determine, warmth rose in his cheeks. Maybe the fact he'd made a silly rhyme out of his answer left him feeling the fool.

Arnie set the milkshake, mounded high with cream, adorned with a bright red cherry, on the counter in front of the woman. "Here you go. Anything else?"

She smiled at Arnie. "Oh, my, that looks delicious."

He arched his brows at Tom before turning his back to wash up.

"Mr. Franklin, I'm Rose Ella McCoy. It's two names: Rose, Ella. But most folks call me Rosella. My brother and I have recently moved to Trenton. He's getting ready to build a warehouse over on Tenth Street."

Tom already knew most of this information, but he gave her a polite smile. "Welcome. I hope you'll like our town."

"Oh, I already do, so much." She spooned some of the whipped cream into her mouth. "Oh my, there is nothing in this world like the taste of fresh whipped cream. I do love it so."

Tom made himself busy, checking and re-checking his inventory. Would she notice he'd counted the same items more than once?

Miss Rose Ella was halfway through her milkshake when Bo entered. Not a day went by when Bo did not visit. He sometimes stayed all day. Tom always wondered what the man did on Sunday when the store was closed.

Bo gave Miss Rose Ella a head-to-toe once over. She was sitting on his usual stool. However, he said nothing, just planted himself on another while glaring at Tom.

Arnie set a cup in front of Bo and poured the coffee. "You're late, old man."

Bo slapped the counter, making Miss Rose Ella jump.

She glowered at him.

Bo chuckled. "What you mean, calling me an old man?" He busied himself stirring sugar into his coffee. "I'm gettin' around pretty good today, and you go and insult me."

Arnie rested his hands on the counter. "I'm not gonna argue with you this morning, Bo." He turned to Miss Rose Ella and asked the question Tom wanted to ask as soon as he got the chance. "What sorta warehouse is your brother building, Miss McCoy?"

This got Bo's attention. Thank goodness, he had the sense not to interrupt.

She toyed with her spoon. "He'll rent out space to a manufacturer looking to cut down on shipping costs. They're going to store a good bit of their inventory in the warehouse and ship it out to buyers in this part of the country. Of course, I'm not free to say who the manufacturer is."

"Huh." Bo sipped his coffee while the woman took a breath.

"It's moving along fast. The foundation has already been poured. Soon enough, everyone will know who it is. My brother has connections, you see. Important connections."

"Huh." Arnie polished the counter with his rag. "Will he be hiring? Folks around here could use work."

She finished off her shake and touched her lips with a napkin. "I'm not privy to that information, but I'm sure they'll need some workers once the facility has been built. To load and unload—that sort of thing. My brother will run the place, of course." She unclasped her pocketbook and removed a familiar card.

Tom recognized his *Welcome Wagon* certificate.

She handed it to Arnie. "I believe this will cover the cost of that delicious shake?"

Arnie accepted the ticket. "Yes, ma'am, it will. Welcome to Trenton. I hope you'll stop in often."

She dug in her purse then laid a couple of coins on the counter. "Bless you, sir."

Arnie gathered the coins and dropped them in the tip jar near the register. "Thank you, Miz McCoy."

With great care, Rose Ella dismounted the stool. Then, to Tom's dismay, she approached him. "I'm pleased to make your acquaintance, Mr. Franklin. I expect I'll see you again soon. Lincoln—that's my brother—is in this for the long haul. He means to make Trenton his home. I'll be here as long as he needs me."

Tom swallowed. His head spun from the sheer

speed of her words. Way too much information in too short a time. He gave her a polite nod. "Well, I wish you both the best."

Her answering smile reminded him of a big gulp of too-sweet tea, like drinking syrup straight out of the bottle. How'd she do that? He couldn't help a comparison to Annabelle, whose warmth and genuine grace penetrated the darkest regions of his heart. Made him want to close the store, head on over there.

Somewhat distracted by thoughts of Annabelle, he watched Rose Ella sashay out the door. He had the sinking feeling she was right. He would see her again. Probably too often. He'd have to watch out, because this woman had wiles, and she knew how to use them.

Betty Thomason Owens

Chapter Five

March 16, 1957
Memphis, Tennessee

Annabelle waved as her sweet family stepped down from the train car. She wanted to bolt toward them, but she held back to allow Lillian first dibs on the baby. He jumped in Alton's arms when he caught sight of his Grandma Wade.

Connie made a beeline for Annabelle, threw her arms around her neck and hugged. "Oh, Momma, how I've missed you."

Joyous tears overflowing, Annabelle kissed Connie's cheek before greeting Alton. "I'm so happy to see y'all. Look how tanned you are."

Alton slid his arm around Annabelle in a sideways hug. "That island sun browns your biscuits."

Joseph clapped his hands and grinned when he caught sight of Annabelle. "Granny!"

Lillian handed him over. "Your turn, Granny."

Annabelle snuggled him close. Was there any greater joy in all the world?

Tom's voice caught her attention as he spoke with Alton about the luggage. "Looks like you brought back one of the islands."

Alton guffawed. "We had to buy another suitcase to hold all the souvenirs." He grabbed a couple of the bags and headed for the car. "I'm glad you drove Mother's car. We're going to need the extra space."

Close as they could be without embracing, Annabelle, Connie, and Lillian followed the men to the car. Joseph insisted on walking, so Connie held tightly to his hand, lest he cut and run. He had gone straight from wobbly-walking steps to running and was now quite adept.

The three women sat together in the back seat so the men could talk. Joseph crept from one lap to the other until he finally settled. He fell asleep on Annabelle's.

After admiring a new bracelet on Connie's arm, Lillian plied her with questions about the trip. "How's your Daddy doing?"

Connie's eyes lit. "Oh, he's wonderful. He's gone into the touring business. It's turned out quite well. He was the only guide in the beginning but has since been able to hire three more. They're booked solid for the summer."

Alton pivoted to look at them. "He's fixing to buy a couple of boats, too. He'll add offshore tours and fishing excursions."

Lillian arched her brows. "Mac will be raking in the dough."

Connie laughed. "That's what I told him, but he said he'll keep investing the surplus in the business."

"Well, I think that's wonderful." Annabelle couldn't be more pleased for Mac Pruitt. He'd had a difficult time of it. When she looked up, she caught Tom's glance in the rear-view mirror. He hadn't said much, but she gathered he was happy to be included in the family. It was nice how well he fit. His knowing how to stay quiet and give more importance to others was one big reason for that. She pressed a kiss to Joseph's forehead. Yes, there was a lot to admire about Tom Franklin.

The return drive seemed much shorter. Now that Connie and Alton and little Joseph had returned, Annabelle had joy down in her soul. She'd sing it out loud, but she didn't want to wake Joseph. Instead, she gave a contented sigh, drawing Connie's attention.

Connie snuggled close to Annabelle. "It's so good to be home."

Tom leaned against the fence. He gazed into the distance beyond the few acres he'd bought from Annabelle. After leaving the family at Sutter's to settle in, he'd made a polite exit. They'd invited him to stay to supper, but he still felt like an intruder. Besides, his house needed every spare moment of his time.

Peering at the woods that lined the pasture, he ticked off the months. From the day they'd poured the foundation, he'd worked nearly ten months. Seemed too long to wait on a house, but he'd saved a mint doing most of the work himself. With Riley's help, of course.

He'd hired a bricklayer and a concrete guy who'd prepared and poured the foundation. He'd also helped Tom build the framework for a corner cellar. The concrete-lined room lay beneath the kitchen, but you could only enter from the outside through a sloped door. That way, it was available to neighbors in case of a tornado.

He'd lined the walls with wooden shelves for canned goods, leaving room on one side for a long bench where folks could sit and wait out the storm. He'd installed boxes beneath the bench for root crops like potatoes and yams.

Riley had scratched his head and wondered,

"What's an old bachelor like you gonna need with shelves of canned goods, or boxes of root crops? You ort to bring in one of those billiard tables. Plenty of room for it. That'd give the folks something to do whilst they wait for the storm to pass."

Tom had laughed, but he understood why Riley asked such a question about storing food. Tom had seldom cooked when he lived alone, other than the fish he'd caught. Most times, he'd brought home a sandwich from the store.

He couldn't talk about it to Riley, the man would yap it all over town, but Tom reckoned Annabelle would have a lot of use for a root cellar. He'd seen her pantry shelves lined with jars of vegetables, jams, jellies, and pickles.

He breathed out a sigh. Last week, as he enjoyed lunch with Brother Nathan, the man had given him one of those piercing looks that seemed to plumb the depths of Tom's soul.

"Tom, the Bible says hope deferred makes the heart sick."

Tom had quirked an eyebrow and stared at the man. What could he possibly mean by that? "Do I look heartsick?"

Brother Nathan laughed. "I'm giving you fair warning. Don't drag your feet too long."

Then Tom wondered whether he meant getting his carcass back to church, or was he talking about something more personal, like Annabelle? Tom wasn't so sure he wanted to know which it was, so he'd tried to change the subject, but Pastor wouldn't let go of it.

"A dog can only guard a bone so long. Sooner or later, he's gonna take his eyes off it, and in that moment, a hungrier dog's gonna steal it."

After that, Tom was sure enough puzzled, but he smiled and acted as though he understood. It worked, Brother Nathan got to talking about other things and then lunch was over. Long after the man had gone, Tom ruminated his words. He was pretty sure the pastor was counseling him to secure things with Annabelle. Even now, Tom's insides tied themselves into knots at the thought.

A whippoorwill's call startled him. Was it that late? He turned toward the house. Dodging the worst of the mud that was his backyard, he headed inside. Alton was sending Willie over this week to plow the garden and smooth out the rest so Tom could plant grass. It was all coming together. Soon, there'd be no more excuses.

Leaving his muddy shoes on the concrete back porch, Tom entered the house. It still smelled new, like fresh-cut wood and the stain Riley was using on the floors. Flipping on the light switch, Tom admired the new fixture he'd installed in the kitchen. It bathed the entire room in warm light, but also made it easy to see all the dust on the cabinets.

Thelma had offered to bring the kids over to do some cleanup. He'd half a mind to let her, since that meant Annabelle would come over, too. The thought stirred something in his chest.

Did she have any idea how much he wanted her here, sharing this house with him? Making it a sweet home, filling it with love? Had he any right to dream of such things?

After another sigh, he figured he'd better get busy. Picking up a rag, he swiped at the dust on the counter. Yep, it was past due for a clean-up. Then he could start thinking about paint. That meant having Annabelle over. He made a mental note to stop in at the hardware store this week to pick up some paint chips.

He probably wouldn't see her tomorrow, it being Sunday, but maybe one evening next week, he'd stop by to let her know it was time.

What would she think of the recent work they'd done? The shiny, new floors. Bright, white tile gleaming in the bathroom. He was especially proud of that. He knew lots of folks preferred the new pink, aqua, or blue tiles, but he had a feeling they'd be outmoded in a few years. Maybe he was old-fashioned, but he loved the white. It looked clean.

He glanced around, trying to see the place through her eyes, then smiled to himself. It was no use. He knew so little about women, it was too hard to predict what she'd say or think. According to Riley, whatever a woman said, it would be something different the next day.

He folded the cleaning rag, set it near the sink, then dusted his hands. Might as well go on back to town. He'd get a good night's sleep and be ready to work all the harder tomorrow. Or maybe he'd put in an appearance at church. That would make two people happy. Pastor, and Annabelle. Yep, he might just do that. He could use a couple points in his favor.

The pixie sat at the well-worn, upright piano, running a lacy handkerchief over the keys. Annabelle turned her gaze away. Why did the woman rankle her so? Maybe because she was everywhere, into everything. She'd already insinuated herself into the choir, taken the pianist's position, among other things. Of course, Hattie Overton, the former pianist, was only too happy to give it over. At ninety-two, she was ready to retire.

Annabelle had stifled a twinge of disappointment when Rosella never hit a sour note. Every song, even the most difficult came out perfectly.

It didn't help to hear such words as "effervescent" used to describe the newcomer. *Effervescent.* Made her think of those seltzer tablets you used for an upset tummy. Something Annabelle could use right about now.

Thankfully, Lillian slid in beside her as the music started. Everyone stood for the Doxology. Annabelle did her best to let go of her ill feelings toward the pianist. She managed to keep her thoughts away entirely. She did not want to contemplate the reason for her attitude.

Thank goodness Pastor Nathan hadn't discerned her state of mind. His sermons of late were taken from the parables of Jesus. This morning's was the widow's mite. A safe topic, as far as she was concerned. Annabelle was always careful to tithe on whatever increase she received, which wasn't much.

Not long after the sermon began, Lillian's elbow found its way into Annabelle's ribs. Annabelle drew back to settle a glare on her. The woman kept nodding her head toward the rear of the sanctuary. Well, Annabelle was not about to draw attention to herself by turning to look back there. Whatever it was, it could wait until the sermon had ended. When everyone stood for the altar call, she could look without anyone noticing.

Lillian shrugged and shook her head, as though exasperated.

Annabelle lifted her chin and kept her eyes pinned to the pastor. He was going into detail about moving all the furniture in the house to find a missing penny. Annabelle reckoned she'd missed a line or two of his narrative, thanks to Lillian.

Rosella's pudgy fingers trilled out the opening to *Just As I Am*. The congregation stood and began to sing. Annabelle cast a glance over her shoulder as the sanctuary door closed. Someone was in a powerful hurry to get out of there. Maybe a sinner unable to face another altar call. Or a deacon needing a smoke. She stifled a giggle before joining in on the second stanza. "Just as I am, and waiting not to rid my soul of one dark blot; ..."

There certainly was a dark blot on her soul this morning. Jealousy. That's what it was. The green monster gnawing away at her heart. Annabelle paused her singing long enough to mentally utter a prayer of repentance, asking for forgiveness.

The song ended, Pastor prayed a benediction over

his flock. "Lord, help us to forgive others as you have forgiven us. If any of us holds anything against our neighbor, give us the strength to make it right. In your Holy Name, we pray, Amen."

Annabelle opened her eyes to peer at Pastor Nathan. Maybe he had discerned a thing or two. Or maybe, it was chance. Or possibly the Lord speaking through him. But he wasn't looking at her. He was studying the back of the room. The look on his face hinted at disappointment. What was he disappointed about? She drew a breath and let it out with a gasp as Lillian jabbed her in the ribs again.

"Why didn't you look when I told you to? Tom was here."

Annabelle widened her eyes to peer around the sanctuary. "Where?"

"He's done gone. You should of looked. That'll teach you to ignore me when I'm trying to tell you something."

"You weren't telling me anything. You jabbed my side."

"I was trying not to draw attention."

Annabelle chuckled.

Lillian laughed too. "You've waited so long for that to happen. When it did, you missed it. Come on, maybe he's a-waiting outside."

Her heart all aflutter, Annabelle hurried to catch up with Lillian. But Tom was not outside the church. Most likely, he'd already headed over to the house.

Ilene Nathan caught hold of Annabelle's arm. "Miss Annabelle, Miss Lillian, I heard Alton and Connie are back home. How are they?"

Annabelle smiled. "Fine. They got in late yesterday evening, so they stayed home to rest."

"Oh, of course. What a long trip that is. You give them our love and tell them we hope to see them real soon."

Lillian nodded. "Thank you, Ilene."

A trill of feminine laughter sent shivers up and down Annabelle's spine. The pixie was on her way out. Turning toward the parking lot, she set off at a quick pace.

"Where're you going in such a hurry?" Lillian rushed to keep up. "Is it a fire?"

Annabelle shook her head. "I just want to get home, that's all. I'm thinking of that barbecued roast beef you told me about on the way in."

"Huh. Well, I could've sworn, if I made a habit of swearing, that you were running from a certain somebody."

"Ha ha ha." Annabelle was not about to admit to any such thing. Her conscience was giving her fits, though. Hadn't she just repented a few minutes earlier? Now, she was avoiding the object of her discontent. How would God look upon that? He'd probably much rather she faced her trouble, show kindness and mercy. After all, the woman was new in town. Surely, she could use a friend or two.

As Lillian pulled out of the parking lot, Annabelle caught sight of a clutch of women, and there was that bright blue hat, right in the middle. Closing her eyes, Annabelle sent another silent prayer toward heaven. Oh, Lord, give me strength. Help me overcome my revulsion, find something admirable about Miss Rosella McCoy. Her lips quirked. Rose Ella. Rosella.

Lillian cackled. "You can open your eyes, Annabelle. I'm driving as safe as can be. I daresay I'm driving as well as any after all the practice I've had in the last month.

It started with a giggle and then Annabelle was laughing out loud. She couldn't seem to stop. But oh, how good it felt. Was this God's answer to her prayer? He had definitely answered her other one, about Tom coming back to church.

It was as though a weight had lifted. Even though it was the first time, and he'd sneaked out before anyone could see him and remark on it, hope filled Annabelle's heart. If Tom was coming to church, she could even put up with Miss McCoy.

Chapter Six

April 10, 1957

Tom glanced at the script he'd been handed. Nothing had changed, so he dispensed the pills into a bottle, applied the label and wrote up a ticket. Many of his patrons returned right on schedule for their blood pressure medication or heart pills. He'd noted some of the regulars on his calendar, so he could keep his supplies topped off.

Checking that calendar, he almost sighed aloud. Already halfway through another week. Time does have a way of disappearing on you.

As he reached for the next prescription, the doorbell jangled. He looked up to see Alton remove his hat as he headed to the prescription desk.

"Morning, Tom."

"Good morning, Alton. What can I do for you?"

Alton held out a slip of paper. "I need you to fill

this prescription."

Tom took the script and looked at it. He raised his eyes to Alton's, then gave him a nod. "I have these on hand. It'll only be a few minutes."

Alton nodded. "I'll wait at the counter there. An ice-cold cola sounds real good." He stepped over to the counter and slid onto a stool.

Tom wanted to comment on the prescription, but he held his tongue. Several regulars hung around the aisles or sat at the counter. News like this would soon be all over town. He smiled to himself as he reached for the bottle. Had they told Annabelle yet? Or Miss Lillian, for that matter? Boy, howdy, they'd both be ecstatic.

A few minutes later, he called Alton back to the counter.

Alton pulled out his wallet. "I'll settle up our account while I'm here. Anything on Annabelle's, too."

Tom nodded, though he knew Annabelle's chart was empty. He'd seen to that, himself. He punched the numbers in the cash register and Alton paid. As Tom handed him the change, Alton leaned forward. "We haven't told anyone yet. I know you'll keep our secret."

"You've got my word."

"Oh, by the way, I hope you can come to dinner Saturday evening. I've invited Thelma and Riley and their bunch, too. After dinner, I'll show the movies we made."

"Yes, sir. I wouldn't miss it. What time?"

"Five o'clock. Mother doesn't want to keep everyone late since we have church the next morning." Alton grinned as he settled his hat.

Tom closed the cash register and picked up the prescription. "Sounds good. I'll be there."

After Alton left, Tom filed the ticket, not wanting anyone to see it. He had some mighty nosy customers. A couple of them were in the store this afternoon. He scanned the room before picking up the next prescription. Yep, nosy.

Bo hobbled over. "Somebody sick out at Sutter's?"

Tom raised an eyebrow. "You know I can't talk about that."

"Course not. I'm wondering about it is all." He gave a shrug then lowered his voice. "I'd hate for anyone to be ailing. They could've picked up some bug over there in the islands, brought it back here. We could all get sick."

Tom almost laughed out loud. "It's nothing serious, Bo. Don't you go spreading panic."

Bo chuckled. "Oh, I won't. But you know them things happen all the time. I read about it in the paper last week. A couple came back from Panama. A few days later, he up and died."

"I read that, too. But he was poorly to begin with. It was parasites, the doctor said. Besides, it was Panama—a long way from Hawaii."

By this time, Mabel Shanks had made her way back to the prescription desk. "Is someone sick out at Miss Lillian's? I saw Alton picking up a prescription."

Tom shook his head. "Yours is ready, Miss Mabel." Pretty sure she wouldn't want him advertising what she was picking up, he held the bag for her to see.

She cleared her throat as she reached for it. "Put it on my tab, would you, Tom?" She made a hasty retreat.

Bo chuckled. "Her hemorrhoids must be acting up again."

Annabelle was washing the last of the breakfast dishes when the screen door opened and slammed.

"Aunt Annabelle? You here?"

"Judith?" Annabelle glanced at the clock. It was still early. She hadn't even heard a car pull up.

Riley and Thelma's eldest daughter rushed through the door, her face mottled, as though she'd been crying. The pink of her cheeks magnified the girl's freckles. Her red hair, usually neatly pulled back in a ponytail, hung loose, half-covering those brimming eyes.

Annabelle dried her hands on her apron as she stepped nearer. "What on earth?" She caressed the girl's damp cheek.

Judith almost fell into Annabelle's arms. "Oh, I'm so glad you're here."

"Come sit and tell me what's the matter. Is everything all right at home?" She led Judith to a chair.

"Oh, yes. It's not that. Well, I haven't been there, I guess everything's all right. No, Aunt Annabelle. It's me. I'm in trouble."

Annabelle smoothed Judith's hair from her face, pulled up a chair and sat next to her. "I hope not, child."

Judith sniffed, then shook her head. "No. Not that kind of trouble."

Relieved, Annabelle felt in her pocket for a handkerchief, found one, and handed it over. "Well, you'd best tell me all about it."

Judith swiped at her eyes and dabbed at her nose. "You remember that guy I was going out with?"

"Yes, he's such a nice boy." Annabelle narrowed her eyes. "What did he do?"

"Oh, no, we were friends, really. He met another girl a couple of months ago. He's been going out with her."

Confusion clouded Annabelle's mind. "So, what's the problem?"

"Well, he invited me on a double-date with a friend of his." Her lower lip trembled. "I said I would. We had a really good time, all of us together. Then Preston, the other guy, he wanted to meet up the next day at the library. So, I did. Afterward, we walked all over campus. We talked and talked, Aunt Annabelle. It was like we'd known each other forever." When she wiped her eyes again, Annabelle noticed her fingers trembled.

"You want a glass of tea, sweetheart, or something to eat?"

Judith shook her head, then seemed to think better of it. "Do you have any cookies?"

Annabelle rose from her chair. "I can make some while you finish your story."

The girl nodded. "I've missed your cookies—" Fresh tears flowed.

Annabelle turned her back to reach for the sugar. Best let the child cry it out, so she could finish her tale. Judith was awfully good at telling stories.

"So, we've been spending time together whenever we could. And … and then last night, he told me … he has a calling on his life."

Annabelle drew back. "Well, that's a good thing, isn't it?"

Judith frowned. Tears threatened again. "It would be, I guess."

"What's the problem, then?" Annabelle cracked a couple of eggs into the bowl.

"He's going to the Southern Baptist Seminary next year. He feels called to be a pastor."

Stirring slowly, Annabelle frowned. Was the girl upset that this young man was leaving? "Louisville's not so far away. He can come visit, surely?"

After a couple of dry sobs, Judith twisted the handkerchief. "That's not even it, Aunt Annabelle. If he's going to be a pastor, he could be going anywhere." She shook her head, almost as if she wanted to be shed of the whole thing. "He wants me to go with him."

Annabelle almost dropped the spoon. "With him? I thought you just met him?"

Her head bobbed in agreement. "We've been seeing each other for a little over a month, now."

"That's not long enough to be thinking about— wait—you mean after he graduates from the seminary, or before?"

"Oh no, it'd be after. I have to finish school, too. But … I don't want to be a pastor's wife, Aunt Annabelle."

Annabelle sighed when the blubbering started again. She cleaned cookie dough from her fingers before kneeling to wrap her arms around the distraught girl. When the sobs subsided, she kissed Judith's cheek. "When I was a young thing, all I could think about was getting away from here. I met Ray, and before the month was out, we married and took off for California."

Judith sniffed. "But your life was hard here. Ma told me how folks treated you—those snooty Wades. Well, not all of them. Miss Lillian's good as gold. I can't imagine her ever being ugly to you."

"She never was. Now, let me get those cookies in the oven and we'll have ourselves a treat."

Judith drew in a breath and slowly exhaled. "I'll fix us a glass of tea."

"Thank you kindly, sweetheart." Annabelle finished dropping dough onto a pan and placed it in the oven. She set the egg timer, then filled another pan. Ice cubes crackled as Judith poured the tea. The only other sounds in the room were the egg timer and the ticking of the clock. Judith's relaxed features told Annabelle she felt better. Sometimes, you just need to talk it out.

The girl returned the pitcher to the refrigerator. "Those cookies sure smell good. Oh, how I've missed your molasses crinkles."

The baking done, Annabelle sat with Judith on the front porch, sipping tea and munching cookies.

Ginger lay in the sunshine, sound asleep.

Judith reached to pet the cat. "Any more kittens lately?"

"No, thank goodness. I've about had my fill."

"Maybe she's done."

"I hope so. She had so much trouble with that last litter. So, are we all finished talking about that young man? What was his name?"

Judith pulled in a breath and let it out slowly. "Preston Weatherby."

"Well, that's certainly a dignified name." She leveled a frown at the girl. "Why wouldn't you want to be a pastor's wife?"

Judith leaned back in her chair to gaze toward the porch roof. "I've always had the idea that if pastoring is a calling, then a pastor's wife ought to also be called. I think anything less could spell disaster."

Annabelle rocked slowly, lessening the creak of the old wooden rocker. "That sounds like good thinking, Judith. You're right sure you're not called?"

Judith leveled her gaze at Annabelle. "I think we're all called to one thing or another, Aunt Annabelle. I won't say never, but I sincerely hope not. I only ever wanted to live right here in Trenton. I love it here." She finished the last of her iced tea and then set the glass on the porch floor.

"I know you do. I think that's honorable. I know God hears."

"I know He does, too. Sometimes, though, I wonder if He's not smiling at our utter lack of understanding. He may have in mind to send me far away."

Annabelle giggled. "Oh, I don't know about that." She angled another glance at the girl. "But if He does, you can trust that He'll prepare you ahead of time."

"I know. I'm wondering if that's what He's doing, right now?"

"Do you love this young man?"

"I like him an awful lot. He's the best person I've ever met." Her lip trembled again.

Annabelle decided to give it a rest, not stir up any more emotion. "Well, I reckon you have some thinking to do, but it seems you have ample time to do it."

"I do." She sat forward with a sigh. "Want to ride over to Sutter's with me? I want to see everyone, especially little Joseph. I'll bet he's grown."

"He certainly has. He chatters a mile a minute. You'll be completely distracted." Annabelle bent to pick up her empty glass and stood. "It'll take me a minute to run a comb through this unruly mop of mine." She peered at Judith, hoping the girl would take the hint.

"Oh, my goodness!" Judith drew her fingers through her errant locks. "Thanks for saying that. I didn't even take time to brush my hair before I left this morning. I must look a sight."

"Oh, you're a sight, all right." Annabelle tweaked Judith's cheek before heading to the kitchen.

Samson barked a greeting as Judith pulled into the drive at Sutter's. Annabelle laughed to see the dog's exuberance. "I believe he's missed you."

Once out of the car, Judith greeted the dog. "I've missed you, too, boy." She straightened as Connie stepped out onto the back porch.

"What a wonderful surprise!"

Judith approached the porch where Connie caught her in an embrace. "Is it Spring Break already?"

Annabelle followed along behind the younger women as they entered the kitchen. She hadn't realized Judith was probably home on break. How had it gotten so late in the year?

Joseph trotted into the room, a small red truck in one hand, a toy soldier in the other. He halted when his gaze landed on Judith. "Juju!"

Judith caught him in her arms and nibbled at his

neck until he giggled.

After the noise died down, Regina waved a spoon at the young woman. "How you doin' Miss Judith?" Barely waiting for an answer, she addressed Annabelle. "Y'all stayin' for dinner? Got aplenty."

Lillian scuttled in, carrying an armload of folded towels. "Of course, they're staying. We're clearing the pantry, so we have a variety of vegetables."

Regina nodded. "I made cornbread, Miss Judith. I know you like my cornbread."

"I sure do. I can't wait."

"Looks like you could use some vittles," Regina went on to say. "Down to skin and bones. Don't they feed y'all at that school?"

Connie's laughter bubbled.

Annabelle looked her up and down. Eyes sparkling, roses in her cheeks. A faint suspicion worked its way into her mind. Could it be?

Connie caught Annabelle looking at her. Her gaze warmed as she moved forward to give her a kiss. "Good morning, Momma."

"Morning, pumpkin."

Lillian returned empty-handed. She patted Judith's shoulder. "We're having all your family over Saturday night, sugar. Alton's planning to show the movies he made in Hawaii."

Judith set the squirmy boy down before answering. "That sounds wonderful." She pivoted toward Connie. "I was hoping y'all got off the islands before the earthquake hit."

Annabelle pressed her hand against her chest. Her breath caught in her throat as she stared at Connie. "What earthquake?"

Betty Thomason Owens

Chapter Seven

April 12, 1957

Annabelle glanced from one face to another. Why had she heard nothing about this earthquake in the Hawaiian Islands, so close to the time when Connie, Alton, and little Joseph had visited there? When had it happened? How bad was it? What if they'd been delayed? Feeling the need to sit, she tugged a chair forward and sank into it.

Connie shrugged, as though it was nothing to be concerned about. "We were already in San Diego when we heard the news. The main quake happened two days after we left. I called Dad as soon as I could. He and all the family were fine. Apparently, most of the damage came from a tsunami. He happened to be inland on the Big Island that day, so he was safe."

Regina spoke up. "Soo … nami? What's that?"

"A big wave caused by an earthquake," Judith told

her.

Annabelle shook her head. "Why am I just now hearing about this?"

Connie touched Annabelle's arm, and spoke in a calm voice, "I had a letter from my sister Pat yesterday. Dad didn't have much information when I called, except to say he was fine, and he believed my sisters were okay. Pat said it was a strong quake, but they are used to them in the islands."

"Along with volcano eruptions," Judith said.

Annabelle scowled at the girl. "You're not helping, Judith." She faced Connie. "I'm glad y'all left when you did. Amazing, now I think of it, how you got out in the nick of time. Then your dad happened to be somewhere safe."

"Praise the Lord Almighty!"

Annabelle startled at the sound of Alton's voice. She hadn't heard him enter. From the looks on their faces, no one else had, either.

He removed his hat and hung it on a wall hook beside the kitchen door. "That's what I have to say about it, Annabelle."

"I'll second that," Lillian added. "Now, y'all wash up for dinner."

After dinner, Judith planned to visit her family.

Annabelle walked with her to the car.

Her hand on the door handle, Judith paused. "You need me to run you home, Aunt Annabelle?"

"A nice walk would be just the thing, after such a nourishing meal. I may have to let my waistband out another inch or two if I dine often at Sutter's."

Judith giggled and patted her midsection. "I know what you mean." She gave Annabelle a quick kiss on the cheek. "I may stay the night at Ma's. If so, I'll see you in the morning."

Annabelle waved as the girl drove away.

"Come sit a spell," Lillian called from the porch. "What's going on with that one?"

Annabelle figured someone was bound to ask that question before the end of the day. She'd expected it from Connie. Straightening the skirt of her favorite day dress, she relaxed in the porch swing. Judith wouldn't want her private business broadcasted, so Annabelle kept her voice light. "Stress from finals, that's all." It was not really a lie. The girl had mentioned it. "I reckon it'll get worse before it gets better. She chose some tough courses."

"Well, then, she'll be all right. I was afraid that young man of hers had broken her heart. He didn't seem all that interested in her."

"Turns out he wasn't, but she wasn't either, so it didn't matter. She said they were friends, is all."

Lillian nodded as though she understood.

Annabelle opened her mouth to ask about Connie when Lillian raised her arm to wave at someone.

A young boy sidled up the drive, his shoulders hunched and nothing but the top of his curly black hair showing on his head. He cut a glance toward them and nodded as he passed by on his way to the back of the house.

After he had gone, Annabelle looked at Lillian. "I didn't know Hero was still coming over."

Lillian nodded. "Today's his first day back. Connie said he'll come a couple of days a week through spring and summer, to keep up with his lessons."

Annabelle toed the floor, pushing her swing. The boy had seemed a little down, which was unusual for Hero. "I'm still amazed that Marla would offer to pay for that boy's tutoring."

Hero was the grandson of Lillian's former cook, Edris. She had remained at the mansion in town after Lillian's elder son, Jensen and his wife, Marla, moved in. Annabelle shook her head, musing over the situation. Did Jensen know about the arrangement? That was not a subject she wished to bring up with Lillian. It was none of Annabelle's business, either.

Sitting forward to stop the motion of the swing, she smoothed the hair back from her face. "Well, I hate to part from good company, but I need to get back home. Chores are waiting."

"Are you sure you don't want Alton to run you home?"

Annabelle stood. "No, I can use the walk. Creek's running low again, so I'll take the wagon road."

Lillian rose to walk with her, around the corner of the house.

Here, they could see Connie seated on the porch next to Hero, pointing at picture cards on the back porch.

Annabelle kept her distance. She didn't want to disturb the boy's lesson. He seemed thoroughly absorbed, not even noticing when Connie raised her hand to wave.

Annabelle returned the farewell with a nod and a smile, then trod down the slope toward the creek. Since the sun had taken cover behind a cloud bank, a light breeze felt cool on her back and arms as she crossed the sandy bottom. Overhead, a cardinal's song rang out from its perch on a still-barren branch. Soon enough, these trees would provide a deep canopy over the creek, a cool respite from the heat of summer.

Annabelle rubbed her arms as she followed the old

wagon road on the opposite side. How many times had she made this crossing? Each time, her imagination brought back sounds of a wagon's wheels grinding, its floorboards creaking, the jingle of harness and tack. Old memories ebbed and flowed, one day bringing joy, the next, melancholy.

Today, her heartbeat quickened, as she contemplated the possibility of a new baby later this year. Though she hadn't had the chance to talk to Connie, she was convinced the girl was in the family way. She'd noted all the signs she missed the first time—the bloom in her cheeks, the softness of her eyes as she gazed at Alton, the overall glow of health.

Her mind thus occupied, the walk seemed shorter than ever. Topping the hill, she caught sight of Alton's farmhand, Willie, plowing Tom's back lot. Soon, she reckoned, Tom would have a green lawn instead of mud. The house would be occupied every night, instead of standing empty from late evening until the next afternoon.

What a long time it had taken to finish. It was well-built, that was for sure. She paused next to the wide gate Alton had installed in her back fence, so he could gain easier access to her garden. He'd plowed it this year since Riley had been busy at Tom's house.

She paused another moment, arrested by the sight

of a small white car driving slowly past the new brick home. Folks tended to do that. It wasn't often someone built a new house out this way.

After the car passed, Annabelle stepped through the gate.

"Paint it all one color." Riley punctuated his statement with a goofy chuckle.

Tom shook his head. "It won't look right. I have some ideas, but I'm planning to get another opinion."

"Yeah, I can guess whose opinion you're going for." With a wink, he nodded toward the kitchen window.

Tom peered out the window as Annabelle passed through the new gate into her garden. Now might be a good time to check with her. Maybe she'd have a chance to come by one day. Then he could order what paint he needed. He slipped his shoes on before opening the door. "Be right back."

He closed the door before Riley could make further comment. Sometimes, the man got on his nerves, but Riley was still Tom's best friend. Close quarters for almost two years, however, tended to strain even the closest friendship. Even those who'd been friends since the cradle.

Dodging dirt clods, Tom quick-stepped across the field to the gate, where he paused a moment. He didn't want to sneak up on the woman and startle her. "Evening, Annabelle."

She turned from gazing out across Alton's fields. "Tom, how are you?"

"Doing well, and you?"

"Very well, thank you."

Small talk over, he plunged in before he lost his nerve. "I was wondering if you'd be able to come over one day and look at those paint colors." He propped an arm on the fence post, hoping to seem nonchalant.

She shielded her eyes with one hand and peered toward his house. "I reckon so. Meant to do it sooner, but with everything that's been going on …"

"Oh, I know. You can do it during the day. Write down your choices—I mean suggestions." He watched her, waiting. Had he overstepped? Would she think he was rushing her again?

She stepped closer, her eyes on his. "I'll try to get over there soon." She chewed her lip. "Maybe I can get Connie to help."

"Good idea." He took a backward step. "Well, I won't keep you. I'd best get back to work. Riley will think I'm shirking."

A bright smile lit her eyes. "Oh, he knows better than that. Y'all need anything? I've got fresh cookies baked."

"I won't turn down a few of your cookies, Annabelle. That'd be plumb crazy."

He loved watching the rise of color in her cheeks.

She turned aside. "I'll be over in a few minutes, then."

"I can wait if you'd rather. I hate to put you out."

"It's no trouble. I'll bring them by."

With a nod, he turned away. As he started back across the pasture, he prayed, "Lord, I sure hope you know what you're doing. This waiting thing is wearing me down."

Willie called out. "All finished, Mr. Tom. You want to take a gander?"

Tom strode over, laying a hand on the nearest horses' bridle. "These are some fine animals."

Willie removed his hat. "Yes sir, they sure enough are. Mr. Alton, he keeps the best." He turned toward the newly tilled plot. "Garden suit you all right?"

"Looks good. Plenty of room here."

"Yes sir, it's a fine size. Me and Anthony will come over tomorrow. We'll cast the grass seed for the lawn."

"That'll be good. I read that rain is expected early

next week."

Willie swiped at his forehead before replacing his hat. "Don't know how they can guess that so well, do you?"

"Nope. Something about atmospheric pressure, cloud cover, winds, and such."

"If you say so. They right sometimes. Almost as accurate as the ache in Miss Lucy's knee." He chuckled, then touched his hat's brim. "You have a good evening, sir." He climbed into the plow's seat and took up the reins. The horses turned in unison and then set off across the yard toward the old wagon road.

Annabelle stayed long enough to drop off the cookies, along with a jug of sweet tea. She didn't want to disturb their work any longer than necessary. Shortly after settling into her favorite chair, loneliness set in with a vengeance. Maybe she should have offered to sweep up or clean something.

She leaned her head back with a sigh. They'd probably end up talking instead of working. She'd get the blame. It was just as well she returned home.

Ginger jumped into her lap and settled down. Annabelle rubbed the cat's downy head. This would have to be enough company for now. Could she endure years of living alone?

"I don't know, Ginger, what do you think?"

The cat opened one eye but didn't move.

It's possible she drifted off to sleep, Annabelle didn't know for sure, but the sound of a vehicle in the drive brought her fully awake.

The cat jumped down from her lap.

Annabelle stood to peer out the window, expecting to see Judith's car, but found Alton's truck, instead. She stepped onto the porch as Connie got out.

Annabelle smiled a welcome. "What're you doing out this time of night?"

Connie laughed. "It's only seven-thirty, Momma. We didn't get time to talk today, so I thought I'd come visit. Is that all right, or is it too late?"

Annabelle waved her hand in the air. "Oh, come on in. Can I get you a glass of tea?"

"Maybe some ice water, but I can get it." She bent to scratch behind Ginger's ears, then followed Annabelle into the kitchen. "Judith seemed troubled, is she okay? I thought maybe she'd be back by now."

"She said she might stay in town tonight. She's fine, finishing her finals. It's kept her a little stressed."

Connie slid past Annabelle to get a couple of glasses, which she filled with cold water from the icebox. "I thought it might be something more. Don't know why I'd ask you, though."

Annabelle set the remaining cookies on the table. "What do you mean by that?"

"If you know something, you'll never tell. That's a good thing, Momma. That means we can trust you with our deepest secrets." She eased into a chair, picked up a cookie, and bit into it.

Annabelle sat across from her. "Your deepest secrets, huh? Like the one you're carrying right now?"

Connie grinned. "I figured you knew. That's really why I came. Alton and I wanted to tell you earlier, but we didn't get a chance."

Annabelle covered her mouth with both hands. Not that she was surprised, but to keep herself from shouting hallelujah so loudly, she'd disturb the neighbors.

"I hope it's welcome news, Momma."

"Oh, my darling girl, it's more than welcome." She reached across the table to squeeze Connie's hand. "You're happy about it, aren't you?"

"Oh yes, Momma. Alton's about to bust. He intends to make the announcement Saturday evening." She let go of Annabelle's hand, sat back, and sipped her water.

"Well, we don't have to wonder whether he'll

make a good daddy. He's sure proved himself there." Annabelle helped herself to a cookie.

Connie beamed. "He's been wonderful. He loves Joseph like his own."

"In a way, Joseph is his own. That boy has never known another. From his birth, he's only ever seen Alton's face, known Alton's voice, and loving touch."

"You're right about that. I don't know why, but I was concerned that you might worry about this new baby."

Annabelle sat back in her chair. "Why?"

Connie shrugged. "You might worry that Alton will give preference to his own flesh and blood."

"Are you thinking he will?"

Connie shook her head slowly. "He's told me he never will. As soon as we knew this one was coming, he took the time to reassure me. He said Joseph will always be his child."

"That was good of him. I would never worry about it. I know his heart. He's a good man, loyal and true."

Connie grinned. "He really is, Momma. I love him so much sometimes."

"Hearing you say that gives me great joy, sweetheart."

After she walked Connie to the truck, Annabelle stood outside for a good while, gazing at the brightening moon. Joy threatened to overflow her heart. She almost danced a jig right there on the front lawn.

Tom sat directly across from Annabelle as they watched the filmstrip of Alton and Connie's vacation. Her expressions interested him far more than the black-and-white scenes on the pull-down screen. He tried to be inconspicuous, but she caught him and smiled.

Moments later, her attention moved to the window and she laughed.

Several dark faces pressed against the window screen. Miss Lucy's grandkids, no doubt, enjoying the movie along with the rest of them. When the final scene played out, everyone applauded. Even the three or four children outside the window.

Tom's attention returned to Annabelle's face, now wreathed by a smile that lit her eyes. What was she thinking about?

Alton stood amid the group and held out his hands. "I hope you enjoyed the scenes and weren't too bored by my constant interruptions. I believe Regina has our dessert ready if you'd like to return to the dining room. But first, Connie and I would like to thank all of you for coming tonight." He turned to take Connie's hand. She stood and moved closer. "And we would like you to be the first to hear our good news."

He put his arm around Connie. "We'll welcome another family member late summer or early fall."

Tom clapped and smiled, though he had known since Alton's visit to the drugstore. About time they shared it. He was tired of watching his tongue, though judging by the look on Annabelle's face, it was no surprise to her either. A moment later, another thought struck him. If this child called Annabelle grandmother, wouldn't that mean he'd finally be a grandpa?

Betty Thomason Owens

Chapter Eight

May 1, 1957

Annabelle flipped the calendar on another month. Hard to believe April had already ended. It was past time for a visit next door, to look at those paint chips. She'd promised Tom, but doubts crowded her mind. How did she know what colors he'd like?

She should have waited for Connie. The girl had a good eye for decor but a busy week, so Annabelle hadn't said anything to her about it.

"I reckon this is something I need to do myself." She hung her apron on a hook near the door.

She weighed Tom's house keys in her hand. Why did this jangle her nerves so? He'd asked for suggestions, not choices. If he didn't like the colors she chose, he didn't have to use them.

Tom had been at church again on Sunday. Though he'd sat in the back, and left early, she felt he was warming up to it, making progress. Perhaps one day soon, he'd sit with her, and make his feelings known to all. At first, she smiled at the thought, then she gave her head a shake. She was much too level-headed to partake of fantasy. After one more glance in the mirror, she stepped onto the porch, easing the screen door shut behind her. Such thoughts are fine for the young, but not for forty-something grandmothers.

The dirt patch that was Tom's backyard was already beginning to show signs of green as new blades of grass found their way to the sunlight. Annabelle stepped carefully to avoid the new growth, thankful that Tom had laid a path of flat rocks from the gate to the porch. That man was certainly thoughtful.

The house was silent. For some indeterminate reason, she found that sad. "Too long empty." Her words echoed in the barren interior, where she stood looking around, trying to determine the source of light in the ample front room. What color would suit it best? Tom said he intended to keep this room for company, so it would be a bit more formal. Maybe a light blue, a relaxing color, easy on the eye.

She found the paint chips right where he said they'd be, in the kitchen near the sink. Turning toward the window, she fanned them out on the counter. After placing a neat little "x" on her favorite blue, she located the notepad and pencil. She jotted down her choice for the front room. If she gave him a couple of possibilities for each room, then he could make the final decision. That might take some of the pressure off her. So, she included a second choice in her neat script.

He'd mentioned how he loved a yellow kitchen. "It's such a bright, welcoming color," he'd told her. "Long as it's not too bright. Maybe like fresh butter."

She found the perfect one and settled on it. He wouldn't need a second choice there. After the kitchen, she wandered from room to room, making similar determinations. Through their conversations, she had realized that Tom was a bit old-fashioned, but he didn't care for wallpaper. He wanted each room painted. Sensible man. That way, he could easily change the color if he wanted. She did her best to blend the hues, so no room would clash with another.

She had nearly completed the job when she heard a car door slam. Peering out the bedroom window, she saw a red and white car in the drive. Who could that be? Tom hadn't mentioned anyone coming by.

She headed to the foyer, expecting to hear a knock at any moment, but whoever it was didn't even bother, just opened the door. "Yoohoo! Anyone in here?"

Oh, Lord, no! Please, God, don't let it be. Annabelle's desperate prayers came too late.

The door swung wide, and Rosella stepped in.

Instead of her usual blue pillbox, Rosella wore a neat straw hat, trimmed with red ribbon and a couple of white daisies. The hat matched her outfit—a white blouse with daisies embroidered on the front, topping a red skirt. She had on red shoes, too.

Feeling rather frumpy in her everyday dress, Annabelle looked the woman up and down, wondering how she could always seem so put together.

Rosella eyed Annabelle. "There you are. I've been looking all over for you. Brother and I visited Tom last evening. He gave us the grand tour. You know my brother is hunting for a house. We've looked all over Trenton, and he hasn't found anything that suits him, so we were thinking, maybe he should look into building. Tom said he had done it and was almost finished." She glanced around. "Of course, it's not quite my brother's taste. He likes something a bit higher on the grand scale, and he'd have to live in town, or at least closer in than this."

Annabelle stared. The woman hadn't even taken a breath. How on earth could anyone think as fast as she was talking? Annabelle had a time keeping up.

"One thing led to another, and Tom mentioned that you were helping him choose the paint colors. So, of course, I told him I have a certificate in home decorating. So, I'm up on the trends. I can advise him and see that he doesn't make any unfortunate mistakes." She grinned.

Annabelle opened her mouth, but before she could comment, Rosella started up again.

"I wish he had asked me before he ordered those white appliances. Big mistake. I asked if he could return them, but he didn't seem interested in doing that. Pink is the ticket, or aqua. Those are the colors that are in right now. But he just stared, you know, in that way men do when they don't get what you're trying to tell them. So, here I am." She glanced around the room. "Where are those paint chips?"

Annabelle lifted the colors she held in her hand. "I've been through most of the house already."

Rosella stepped closer and took the slips of paper, lifting them toward the light. "Is this all there is?"

Annabelle nodded.

Rosella strode to the kitchen, her heels clicking on the new tiles. "It's possible you can't even get what's in vogue this far out in the sticks." She stopped a moment to toe the floor, shaking her head. "Humph. Black and white tile. Five years ago, maybe."

Annabelle liked the black and white tiles. They looked clean and cheery. She started to say so but missed the interval.

"This the pad you're using? Oh no! Not yellow. No, no, no."

"Tom likes yellow. It's the one color he asked for."

"Big mistake." She marked through the creamy yellow Annabelle had chosen. "No. Too drab. He needs something perky. Something to wake him up of a morning." She rifled through the colors. "Here you go, this will do." She wrote something on the paper, nodding all the while. "Tangerine. That'll do the trick."

"But—"

Rosella gave her a look that said, you know nothing. I'm the expert.

Annabelle pursed her lips and tried to dilute the irritation building in her chest. Being a good Christian woman, she did her best to keep the peace and return loving answers, even when it hurt.

"Oh, no! Blue will not do for a formal living room." She leveled another knowing gaze at Annabelle. "I think I'm starting to see a pattern here, hon."

Annabelle clamped her mouth shut. Would it be impolite to make some excuse and head home?

Rosella's hands went into action, as though she

was on a podium, giving a speech before hundreds of town folk, instead of one offended woman. "Now, I understand you've known Tom for a number of years, and you believe you're doing what's best by being conservative, but you have to consider, Tom's an important man in town. He's a business owner, and as such, will need a place to entertain guests. I'm quite certain he'll want his home to be a showcase. A place folks walk into and say, 'Ahh!', not, 'Oh, no.'"

Annabelle had no words. True, she had not considered Tom's place in the community, or that he would ever have such guests in his home. She figured he'd want the house comfortable, so he could relax, after a long day's work.

"No. No. No." Rosella slashed more colors. Then, she sashayed into the living room, a thoughtful look on her face. "Lilac is the ticket." She waved her tiny hand in the air. "It's practically regal." She tucked the pencil in her hair and set off at a trot. "Kelly green in the study. That's a manly color. And a deep gold for the dining room. Too bad he's so dead set against wallpaper. The dining room should have wallpaper, don't you agree? I'm sure you do. I saw wallpaper in your house. Of course, it was white and all one color throughout, but you being a widow, I suppose that was all you could manage. Nothing wrong with it."

She'd been in Annabelle's house, walking around, judging her decorating choices? Steaming, Annabelle bit down on her lower lip to keep from releasing a rant. She would not give in to her emotions. Oh, but this little woman could get on a person's last nerve.

"White in the bathroom! Oh, my goodness, gracious. We need a bold color. What on earth made that man choose white tile? At least it has that little pattern in it. Navy on the walls! That's it." She gave Annabelle a triumphant grin. "He's going to be so pleased."

Annabelle hung back. "I'm not so sure about that."

"Hah! Oh, yes, he will, you'll see—especially when—" She stopped speaking, lifted luminous eyes to Annabelle. "When he finds that perfect someone to share it with him."

Annabelle held her breath a moment. Did this woman know he was sweet on her? Had Tom mentioned it? She couldn't quite see him saying such things to strangers. Well, almost strangers. "I'm not sure. He's pretty old fashioned and set in his ways."

"The right woman can change all that." She adjusted her hat. "He's quite a catch, you know. I noticed that right off."

What was she saying? Annabelle forced herself to swallow, then breathe, then speak, "You did?"

She jotted down another color, finishing with a flourish. "There. We're done. That didn't take long. But you wait and see. I … am going to do my level best to talk him into wallpaper. A man needs a little encouragement, and I'm just the woman to do it." She fluttered her eyelashes.

A move that might work with men, but it curdled Annabelle's stomach. If she didn't get out of here fast, her temper would boil over. That would not be a good thing.

Tom's long day ended, he tidied up his desk before grabbing a sandwich and heading out the door. Along about four o'clock, he'd gotten a call from Miss Rose Ella. With great pride, she'd informed him that she had helped Annabelle choose colors for the house. "You're going to be so pleased with what we picked out."

Tom wasn't so sure. Though she had emphasized the "we", he couldn't help wondering whether she'd allowed Annabelle a say in the matter. Though small, Miss Rose Ella tended to cast a long shadow. Would Annabelle be bold enough to veto bad choices?

He climbed in the truck and turned the key in the ignition. Thinking about those colors set his teeth on edge. He trusted Annabelle, but Miss Rose Ella … kind of scared him, little as she was.

Riley was going to be late, so the house was dark when Tom arrived. Once inside, he headed straight to the kitchen, intending to look over the notes while he ate his sandwich. However, a first glance stole his appetite away.

"Tangerine?" He tossed the pad down. Not doing that. He'd told Annabelle he wanted a yellow kitchen. Had she forgotten?

He picked up the pad again. There was the tail of a "y" beneath several dark lines. Picking up the pencil, he used the eraser, but it smeared, making what was under the lines even less legible.

Then he noticed that most of the list began with something marked out. He believed those were written in Annabelle's hand. "Hah!" So, she had let the little woman overrule her choices. When he examined the paint chips, he found neat little exes on several, including one called, "Butter Yellow."

Feeling better, he unwrapped his sandwich and bit into it.

About that time, he heard Riley's car in the drive.

Riley sauntered in, a bottle of pop in one hand, a brown sack in the other. "Good, we can chow down together." He grabbed a step ladder and plopped down.

"What're you smiling at?"

Tom pushed the pad toward his cousin. "I have my colors all picked out."

Riley fumbled for the glasses in his pocket, set them on his nose, and squinted at the list. His brow furrowed. "You've done had too many of them ham sandwiches, Tom." He pushed the pad away as though it repulsed him. "I liked you better as an old bachelor. Gave me hope. I was looking forward to having a place to come cool my heels, away from all the females. You're gonna ruin that."

Tom grinned. "It's only paint, Riley."

"Only paint now. Next thing you know, it'll be flowered couches and frilly curtains. You wait and see." He pointed to the list. "This is only the beginning."

Unable to relax, Annabelle tossed and turned in her bed. She should have told the woman what she really thought about those colors. Now it was too late.

She'd half expected Tom to come over. Surely, he'd know those weren't her ideas? Then another thought struck her. Maybe he liked the choices. Maybe he knew whose ideas they were, and he liked that, too.

She sat up in bed. Could be she'd waited too long. He'd already transferred his affections to a more willing party.

"More willing!" She was practically moving into that house already, planning what wallpaper she wanted in the dining room.

Wide awake, Annabelle got up, threw on her robe, and found her slippers. Padding into the kitchen, she filled a glass with water. After an exasperated breath, she took a drink. On the way back to bed, she stopped to peer out the window. Was it only this morning, she'd been so happy? She'd entertained thoughts of living in that house next door? Mercy be, Annabelle. When are you going to learn?

All these emotional ups and downs reminded her of a roller-coaster. She didn't like it one bit. She craved peace and tranquility.

It was no use going back to bed to toss and turn some more. She plopped down in her rocker and gave it a push, working off the frustration. What she needed was something to do. A way to keep busy now that her house was empty. She'd gotten her garden planted, given the hen house a good clean out. There'd be a lull until the garden produced enough to put up.

Judith had already gone back to school. Probably longing to see that fella. Thoughts of her calmed

Annabelle's nerves a little. That precious girl was so dead set against becoming a preacher's wife, she'd probably end up as one. She'd make a good one, too. She was a hard worker, and stubborn as a mule. Annabelle smiled. That was a good combination for the clergy.

Two chimes of the clock made her sit up straight. How had an hour passed so quickly? She must have drifted off. But at least her heart felt lighter as she started back to bed. That is until she passed the window, where something caught her eye.

Away over the fields to the north—was it a house afire? She looked harder, trying to discern the direction. Hard to tell in the darkness.

"Lord, I pray for the safety of all those involved." She shook her head as memories surfaced of her childhood when a nocturnal fire could mean death to all those living in the house. Then another memory crept in, niggling at her heart. Sometimes those night fires had been set.

Surely, those days had passed. There hadn't been an incident in nearly two years.

Betty Thomason Owens

Chapter Nine

May 2, 1957

The pharmacy's back door opened. A young man in a black and gold letterman jacket entered. Tom nodded a greeting. "Afternoon, Fred. How was school today?"

Fred hung the jacket on a hook and made his way to the counter. "Not bad. Y'all hear about the fire?"

Tom paused, giving his full attention to the young man. "What fire?"

The front door jangled. Fred took one look and headed for the soda fountain where he put on his apron and began to clean up.

A moment later, Stu stepped up to Tom's desk. It was rumored Stuart Fox led the local "racist" activities, which led Tom to believe the fire Fred was fixing to tell him about was not accidental.

"What can I do for you, Stu?"

"Doc called in a script for Ma?"

Tom nodded. "He did. I'll get it for you." He turned to a shelf where several small, white bags waited for pick up, and chose one. "Here it is. You want it on her account?"

Stu cleared his throat. "No, I'll pay for it." He pulled out his wallet and removed a couple of bills.

Tom handed him the change.

The bag in hand, Stu turned away. He tipped his hat to Bo and Fred on the way out the door.

Of course, the conversation resumed at once. Fred placed his long-fingered hands on the counter and leaned forward. "It was all over school today. The Dawsons' house burned to the ground. They lost everything. Only Hero and his mama were inside at the time, but they got out. They're staying in town."

Tom knew where they must be staying. Ironic, really.

Bo faced Tom. "Reckon they're staying at the Wade mansion? Wouldn't that be something?"

"They are," Fred said, giving the counter a good swabbing. "Miz Marla Wade took them in. Drove over there and picked them up herself, is what I heard."

Tom thumbed through his sales tickets. "Ought not to listen to gossip, son."

Fred rinsed the towel and wrung it out. "Ain't

gossip, it's gospel. Ben Clark lives down the road from Dawson's, he saw that light blue convertible drive by, and them in it. No mistaking that car. No, sir."

After a slow intake of breath, Tom placed the stack of tickets in his drawer and closed it. "Well, good for Miz Wade, then. Edris would've been beside herself, worrying about her daughter and grandson."

Bo humphed.

Tom eyed the man. "Keep a civil tongue in front of the boy, Bo." He could guess what Bo was about to say. It, sure enough, would be gossip. No gospel to that at all. The scuttlebutt had been thick the last few days. Hero's daddy had mouthed off to the wrong folks and lost his job at the hosiery mill. He'd been unable to find work anywhere because word got around too fast. Now his house had burned to the ground. That was not happenstance or bad luck. "I'd be willing to place a wager on that," Tom muttered as he closed a file drawer.

Fred poured more coffee in Bo's cup. "Everybody already knows, sir. It's the talk at school, too. They're all pretty upset over it because we all like Hero."

"Everybody loves that boy." Bo's head bobbed in agreement.

Tom couldn't help but smile. It was true. Hero's upbeat attitude and obvious joy over being alive was downright contagious. Tom had to wonder. How would this incident affect his outlook?

Annabelle had barely finished her coffee when she heard a vehicle in the drive. "Who could that be at this hour?"

She stepped to the open door and peered through the screen. Alton's truck. But not Alton. Connie opened the door and hopped down, a wide smile of greeting on her beautiful face.

Annabelle opened the screen door and walked out. "What are you doing here this early of a morning?"

"Aren't you happy to see me?" Connie climbed the steps.

Annabelle welcomed her with a hug. "I'm always happy to see you."

"I'm headed to town, running errands, and thought you might like to ride along."

"You thought right. Sounds like fun. Give me a minute to make myself presentable."

"Only a minute?"

Annabelle giggled. "Well, it might take a little longer."

Connie followed her into the house. She sat on the

bed while Annabelle changed her dress and combed her hair. Annabelle glanced at Connie in the mirror. "What all do you have to do today?"

As usual, Ginger had found her way into Connie's lap.

"First, I need to drive over to Milan to pick up some kind of special wrench from Allen's Machine Shop. On the way back, I have a list of groceries to buy, a deposit to put in the bank, and a payment to drop off."

"Sounds like a busy day. It's been a long time since I've been to Milan. It'll be nice to see what's going on over there." She set her brush down, chose a hat, and then faced Connie. "Am I presentable?"

"Shiny as a new penny."

Annabelle laughed. That was how Ray used to respond. She hadn't thought of that in a long while.

Connie glanced around. "Where are all the pictures?"

"I figured it was time I learned to live on my own, without Ray and the boys looking on."

Connie slipped her arm around Annabelle's waist. "I know it's been hard for you, Momma."

"It gets better every day." She patted Connie's cheek, then stepped away to close the back door and pick up her purse. "Shall we go?"

Settled in the truck, Annabelle looked at Connie. "Did y'all see that fire last night?"

Connie sighed. "Alton said it was Hero's house."

"Dawsons'? Is everybody all right?"

Connie nodded. "The house was a total loss. Hero and his mother are staying with Edris." She gripped the steering wheel and shook her head. "Oh, Momma, it's been so quiet, I hoped all that was behind us."

"Not much chance of it, outside of a miracle. Especially now, with all this desegregation talk going on. I see trouble ahead." Annabelle felt Connie's gaze before she turned to look at her. "What?"

"It's not like you to be negative."

Annabelle examined her fingernails. "This has me worried, is all."

"Alton said it was Lester's fault. He lost his temper at the wrong time. That's the shame of it. A man of color isn't free to express his opinion, even if it's right."

Annabelle laid her hand on Connie's forearm. "Be careful, Pumpkin."

"I know. I'm not free to say what I think, either."

"It's all right talking to me but take care who hears you."

Connie's stern expression kept Annabelle quiet the

rest of the way. The familiar sights soon grabbed her attention. There was a time, she'd known most of the folks who lived along this road. Some were kin, others were friends she'd met along the way. Like most places, however, the years had brought change.

A new subdivision sprawled over former cornfields outside Milan. "We used to drive over here to go to the movie." She hoped to brighten Connie's expression with her memories. Connie loved to hear the stories from Annabelle's youth. "One of my friends had a crush on an usher. He played football at Milan High School."

Connie smiled as she slowed to cross the railroad tracks. Milan had a lot of railroad tracks. Two blocks in, she down-shifted before pulling into a parking spot near the machine shop.

The owner of the shop sent his son out with the wrench. "That thing weighs a good bit," the owner told them, wiping his hands on a filthy rag before accepting the money Connie handed over. "You tell Mr. Alton hello for me."

A sudden gust nearly took Annabelle's hat right off her head. She made a grab for it. "We'll do that."

Connie thanked the man's son, then climbed into the truck. "One down. That was quick."

Annabelle eyed the horizon. "It's clouding up,

looking like rain. I hope we finish our errands before it decides to come a downpour."

"Maybe it'll blow over, or at least hold off until evening." Connie backed the truck around and drove out.

Annabelle held on as they clattered across the tracks. "Farmer's Almanac says it's going to be a stormy spring, tornadoes likely. I don't like the sound of that."

"If a tornado is anything like a hurricane, I'm in no hurry to meet one."

"At least y'all have a good cellar over at Sutter's. All I have is that hole in the hill they call a storm shelter. Gives me the creeps. We used to send the men on ahead to clear it out first."

"Clear what out?"

Annabelle shook off a tremor. "Spiders. Snakes."

Connie grimaced. "Eww. Why don't they keep it cleaned out this time of year?"

"Well, I reckon they used to. I haven't seen a soul near there, though. I doubt anyone's used it in years."

"Didn't Tom build a cellar? You ought to go over there in bad weather."

Annabelle nodded. She had already considered going to Tom's. She didn't reckon he'd mind. "It would be handy. Maybe no critters waiting inside."

At least the dicey weather kept the crowds down at the five-and-dime. Annabelle fingered a cute apron. She liked it, but a quarter dollar was a bit pricey. She could easily create a copy with scraps of material she had at home. After Connie found what she needed and made her purchase, they crossed the street to the pharmacy.

Though the girl tried to suppress the impish grin on her face, Annabelle saw right through it. She had the nerve to blame it on the baby. "I hope you don't mind, Momma. The little one has a craving for a chocolate milkshake."

"Uh-huh." Annabelle stayed close behind Connie, hoping to sneak in without being seen, but she needn't have bothered. Tom wasn't there. At least, not out in the open. She pressed her lips together. The place seemed empty without him.

Bo sat in the fountain area. Annabelle nodded to him as she chose a spot and took a seat. She loved the bright red stool cushions. They lent merriment to the atmosphere, or maybe it was the promise of a special treat, the deliciously cold milkshakes and root beer floats.

The young man behind the counter smiled at them.

"What'll it be today, ladies?"

After placing her order, Annabelle allowed her gaze to wander. Tom and Riley had fashioned the soda fountain after the one over in Milan, which had been the first in the area. It wasn't long before this became a hub of activity in town. Attorneys and city officials stopped in for lunch, along with folks from all over the county. Tom had made another brilliant business decision. Annabelle smiled as she breathed in the heady aroma of chocolate and malt.

Halfway through their refreshments, a door opened in the back. Tom removed his jacket and hung it on a peg before donning his lab coat.

Annabelle couldn't resist watching him. She loved how his eyes lit when he noticed her.

"Well, this is a surprise. What brings you two lovely ladies into town on this blustery morning?" He leaned an elbow on the counter and looked from one to the other.

Connie looked at Annabelle. "We're out running errands. So, of course, we needed to treat ourselves."

His hazel eyes twinkled. "Well, you're in luck, because milkshakes are on the house today."

Bo lifted his cup. "For everyone, or only the ladies?" He cackled, then sipped his coffee.

Chuckling softly, Tom shook his head. "I've been

over at the high school. I'm sponsoring a float for the Strawberry Festival parade this year."

"Really?" Annabelle set her spoon down and looked at Connie. "We ought to go to that. I've never been."

Tom pushed his hands into his pockets. "I won't be able to make the parade since it's on Thursday, but I'd love to go to the carnival." He leaned closer, his eyes on Annabelle. "I hope you'll be my guest this year—at the carnival, that is."

Connie outright grinned.

Drawing her eyes away from her daughter-in-law's face, Annabelle concentrated on her chocolate shake and keeping her trembling fingers out of sight. There was no denying the feeling in her heart. She had fallen in love with this man.

Connie touched Annabelle's hand. "That sounds really nice, Momma. Maybe Alton and I can go, too. We can make it a family outing."

Connie to the rescue. Annabelle eased out a breath before lifting her gaze to Tom's. "I'd like that."

The doorbell tinkled, breaking the spell. Tom straightened, as the light faded from his eyes.

Annabelle turned to see who had entered, but she needn't have bothered. The voice that rang out identified its owner before Annabelle's gaze found the woman.

"There you are, Tom! I tried to get your attention as we were leaving the high school. I have a suggestion to make regarding the design of that float."

Annabelle turned back to Tom in time to witness the change in his expression as he pushed his lips into a fake smile. She knew that look. It was so satisfying.

"Hello, Annabelle, Miss Connie … Bo." Rose Ella set her pocketbook on a nearby stool but made no attempt to climb aboard. The stools were a bit high for her.

Annabelle slurped up the dredges of her shake.

Connie giggled, then poked Annabelle's arm. "Time for us to go. We still need to get the groceries."

Tom stepped near to help Connie down from the stool.

She pressed a quick kiss to his cheek. "Thank you, Tom."

Annabelle gave him an apologetic glance before she pivoted toward the newcomer. "Nice to see you, Rosella." She loved the slight irritation caused by the abuse of the woman's name.

Rose Ella's lips twitched with the need to correct her, but she fake-smiled instead. "Y'all have a good day." Her compliant dismissal spoke volumes. She wanted them out of her way.

"Talk to you later, Annabelle," Tom said. "Always nice to see you, Miss Connie."

The doorbell tinkled again as Annabelle followed Connie out, but she didn't miss Rose Ella's parting shot, spoken loudly enough for all to hear. "I'm so looking forward to the Strawberry Festival! It's going to be such fun, especially knowing I've had a small part in the planning of it."

Outside, Connie took hold of Annabelle's hand. "Deep breath, Momma. I know that woman riles you, but you're an overcomer."

Annabelle sighed. Was it so obvious, her dislike of that woman? Shameful, really. "I'm sorry, Pumpkin. I shouldn't let her get to me."

"No, you shouldn't. She's the clanging cymbal, and you're the love, Momma. Remember that."

Betty Thomason Owens

Chapter Ten

May 4, 1957

Jensen's car in the drive at Sutter's with no Jensen in view meant he was inside the house.

Annabelle's steps faltered as she started up the slope toward the back porch. What life-changing event had prompted such a visit? Closer to the house, she noticed Samson sitting at the back door, his ears alert. The dog barely acknowledged her approach.

Gripping her basket of freshly baked cookies, Annabelle trod past the old pump. When the screen door burst open, the dog jumped and yipped in excitement.

A young, blond-headed boy stepped out on the porch, dodging the dancing hound. "Aunt Annabelle!"

Chase Wade's bright-eyed greeting sent warmth clean through Annabelle. She couldn't hold back the laughter as the lanky twelve-year-old and the dog bounded off the porch toward her.

"Land sakes look how you've grown. You'll soon tower over me." She held the basket aloft as Samson bulleted past, made a large circle, then headed back.

Chase's laughter echoed in the backyard. "Look out, Aunt Annabelle." He took hold of the basket and sniffed the contents. "Molasses cookies? My favorite!"

Annabelle beamed as Samson sped past, barely missing the porch steps when he arced into another circle.

Annabelle hadn't seen the dog this excited in quite some time. Maybe the last time Chase was here.

Basket in hand, Chase accompanied her to the door, leaving a crestfallen dog on the back step.

Inside the overly warm kitchen, Regina grinned as she took the basket. "I can guess what that is. Come on in, Miss Annabelle. Get you a glass of iced tea before you join the folks in the front parlor. They's a waitin' in there for me to announce dinner. You can tell 'em it's about ready."

Chase set the basket down, then stepped back outside where Annabelle noticed him darting about the yard with Samson.

She helped herself to a glass of tea before heading toward the wide central hall, and the door to the formal front room. Low voices, followed by a spate of laughter reassured her all was well. When she paused in the open doorway, Jensen and Alton stood to greet her.

"Good afternoon, Annabelle." Jensen's polite greeting always set her teeth on edge. She wanted to trust her elder cousin, believe he was on the up and up now that he was a Councilman, but he'd yet to prove himself. A twinge of familiar guilt stung her conscience. It was wrong of her to hold the past against him, especially in the face of such a kind greeting. She forced her lips into a curve. "Afternoon, Jensen." Her eyes moved past him to his attractive wife, perched on the edge of the tufted green sofa. "Marla, good to see you."

She gave a barely perceptible nod. "Annabelle."

She'd been so preoccupied with Jensen and Marla, Annabelle hadn't noticed Connie's approach.

"Come sit by me, Momma." She led the way to a wing-backed love seat near the empty hearth.

Alton dropped a kiss on Annabelle's cheek. "I'm glad you could join us." He lowered his wiry frame onto a velvet-covered dining chair near his mother.

"Wouldn't miss it for the world." Annabelle gave her attention to Lillian. "Regina said dinner's almost ready."

"Good." Lillian's bright smile sent another guilty pang deep into Annabelle's heart.

Annabelle glanced from one face to another, wondering what had brought on this momentous event. Both Wade brothers in the same room, smiling and occasionally laughing. Before she could speak, a low thump overhead preceded Joseph's loud laughter, followed by running footsteps.

Connie leaned close. "Landers is upstairs with Joseph."

"Ah." Annabelle sipped her tea. Chase's younger brother, Landers, must be about eight years old by now. She'd not seen him lately, other than sitting beside Marla at church. She reckoned he'd be some taller, too.

The door at the end of the parlor swung open. In her most polite voice, Regina announced, "Dinner's on."

"Thank you, Regina." Lillian stood, then allowed Alton to lead her from the room.

Jensen followed with Marla, then Annabelle and Connie.

Annabelle almost envied the children, who ate their dinner in the kitchen. It would be far more comfortable in there, even with the heat of the stove.

She usually preferred the beautifully appointed

dining room, but today, not so much.

Jensen dominated the conversation. Of course, it was all about politics. He dropped several important names as he told of his recent trip to Nashville, where he'd hobnobbed with state legislators and even the governor himself.

Annabelle eyed him. Jensen was on his way up. How far, and to what end? She was quite certain that freckled, balding pate held a plan. Though her conscience plagued her, she couldn't let go of the past and feel easy about it all.

"Annabelle, I heard you've been keeping time with Tom Franklin."

Her jaw went slack as she gazed at Jensen.

Connie barely concealed a smile.

Alton cleared his throat. "He is about to be her next-door neighbor, so of course, they've been seen together. You know how folks talk."

"More than talk, I'll wager." Jensen dabbed the corners of his mouth with a napkin. His eyes danced with mischief. "My hat's off to you, Annabelle. He's a fine man, our town pharmacist."

If she hadn't been so hungry, she'd consider excusing herself and setting off for home. Instead, she chose to redirect. "What do you think of the newcomers, Jensen?"

He sat back. "McCoys, you mean? He's a good man. Bringing jobs to our town. His sister seems keen to involve herself in municipal interests." He glanced toward Marla. "Though my wife chafes at the idea."

Marla didn't even flinch. "That woman talks too much."

Annabelle wanted to laugh out loud at Marla's most unexpected remark.

"Hah! My thoughts, exactly." Lillian clapped her hands. "But you have to admit, she'll keep the meetings lively."

Jensen chuckled. "Yes, she will."

"Unfortunately," Marla continued in an even voice, "she has already rankled the president of the WMU."

Lillian widened her eyes at Annabelle. "What did she do?"

Marla clamped her jaw shut.

"She's a notorious flirt." Jensen set down his fork. "Alton let's go see that new heifer you were telling me about earlier."

Lillian folded her napkin. "Anyone like to join me on the front porch?"

Marla waited for Connie. "I want to talk to you about Hero's lessons." With a glance toward Annabelle, Connie led the way to the front door.

When Annabelle stood and brushed at her skirt, she detected a rough spot. Moving into better light, she found an ugly gravy stain on the front of her second-best dress.

"Oh, dear." Lillian brushed at it with her napkin. "Go get Regina to help. She's wonderful at getting out the odd stain."

Regina reduced it to a barely visible spot with a bit of dish detergent and some baking soda.

By the time she joined the others, Annabelle found Connie seated on the double swing next to Marla, who spoke to her in a low, even voice.

Lillian patted the seat next to her. "Sit here, Annabelle. We've a good view of the children playing. I enjoy watching them toss that football back and forth. Chase has some skill, I think."

Annabelle sat, but her attention stayed with Connie and Marla, though she couldn't hear much of what was said. She leaned her head back and tried to relax. If she was supposed to know, Connie would tell her later.

Beside her, Lillian rocked and hummed.

Annabelle noted the peaceful contentment on her friend's face. What a blessing to see, after all she'd been through with her pig-headed elder son. Was it over? Would he keep to the straight and narrow this time?

When Marla sat forward, her voice carried. "You tell Miss Lucy I said it was all right."

Connie glanced at Annabelle, then back at Marla. "Please keep us informed."

"Oh, he'll still be out for his lessons, even if I have to bring him myself." Marla glanced at her watch. "Where are those men? We need to get home."

Lillian stirred. "We haven't had our cake yet. I'll go get Regina."

Marla stood. "I'll go find the guys. As soon as we've had dessert, we need to go." She set off at a clip around the corner of the porch.

Connie leaned back and gave the swing a slight push. "What a wonderful Saturday afternoon we've had."

"I take it whatever you two were talking about is good news, then?"

"Oddly, yes. I'll tell you all about it later."

"Won't you stay and watch the *Grand Ole Opry* with us, Annabelle?" Anticipating a negative answer, Alton reached for his hat.

"I've got to get on home, take care of the chickens. I can listen on the radio." She took the covered plate

Connie held out and followed Alton outside. She was about to step up into Alton's truck when Tom pulled in the driveway.

He leaned out the window. "You headed home, Annabelle? I can take you." He opened the door and got out.

Annabelle's heart started that silly thumping again. Her mouth had gone plumb dry.

Alton stepped over to clasp Tom's outstretched hand. "That'd be mighty neighborly of you."

Tom looked at Annabelle.

She managed to form words. "I reckon that'd be all right."

He led the way around to the passenger side and helped her into the seat.

Alton strolled to the back steps. "I tried to talk her into staying to watch the Opry, but she insisted the chickens needed tending."

Tom pushed the door closed. "Good thing I happened along then. Wouldn't want you to miss the opening number."

Connie stepped outside. "We've got plenty of leftovers if you're hungry, Tom."

He patted his middle. "I just left Saturday dinner at Thelma and Riley's."

Connie laughed. "Oh, well, never mind."

Annabelle's tummy twisted into a knot as Tom turned the truck around and headed down the drive. It would only take about five minutes to reach her house. She examined the face of the man beside her. Though she'd known him since they were children, he sometimes seemed like a stranger.

Probably sensing her eyes on him, he turned to look at her. His expression relaxed into a grin. "What?"

Should she tell him what she was thinking? That she didn't really know him at all? Or, wait and let the pieces fall where they may? The kink in her stomach twisted tighter. Maybe talking would help. "I was thinking how little I really know about you."

He sent another glance in her direction. This one held a question. At least she thought it did.

"I hope to remedy that situation, Annabelle, starting next Saturday." He let loose another grin as he pulled into her drive. "That's the whole purpose of dating a person, isn't it? Getting to know them?"

He turned off the engine but didn't get out, just sat there, holding her captive in a smoldering gaze.

Had Ray ever looked at her like that? She reckoned he had but couldn't remember when.

Tom gave a low chuckle before opening the door and hopping out. She watched as he rounded the front of the truck. After a slow intake of breath, she eased herself off the seat, taking care where she set her foot. It was a delicate operation, climbing down from the truck. She almost wished she could wear pedal-pushers or blue jeans like Connie and Judith. She needn't have worried, though. Tom was a perfect gentleman. He took her hand and helped her down while keeping his eyes averted.

Should she invite him in? It was getting late. What would Rose Ella do? Why was she thinking about Rose Ella?

Tom cleared his throat. "I hope you don't mind if I rush off. I've got to get over to the house to check on a few things, then head back to town." He held the screen while she opened the front door. "Otherwise, I'd stay and help you with those chickens."

She tried to picture him in the hen house. "Oh, that's fine, Tom. I'm grateful for the ride."

He turned back before stepping off the porch. "I reckon I'll be at church in the morning." He gave her a sideways grin. "At the back, of course."

Annabelle couldn't stop the smile. "One of these days we may meet halfway."

He laughed outright.

She loved the sound of it, tucked it away in her heart to remember after he left.

Smoothing his hair back, he looked down at her.

For a moment, Annabelle feared he may kiss her. Was she ready for that? Land sakes!

"We may do that one day, Annabelle." He turned to go, leaving her mulling over his words.

Her throat dried up again. Her tongue felt like sandpaper. Do what? Had he read her mind? Had he guessed she was half expecting him to kiss her? Her brain kicked into gear about the time he put the truck in reverse and backed away.

As he passed by on the road, she raised her hand in farewell before stepping inside the house. "Of course, he was talking about meeting halfway in the church, you ninny!" She hung her hat on a hook. She set her purse on the table, changed her shoes, and tied on her apron. The chickens needed attention and she needed to clear her silly head.

Tom chuckled as he parked the truck in his driveway. A few quick steps carried him to the porch where a soft light attracted moths. Annabelle's expression followed him inside. She thought he was going to kiss her, he'd almost bet on it. Another chuckle rumbled in his chest. He'd wanted to. He could have, but it wasn't time—not yet.

The fragrance of fresh paint and new wood mingled with another scent. What was it? He wandered through the empty rooms, flipping the switches, bathing the entire house in warm light. Last of all, he entered the kitchen. There on the counter sat a bouquet of buttercups and lilac. He pursed his lips. He'd locked all the doors before leaving last night. Riley and Annabelle were the only ones with a key. Riley certainly wouldn't bring flowers, so that left Annabelle.

Tom glanced around the room. Had she noticed the paint he'd settled on? He'd wanted to show her, see whether she liked it. Annabelle was too polite to say if she didn't like something, but her expressions were easy to read.

He fingered the blooms. A row of bright yellow daffodils lined her front yard, but he'd never noticed a lilac bush. Had they come from Sutter's? Maybe Connie brought them to Annabelle.

He walked to the window, looking out into gathering darkness. Oh, well. So much for his surprise. He switched off the lights, so he could watch the sunset. It was a beautiful night with a few clouds gathered on the horizon. Clouds were what made a sunset truly glorious. They picked up and reflected the sun's parting rays.

If Annabelle wasn't pleased with the colors he'd

used, she could change them down the road. It didn't really matter to him one way or the other, as long as she was happy. He wanted more than anything to make her happy.

He stepped away from the window. On a whim, he crossed the kitchen to check the back door. He wasn't sure why. It was always locked. But tonight, it wasn't. Pulling it open, he stepped out onto the concrete slab porch and looked toward the spot where he hoped to build a barbecue pit one day. Maybe later this summer or fall. He and Annabelle could invite all their friends and family.

Somewhere over the fields, a cow bellowed for its calf. The sound echoed in the valley, the only significant noise. All was quiet in between. One of the main things he liked about living out here. Back inside, he closed the door and turned the lock, still puzzling over how it had come to be open.

Most folks out this way didn't even lock their doors. He'd never bothered in the old house. But he didn't want anyone coming in here while it stood empty. He and Riley had worked too hard. Those materials were dear. He'd spent most of his savings building this house.

Walking through the other rooms, he found nothing amiss. He shut off all the lights, then let himself out the front door, locking it behind him.

He'd half a mind to stop back by Annabelle's, ask her right out if she'd come in the house and brought the flowers. Had she left the back door unlocked, intending to return, then been distracted? But she'd said nothing about bringing the flowers.

Standing beside his truck, he could hear her singing out back. Her voice carried in the yard as she tended her chickens. He smiled. What did it matter? No harm done. Knowing Annabelle—and he knew her well—if she didn't like the paint he chose, she'd never say so. She'd respect his choice. That was one of the things he admired most about her.

Thelma wouldn't let it go. She harped and complained until Riley did whatever it was she wanted. Rose Ella McCoy wouldn't leave it alone, either. That woman would march right in there and—no—she'd pick up the phone, find someone to come out and repaint. That's what she'd do. She was all about issuing orders. She liked to say she was part of things and making it happen when all she was really doing was supervising.

Both ladies had their charms. Thelma could cook like nobody's business. Rose Ella, well, she could sing and play piano. Truth be told, she was good at barking orders. But neither of them measured up to Annabelle.

She was his type, all the way. She had faults, but he could overlook most of those for all the good things that tipped the scale in her favor.

The final glow of the sunset filled his rear-view mirror as he headed toward Trenton. His heart held a warm glow, too, as he thought of the woman he hoped to marry soon. He could easily imagine her occupying that house. Welcoming him from a busy day at the pharmacy. Their home filled with the wonderful aromas of her cooking and the sound of her voice singing a hymn. It couldn't come soon enough for Tom.

Chapter Eleven
May 5, 1957

Annabelle's heart beat faster. Tom sat on the far end of the back pew, where he could plainly see her. If she turned, she could see him, too. She was not about to move and bring unwanted attention. Connie slipped past to wedge herself between Annabelle and Alton. Lillian sat on the other side of Alton this morning. Easy enough to guess why. No doubt, Lillian hoped if Tom saw Annabelle sitting on the end of the row, he'd be tempted to sit beside her.

One day, maybe, but not today. He'd said as much last night.

A hush fell over the congregation as Rose Ella took her seat at the piano. With great exaggeration, she launched into the doxology. The woman liked to showcase her talent. She did at least have talent to show, Annabelle had to give her that. She appreciated a good pianist at the lead. Made it easier to sing. Annabelle did love to sing.

After the service ended and everyone filed toward the door, Connie came to stand beside her. "You're awfully quiet this morning, Momma. Are you feeling all right?"

"I'm fine." She eyed the younger woman, taking in the glow of her complexion. "How are you feeling?"

Connie hooked her arm in Annabelle's. "Better than fine. Not so much nausea with this one."

Annabelle kept her voice low to match Connie's since folks didn't speak of such things in public. "It was like that with me too. I hardly noticed I was carrying, except for swelling up, of course."

Connie snickered. "You're so funny." She patted Annabelle's hand as they walked down the church steps, where they were joined by Alton, holding Joseph.

Alton grinned at Annabelle. "I thought for sure this was going to be the morning."

She looked at him. "For what?"

He side-stepped her question as he led the way to the car, where Lillian waited. After he set Joseph on the back seat, he held the door for Annabelle. "Matter of fact, I lost a bet."

Lillian chortled, shaking her head. "So did I."

Frowning, Annabelle surveyed their faces. She could guess what they'd bet on. "Who won?"

Connie giggled. "I did." She slid into the front seat. Annabelle got in back with Lillian. Joseph plopped himself between them and commenced driving a toy truck over both their laps, complete with sound effects.

Connie turned in her seat 'til she was facing Annabelle. "I knew he wasn't ready. Not yet. But it won't be much longer."

Annabelle looked out the window as Alton pulled into the street to begin their homeward journey. "Good to know. I hope y'all find something to occupy your thoughts in the meantime."

Annabelle figured it was going to be a long week. Whenever she had something coming up, something she looked forward to, or even a thing she dreaded, it seemed like time dragged its feet. Then, when the thing happened and she was in the midst of it, time flew. It was over almost before it began.

She hoped her date with Tom didn't end too quickly. She wanted it to last, so she could savor the moment, pay attention to him. Maybe she really would get to know him a little better, as he had predicted.

But what was she going to wear? That question plagued her so much, she even discussed it with the chickens. They had no opinion, of course.

Maybe she should have ordered one of those pretty dresses in the *Sears* catalog. She'd thumbed through the pages numerous times, even dreamed of herself in one of them. The pretty blue one with the little yellow flowers. She was partial to the color. Ray had always liked her in blue. Said it set off her eyes and made her cheeks glow. But, how would he feel about her wearing blue for another man?

She wiped that thought from her mind. The last few weeks, she'd tried hard to keep her thoughts away from the past, looking to the future. How could she hope to move forward, if she was ever looking back?

Well, it was too late to order in a dress, but maybe she could fix one of her old ones. Make it look new again. Her feet seemed weighted with lead as she trudged the path back to the house from the chicken coop. If she was to marry Tom, she'd need some new clothes. Rose Ella had called him a successful businessman. As such, his wife should look the part.

After slipping off her dirty work shoes, she found her house slippers and padded into the kitchen. She carefully moved the eggs from her apron pockets to the bowl on the table, then washed her hands at the sink.

While it was foremost in her mind, she went to the chifforobe in the spare bedroom to look through her older dresses. There was a black dress with a short-sleeved jacket she'd worn to the funeral. That one, she hoped never to wear again. Two others, both shirtwaists with gathered skirts, had seen better days. Like everything else she owned. Why had she waited so long to freshen her wardrobe?

As she closed the door, her gaze caught on another hanger behind the black dress. She pushed the others aside to find a navy-blue skirt, long forgotten. She pulled it out and looked it over. It seemed fine, so she tried it on. It fit better than it had when she bought it. She examined her image in the mirror. "I guess I've lost a few pounds."

If she could find a suitable blouse, she'd have an outfit to wear come Saturday.

She found three suitable choices among her blouses. Already, her heart felt lighter.

Halfway through the week, Annabelle walked over to Sutter's. She'd cleaned her house, done laundry, and worked in the garden. With too much week left until the parade, and then the date with Tom, she was feeling antsy. A nervous tummy wouldn't even let her eat properly.

The welcoming warmth of her family at Sutter's soon lifted her heart. After a refreshing glass of iced tea, Connie suggested a stroll in the garden.

"Come see the progress I've made with the flowers, Momma." Her expression triggered Annabelle's curiosity.

She wasted no time following the younger woman out to the garden path. Alton had the flower beds installed before his marriage to Connie. With his wife's constant attention and expert planning, it had become a place of serene beauty. A fitting tribute to the paradise where she'd grown up.

Walking arm-in-arm along the path, Connie related her conversation with Marla. "I wanted to know why she was so interested in Hero's welfare. I thought I'd offended her at first. Then I realized she was hiding her feelings from me." Connie paused and gave Annabelle's arm a light squeeze. "Momma, she actually swiped away a tear."

"My goodness. You must've touched a nerve." Annabelle had never seen Marla exhibit any emotion, except irritation and anger. And maybe annoyance. All three of those were closely related.

Connie looked down. "I suppose I did." After a

moment, she continued. "Marla said there was a deep attachment between herself and Hero and Livia. She refused to go into detail, just said she'd let Miss Lucy tell me. She said how she knows you and I talk about everything, so she hoped I'd feel free to share it with you." She looked at Annabelle. "Is that not odd?"

"It is odd." Annabelle couldn't fathom it.

"So, I asked Miss Lucy to stop by on her way home from the field." They had reached a well-shaded area near the center of the garden, where a couple of wrought-iron benches faced a small fountain and birdbath surrounded by roses. "I'm curious to know what she has to say about what Marla told me. Or rather, what Marla didn't say. Why didn't she tell me herself?"

Annabelle shielded her eyes from the sun as she looked out over the yard to see Miss Lucy trudging toward them. "I reckon we're about to find out." After greeting the elderly woman, Annabelle sat down. This was not her conversation, but she wanted to hear whatever may be coming.

Miss Lucy refused Connie's offer of water. "I'm flap-jawed she would want to tell anyone after she swore me to secrecy all those years ago."

Connie perched on the edge of the bench next to Annabelle. "I think it's because Hero's leaving. For some reason, Marla wants me to understand the situation."

Miss Lucy shook her head. "Well, I know it must be true, or you wouldn't ask." She bent to examine a bud on a nearby hibiscus. "Looks like it's gonna bloom early this year. It shore was purty. Never seen anything like it befo'. Too bad it doesn't have a scent, though. I sure do love the smell of summer blooms." A sigh escaped her lips as she sank onto the bench across from Connie and Annabelle.

For a few quiet moments, no one spoke. Though it tried her patience somewhat, Annabelle held her tongue. She had learned from experience, when Miss Lucy contemplated something, she could not be rushed.

The older woman stirred, then fixed her eyes on the fountain. "It was some years ago. I had spent a day and a night with Edris's girl, Livia Dawson. She was in a bad way." Miss Lucy's eyes reflected deep sorrow as she seemed to relive the moment. "One of the hardest I've seen. Baby was born dead—a puny little boy— never took a bref." She sighed again and used the hem of her shirt to mop her brow.

"I was still cleaning up from it when my boy, Orton, come a runnin'. He said as Miz Marla Wade needed me right away. Said I was to get over to the ole Bruster shack by the river." Her frowning gaze settled on Connie. "I couldn't plumb the reasoning. Why was Miz Marla in a place like that? I'd heard there was a squatter in there, so I figured must be somebody needed help." She set a gnarly hand on Annabelle's knee and leaned forward. "So, you can imagine my surprise, Miss Annabelle, when I laid eyes on the squatter."

She removed her hand and sat back. "It was Melva Bennett, Miz Marla's sister, and she was 'bout ready to pop. It wasn't long after I got there, she had the baby. It was a boy, and that weren't all." She moved her dark eyes to Connie's face, then back to Annabelle's. "He was dark."

"Miss Melva was so worn out, she nearly fainted. She never even looked at the chile. So, Miz Marla, she grabbed the babe, wrapped it up, and headed outside.

"She said to me, 'When you finished, come on out here.'

"After I cleaned up and tucked Miss Melva in for a rest, I went outside. Miz Marla, she say, 'You don't tell nobody nothing.' Well, I knowed that was best, but then she say, 'You take this chile and give it away to somebody can raise it. Don't tell nobody where it come from, nor who's the mama.'"

I took the baby, but 'fore I left, I asked her, What about yo' sister?"

She told me, 'If she sees the baby, she'll want to

keep him. You know that's not good. Not for her, and not for the baby. It's better for both this way. I'll tell her he never drawed a breath. You find somebody can take care of him. I'll help, anyway I can.'"

"Well, as it happened, I knowed somebody that needed a child, so I took the boy to Livia. She was most thankful to God for the provision. It about busted my heart. She took to him and raised him like he was her very own."

Connie's voice startled Annabelle. "What about the baby's father?"

Annabelle touched her arm to stop her, but it was too late.

Miss Lucy stiffened and puckered her lips. "He got what was comin' to him. Ain't right, what he did."

Connie gazed at Annabelle. "Rape?"

Miss Lucy leaned forward and spoke in a loud whisper, "Don't matter whether it was forced or given, ain't right for a man of color to be with no white woman. That boy would of paid all his life for bein' raised up by a white woman with folks knowing where he come from."

Connie nodded. "I know you're right, Miss Lucy. He's had a good life. No one would ever say otherwise. I guess I know why Marla's so concerned about Hero now. Why she's taken such an interest in his education."

Miss Lucy relaxed. "Yes'm, she done right by the boy, takin' him under her wing, as she done. Folks around here always believed it's because of Edris being her housekeeper. Three people knowed the truth." She looked down her nose at Connie and Annabelle. "'Til now."

"Three?" Annabelle frowned. "What about Hero's daddy? I mean Lester, of course."

"Lester never knowed about his boy dying. He was in the Army when it happened. Livia didn't have the heart to tell him. I thought it was probably for the best. Less folks knew the truth, more likely it would stay a secret. Better for the chile that way." She angled another warning look at the two of them.

Annabelle nodded. "I agree. Seems like it's going to turn out all right for everyone."

Miss Lucy stood and dusted off her skirt. "It does. Miz Marla got Lester on at that factory away up in Detroit. Soon, they'll all live up there. Hero's going to go to college, that's what I heard. Won't that be something?"

She gave them one of her toothless smiles. "Well, I reckon I'd better get home now. Got to get the food going before the mob hits."

Annabelle slipped her arm in Connie's as they

watched Miss Lucy walk away. "What an incredible story. Most unexpected."

Chapter Twelve

May 8, 1957

Strolling toward home, Annabelle's thoughts kept returning to the story of Hero's birth. She could find no fault in how Marla had handled the situation, though she hurt for the woman's sister.

"Oh, dear Lord." Annabelle's motherly instincts kicked in. Poor Melva believed her baby had died all those years ago. Gazing at the bright afternoon sky, she nearly stumbled on a clump of dirt. Better pay attention, Annabelle. She glanced around. No one around but the cows, and they'd be no help if she fell and hurt herself.

Would Hero ever learn the truth about who he was? Miss Lucy and Marla seemed to agree that he didn't need to know. That was all right unless he somehow came across the truth. How would he feel then, knowing everyone had kept it from him?

One of Alton's cows lifted her head. She seemed to eye Annabelle as she passed.

"I know, it's none of my business." But what a lot of food for thought. Why had the story been told to them? Had Marla hoped for their approval? Or was it something else?

As she went about her evening chores, Annabelle prayed for Melva, wherever she was. She also prayed for Hero, Livia, and Lester. "Lord, bless Marla for the good she's done through the years, looking after that boy. Even stepping in to protect him from harm."

In doing so, Marla had thwarted the efforts of a group of men her husband used to lead. Annabelle couldn't keep from smiling. It was downright ironic. When Jensen set his sights on the political arena, he had been advised to back off from certain activities. Though he'd never made a public statement to the fact, everyone in these parts knew he'd been one of the ringleaders of the … she couldn't even think that word.

When she was a girl, they'd been called the night riders. She'd had nightmares about them. She'd never forget the time she was on the back porch after dark when she'd heard hoof beats. Lots of hoof beats. They'd ridden right through the yard, never stopped. She didn't think they'd seen her, but she always wondered about it. Next day, she heard of a hanging over near the county line.

A chill danced up her spine at the memory. She shook it off. "Shouldn't be remembering bad things, it'll weigh down the heart." Another of her granny's sayings. Granny had kept a joyful spirit through some of the worst of times, so Annabelle guessed the woman knew a thing or two. She'd been the one who taught Annabelle to sing away her troubles.

The chickens all shut up for the night, she slipped through the gap in the fence and plodded toward the house, still thinking about Marla. Perhaps her involvement with Hero had made her more willing to have her oldest boy, Chase, stay at Sutter's every summer. She'd managed to get the boy out from under his daddy's negative influence where race was concerned.

Annabelle had always heard that the Lord worked in mysterious ways. "You certainly do, Lord."

She began to hum, and then to sing, as she walked.

"I wish Tom could've come to the parade." Lillian stood next to Annabelle as another float drifted past. Its costumed occupants smiled and waved. "Too bad he has to miss seeing that float he sponsored."

Annabelle agreed. "He saw it last night, but I guess it's not the same."

Joseph laughed out loud at the antics of a clown dashing by.

When the clown caught sight of the boy, he circled back, offering a bright red sucker.

Joseph bounced up and down on Alton's shoulders. "Hey, calm down, little buddy." Alton grinned at Annabelle. "I believe he likes a parade."

"He's not the only one." She pointed to Connie, who stood enraptured, her hands clasped together, as another band marched past.

She turned to catch everyone looking at her. "What?"

Alton grinned, but the next band passing made conversation impossible.

"Here they come!" Lillian pushed her way to the curb, raising her arm to wave at Jensen and Marla, riding in the back seat of her powder-blue convertible. A sign on the side of the vehicle said, "Vote Jensen Wade for County Commissioner."

Annabelle waved, along with the rest of the family. He was on his way up. She'd heard him telling Alton about his plans, which included a run for state representative, a few years down the line. She reckoned he'd be a good fit over in Washington D.C. He sure did love to pontificate.

After the parade ended, the crowd dispersed. Alton led the way to the car, still carrying Joseph on his shoulders. Annabelle and Lillian walked with Connie.

Lillian linked her arm in Annabelle's. "I don't know about you, but I'm about ready for that picnic lunch."

Annabelle patted her hand. "I could eat."

"I'm always hungry." Connie punctuated her statement with a giggle.

Lillian laughed outright. "Child, you must be carrying another boy."

"Oh, I hope so. A little brother for Joseph. Or, a girl would do just as well."

Annabelle's heart warmed to the thought of a little girl with rich, dark hair like her mother. Or, maybe a little blond like her daddy. Of course, it could be another boy. She reckoned Joseph would have a playmate, either way. How she'd longed for a brother or a sister when she was growing up. She'd dreamed of it. Oh, how she'd envied Lillian's big family.

Alton spread a quilt on the ground near a tree, within easy reach of the playground.

Joseph begged to go play, but Connie commanded him to sit. "Eat first, then play."

"Regina packed us a feast," Alton said. He set the

basket in the middle of the quilt.

Just as Annabelle bit into an egg salad sandwich, a sound like fingernails on a chalkboard assaulted her ears. A trill of laughter that left no doubt, they were about to be under siege from Rose Ella McCoy.

Annabelle used a napkin to make sure no crumbs of egg salad held on as Alton stood to greet Rose Ella and her brother.

"Won't you join us? We have plenty."

Mr. McCoy shook his head. "No, sir, I appreciate the invitation, but we've got to get back to Trenton. My sister couldn't pass you by without saying hello."

"What a quaint little park!"

Before Rose Ella could launch into one of her long speeches, Lillian grabbed the reins. "How did you like the parade?"

"Oh, it was really special. Not at all what I expected of a backwater town like Humboldt. Such a fine showing. And your son and daughter-in-law looked like celebrities riding in that blue convertible. That ought to get him some votes. I—"

"Rose Ella, we need to be on our way and let these folks get back to their picnic."

She closed her open mouth. After a moment, she forced a stiff smile. "Why, of course, Lincoln, I'm ready to go." She turned to Annabelle and Lillian. "My brother is a busy man. He's got to get back to town now. I hope to see y'all on Sunday."

Annabelle widened her eyes as a thought occurred to her. Either Lincoln McCoy knew how to handle his sister's exuberance, or there was some discomfort between the two.

Not long after the McCoys departed, Alton and Connie left to take Joseph to the playground.

Lillian leaned near Annabelle. "What about those McCoys? Did you hear what I heard?"

"Maybe they've had a tiff."

Lillian chuckled. "Wouldn't be the first time a brother and sister argued. Looks to me like they're both lead dogs."

"You may be right." Annabelle's mind held onto the thought for a bit. Maybe that woman wasn't as perfect as she liked everyone to think.

"We're almost there."

Tom glanced at Riley. They'd finished installing the shelves in the study. "I've been thinking about that. Maybe I ought to start bringing the furniture out."

Riley paused to wipe his hands on a rag. "Naw, I was thinking we ought to take a weekend off to go fishing. Been way too long, cousin."

"Huh! Well, I reckon you're right about how long it's been. You've invested almost all your spare time, helping me get this house built. Anytime you need to take off, you just do it."

"Not without my partner in crime. Don't tell me you're going to be too busy for fishing. Or maybe, you've already gotten tangled up in those apron strings." He nodded, as though he'd stumbled on the truth.

"Oh, come on, Riley. That's not the reason." But what was the reason? Tom had to admit the woman next door was pretty high up on his list. He could hardly wait for Saturday when they'd go to the carnival. Out for a night of fun with the woman he loved. A rush of excitement shot through him so fast, he nearly dropped the hammer.

Riley's goofy laugh echoed through the empty rooms. "Admit it, man. She's ringing your bell. Ring-a-ding-ding!"

Tom groaned and shook his head. Sometimes Riley got on his last nerve. Maybe what he needed was time to himself. But Riley would never consider going fishing on his own.

"This weekend is the carnival. Then, next weekend is when I hope to get moved in." He watched his cousin's expression. "That new intern I hired arrives next Thursday."

"Oh, I know your calendar's full."

Tom drew back to look his cousin in the eye. He'd expected Riley to say something about that date with Annabelle.

Riley scratched his chin. "Well, I reckon I can wait. Soon as you get settled in, though, we need to take a weekend off. What do you say about that? Gotta plan ahead if you want my company. Thelma's got a list of chores a mile long."

Tom chuckled. "And you were talking about apron strings. Seems like you're an expert on the subject. She'll be tickled pink to have you back and I suspect you'll be happy to have your evenings off." After a moment's thought, he added, "I really appreciate all you've done to help me get this place built."

"Ah, now don't go getting all mushy, cousin. I only did it to get you out from under my roof." He mopped the sweat from his face and neck with one of the rags they'd been using to clean the shelves. "You gonna get you one of them there billiard tables like we talked about? If you don't want to put it in the cellar, it'd go great in that room yonder." He nodded toward the front room.

Tom shook his head. That wouldn't go over with

Annabelle, though he didn't dare say so to Riley. "I hadn't planned on it, no."

Riley mumbled under his breath as he gathered up the leftover scraps of wood and headed toward the garage.

All Tom could make out were the words, "apron strings."

Chapter Thirteen

Saturday
May 11, 1957

Tom couldn't say when he'd first laid eyes on Annabelle. They'd known each other since babyhood. Maybe they'd played together as toddlers, while their folks partook of Sunday dinners on the grounds at church, or at Fourth of July picnics.

He would never forget the first spark of love he felt for her, though. It was second grade. She had blue bows on both pigtails. Ernie Snyder kept tugging at the bows and untying them. When she pursed her lips and glared at old Ernie, Tom's heart skipped a beat. He'd been soft on her ever since.

After one last glance at his image in the bathroom mirror, Tom guessed he was as ready as he'd ever be. Now, to get out of the house without being teased to bits by the whole Franklin clan. Maybe he should have put this first date off until he lived alone.

"You're looking mighty fine, Tom." Thelma's bright smile reassured him. She winked. "Smell good, too."

Fist to his mouth, Tom cleared his throat, hoping no one had overheard that last remark. "Thank you." But then, he groaned inwardly at the sight of Riley's wiry frame in the doorway, thumbs hooked in his overall straps, grinning to beat the band.

"Look-it you all shined up and ready for your date with Annabelle."

Stevie, the least of Thelma and Riley's brood, gave Tom a gap-toothed grin. "Are you going out with Aunt Annabelle, Uncle Tom?"

Tom eyed the boy. All Riley's kids called Annabelle "aunt," even though she was their cousin. They'd always called him Uncle Tom, for the same reason. It was a term of respect. So, why did it make Tom's heart skip? Was it the fact he hoped to marry her? Uncle Tom and Aunt Annabelle—he liked the sound of it.

He tousled the boy's mop of red hair. "Yes, Stevie, I am."

Stevie fisted the air. "Hot-diggity!"

Tom headed for the front door, nearly stumbling over his niece, Raydeen, the second youngest. She threw her skinny arms around him and squeezed. "If you win any good prizes at the carnival, bring me one."

He kissed her cheek. "I'll do that, Ray." Finally. Outside and on his own, relief flooded his chest. He loved them, but right now, all he wanted was to get to Annabelle.

The drive provided time to breathe. To get his bearings. He fine-tuned the radio in his two-year-old Chevy truck and settled in as Tennessee Ernie sang about working in the coal mine. Working for others lay in Tom's distant past. He loved being his own boss. With the Lord's help, he had made a success of the drug store. All his debt would be paid off soon. When that happened, he could hire another pharmacist—not an intern—so he could take an occasional day off, or even a week or two. He'd need time off when he married Annabelle.

When. Not if. He grinned and thumped the wheel. At some point, he'd changed his way of thinking. No, she'd changed his way of thinking, with her smiles and looks. She'd made him feel this way. She'd said yes to a date with him. An evening date, at that. True, Connie and Alton would be there, but it was still a date. There'd be times when he'd be alone with her. He intended to make the best of those times.

Annabelle checked the clock again. Tom would be on his way by now. She smoothed the front of her skirt, patted her hair, and paced to the window. She'd fed the chickens early, then spent the afternoon getting ready. She'd even remembered to clean her fingernails. Land sakes. When had she become so careless about herself?

Time was, she and her two daughters-in-law had gone weekly to the beauty shop. Since she'd been back home, she'd gone one time. When her hair got too long, she had Connie trim it for her.

Annabelle peered in the mirror. The girl did all right, but maybe next time, she'd make an appointment at the shop in town.

If she was to marry Tom … no. She shook her head and moved away from her reflection. She wouldn't think of it. Not now, when they were about to go out on their first real date. Here she was planning how she'd spend his money. It wasn't right.

If she married him, and that was a big "if," she'd have to be careful, or folks would say she'd married him for his money.

Her nerves all in a bundle, she perched on the edge of a chair. She'd be under a microscope, living in Trenton. Folks would always be watching, because

Tom was an important member of their town. They were proud of him, and rightly so. He'd done well and he tended to share his wealth. He helped support their little league ball team. He'd financed that float for the high school. He'd helped her and Connie, too, when they'd first come to town. She glanced at the refrigerator he'd bought, brand new.

Annabelle had always been proud of him. She had known him to be the smartest of her friends. She'd kept up with him through the years, by way of Thelma's letters. Cousin Thelma had kept Annabelle abreast of all the local news.

The sound of a vehicle jerked her out of her thoughts and brought Annabelle to her feet, but it was a passerby. Whoever it was honked their horn.

She checked the clock again. It was nearly time. He'd be here any minute. She passed through her four small rooms to see that everything was ready. Assembled her purse, checked to see that her gloves were inside in case she needed them, then settled her hat, tucking in a few stray wisps. Last of all, she put on her lipstick. Her fingers shook a little as she blotted her lips. Why on earth was she so nervous? Hadn't she known this man all her life?

Looking down, she realized she still wore her house slippers. "Land sakes!" She rushed to her bedroom to change into her freshly polished loafers. Connie had cautioned her to wear comfortable shoes. These were the best she had.

She heard the truck pull in as she was sliding her house shoes beneath the bed. She stayed still, waiting, not daring to breathe. Then came the sound of footsteps on the porch, and a rap at the door. He was here.

Annabelle smiled a greeting as she opened the door. Tom stood there, holding his hat. He wasn't wearing his usual light blue shirt. He wore a short-sleeved, lime green sport shirt instead. Rather a stylish one. The warm evening was probably the reason, along with the nature of their outing.

He beamed at her. "You look mighty pretty, Annabelle."

Settling her purse on her arm, she closed the door and stepped onto the porch. "You look nice too, Tom. Casual."

He set his hat on his head and offered his arm. "Not too casual, I hope?"

She shook her head. "Oh, no. I like the look. It's quite stylish."

Near the truck, he paused. "Thank you for coming out tonight, Annabelle. I hope you'll enjoy yourself."

"Oh, I'm certain I will."

He opened the door, but before she had time to

move, she caught sight of Lillian's car headed up the road. "Oh, I believe that must be Alton."

Tom closed his door. "I suppose it is best to leave my truck at your house."

Annabelle tried not to think what the neighbors would say about that.

After pulling in the drive, Alton grinned through the open window. "Y'all ready to go?"

Taking a cue from Alton, Tom opened the rear door for Annabelle. She got in and slid over behind Connie, giving Tom plenty of room. She set her purse on the seat between them.

"Are you excited, Momma?" Connie slid closer to Alton so she could turn to look at Annabelle.

"I reckon. It's been a long time since I've been to a carnival."

"It's an especially good one this year, is what I've heard," Alton said. He put the car in reverse and backed around.

Tom looked at Annabelle. "I heard the same from many of my patrons this morning. They were all carrying on about it."

Annabelle settled her hands in her lap. Whatever would they find to talk about all the way over to Humboldt?

Tom watched Annabelle's face as they rocked their way up to the top of the Ferris wheel. Her expression reflected awe as she gazed at the town below. Though she was nearly as old as he was, sometimes she reminded him of a child. Her eyes sparkled, and her cheeks bloomed with color as they faced the setting sun. For some silly reason, the sight made his heart ache. He longed to put his arm around her but didn't dare. He'd hoped to hold her hand, but she gripped the bar tightly and didn't let go.

He was trying hard to be patient with her, but how long should he wait? Would she be offended if he moved too fast?

Too fast. He'd waited a lifetime for her. Now, as the finish line loomed ahead, his will was wearing down. Still, Pastor Nathan had cautioned him not to wait too long. Angst filled his chest. How would he know when to make a move?

Back on the ground, he stayed close to her as they waited for Connie and Alton.

"What a perfect evening," Connie said. "Did you see that sky?"

Annabelle nodded. "It was all aglow. It seemed you could see the whole county."

Alton pushed his hat back. "We were pretty high up. Makes me appreciate having my feet on the ground." He looked at Tom. "What shall we do next?"

They decided on the carousel. Then, Tom challenged Alton to the duck shoot. Each of them won a couple of prizes, so Tom would have something for Raydeen. After the games, they all stood in line for a hotdog, and then found a place to sit to enjoy their snack.

When music drifted their way, Alton suggested they go there. The stage stood near the backside of the carnival, where a pretty good band played some southern favorites. A few couples danced, but most folks stood or sat close by to listen to the music.

If only Annabelle took a lighter stance on dancing. She probably didn't even know how. He watched as she swayed in time to the music. She did have rhythm, at least.

Annabelle covered her mouth to hide a giggle as Alton drew Connie into the circle of dancers.

Those two had no qualms about it. He glanced back at Annabelle. Did he dare?

Before he could move, she touched his arm. "Can we sit?"

They found a seat along the perimeter where someone had created benches with hay bales and planks. When he sat beside her, she leaned close.

"Thank you, Tom. My feet were starting to hurt."

He nodded his understanding. "We can watch the dancers better from here, anyway."

She looked at him. "I remember how you used to love to dance. Do you still?"

He gazed into her eyes, enjoying her attention. "I haven't in some years. No one to dance with."

"Hmm. I don't know if I believe that, Tom Franklin. Maybe you haven't really looked."

What was she saying? Did she want him to look elsewhere? He held her gaze a bit longer. "I haven't had a need to look anywhere but right here, Annabelle."

Her lips quirked into a tremulous smile. "A girl always likes to hear that, Tom. I hope you're not too disappointed, but I still don't dance."

With her so close, leaning against his side, he really didn't care to move, much less worry about dancing. In fact, the whole scene in front of them receded into the background until all he saw was her. He took her hand in his. "We don't need to dance tonight. But maybe someday you'll change your mind."

She laughed, but it wasn't a laugh that disturbed the mood. It made him think she liked the thought of someday dancing with him. She soon verified his suspicion. "Maybe I will."

The song ended. Alton and Connie joined them.

Tom rose so Connie could sit next to Annabelle.

Alton crouched in front of the ladies. "Y'all about ready to head back?"

"I am," Connie said, leaning against Annabelle. "We have church tomorrow." She stifled a yawn.

Annabelle patted Connie's arm. "We need to get you home, Pumpkin."

Offering his hand to his wife, Alton helped her rise. Tom and Annabelle followed along behind as they strolled back through the dwindling crowds, toward the place where they'd parked the car.

Tom's heart swelled when Annabelle stayed close beside him, rather than walking with her daughter. When they reached the car, he held the door for her, then walked around to the other side. As he opened the car door, Tom turned to Alton. "You hear about the special speaker tomorrow?"

"I did." Alton got in and started the engine. "Funny thing, though. Pastor never did mention the man's name."

Tom grinned at Annabelle as he eased in beside her. This time, she hadn't placed her pocketbook between them. He took that as a good sign. "Maybe Pastor wants it to be a surprise."

"What's a surprise?" Connie covered another

yawn.

"The speaker tomorrow. Pastor never said who it was."

Not long after Alton pulled out of the parking area, Connie snuggled next to him in the front seat and leaned her head on his shoulder. Tom figured she was asleep before they crossed the railroad tracks on the way out of town.

In the dim light of an overhead streetlight, he caught the slight curve of Annabelle's lips as she gazed at him. When he reached for her hand, she didn't object but intertwined her fingers with his. Was there a goodnight kiss in his near future?

Tom's insides felt like a jumbled mass of nerves when Annabelle's house came into view.

Alton eased into the drive as though he carried a load of eggs in the trunk.

After a quick, "Thank you," to Alton, Tom got out and strode around to the other side of the car. When he opened the door for Annabelle, she paused to lay a hand on Connie's shoulder.

"Goodnight, Pumpkin."

Tom was barely aware of Alton saying goodbye to them both. Had he responded in a suitable fashion, and thanked Alton for the ride? He pulled in a deep breath to clear his head as he walked with Annabelle to her porch.

She paused at the base of the steps. "Are you all right?"

He stood looking down at her. Would she mind if he answered by sweeping her into his arms and kissing her? He chuckled and shook his head. "I'm fine, just wondering when we can do this again."

"Another carnival? I don't know where we could find one. Maybe this fall at the county fair?"

Her smile assured him she was teasing. "No, I was talking about another date."

"I figured that's what you meant." She turned and headed up the steps.

Panic moved him to follow. He wasn't ready for the night to end. But it was late, and tomorrow was Sunday.

At the door, she turned again.

He stepped nearer. Did he dare?

She laid her hand on his forearm and lifted her eyes to his.

He leaned nearer. He lifted his hand, caressed her cheek. She didn't flinch but lifted her chin as if offering her lips. He kissed her softly, reining in the passion her touch had ignited.

When he drew back, her eyes were still closed. When she opened them, a smile tugged at the corners of her lips.

He took a backward step. "Well, I guess I'd better go."

"Goodnight, Tom." She opened the door and stepped inside.

"Goodnight, Annabelle."

Chapter Fourteen

May 12, 1957

Sunlight streamed through Annabelle's window. "Oh, my goodness, I've overslept!"

She rose and hurried to the kitchen, side-stepping the cat. "Get out of my way, Ginger. I've got barely enough time to feed the chickens and get ready for church before time to go."

Sleep had evaded her far too long the night before. She'd endured those few moments of angst at her door when she'd wondered whether Tom would kiss her, and then he had. It was a light kiss, all feathery-like, but the feelings that went along with it—well, Annabelle couldn't stop thinking about it. Just his fingertips against her skin made her want that kiss more than anything.

She smiled as a glow warmed her chest. He certainly was a gentleman. Ray never would've waited so long.

The joy of it all kept her mind in a whirl. Every time her eyelids closed in sleep, they snapped back open again at the memory. Sleep skittered away.

After tossing out a bit of corn for the hens and a rooster, she rushed back to the house to get dressed. She'd put the finishing touches on her appearance when Alton honked his horn. The screen door slammed in her wake. She didn't even take time to double-check the lock. With little sleep, no coffee and not even a bite to eat her temper held a short fuse.

The church was at capacity this morning, probably because of the special speaker. A fine-looking young man sat beside Pastor on the platform. He seemed quite tall and had wavy, dark hair. He carried a large Bible that looked well-used.

Right before the service started, Judith rushed in all flustered. She slid into the pew beside Annabelle.

"I didn't know you were coming to church this morning."

The color deepened in the girl's cheeks. "Oh, I wouldn't miss this for the world."

Annabelle had no time to think about what Judith meant, as Rose Ella dived into the doxology with a vengeance. The little woman put on her best show this morning, probably trying to impress the guests with her talent.

Immediately following the opening prayer, Pastor Nathan introduced their visiting speaker. "I heard this young man speak at a pastor's luncheon at Union University." His glance swept past Annabelle, to light on Judith. "This is his first visit to our town, but I have a feeling it won't be his last. He is called of God to serve in the ministry, specifically as a pastor. This fall, he'll head up north to Kentucky, where he has been accepted to the doctorate program at the seminary. Ladies and gentlemen, Mr. Preston Weatherby."

As the young man stood, Pastor Nathan's introduction penetrated Annabelle's sluggish mind. This was Judith's Preston. She gripped the girl's wrist.

Judith's grin spread even wider.

Annabelle relaxed. Evidently, God and Judith had come to an understanding about Preston's calling.

From the moment he launched into his sermon based on Philippians 3:14, Annabelle was enraptured. He certainly had a talent for speaking, and he knew how to use that Bible. He told how it had been passed to him from his grandfather, who was also a preacher. "Granddad traveled the mountains of eastern

Tennessee on the back of a mule, preaching the gospel. He won many folks to Christ. I aspire to do the same." He smiled when he looked at Judith. "I probably won't travel the mountains on a mule, but my desire is to reach many for the kingdom of God."

He held the congregation's attention, too. It was so quiet, Annabelle sent a quick glance around, wondering if they were still awake. She found most eyes on the speaker. They were as engaged as she. It seemed only moments before he was ending his sermon.

"Forget the past, along with its disappointments and failures. Face the future with faith and great expectation of good. Press on toward the finish line— the goal—whatever you hope to achieve this day, this week, or in this lifetime. The prize is the upward call of God."

His words sliced through the last of Annabelle's doubt. If she'd needed confirmation, this was it. God knew her situation. When Preston stopped speaking, Annabelle wanted to applaud, but no one made a sound. Judith's young man had left his listeners in awe.

Clearing his throat, Pastor Nathan reclaimed the pulpit. "I reckon you now know why I wanted this young man to speak to you. I believe God has given him a word for this congregation."

Several amens rang out, an unusual occurrence

among Southern Baptists.

Pastor turned to Preston. "I do hope you'll return a time or two before you leave for seminary."

"I'd like that, Pastor Nathan. You have a fine church here."

"I'm going to give our congregation the opportunity to invest in your education." He faced the front. "If you'd like to help Preston, you can place your offering in the plate on the table up front. Now, please stand for the closing hymn."

He stepped aside to allow the song leader's return.

Rose Ella played the opening chords for "Turn Your Eyes Upon Jesus."

As Annabelle sang, she noted the sparkle in Judith's eyes. The sight warmed her heart.

Hoping to meet Preston, Annabelle stayed close behind Judith. Before they could get to the young man, Rose Ella McCoy drew her aside.

"You have been blessed with a truly wonderful voice, Annabelle. You ought to use it for God's glory."

Annabelle grabbed the nearest pew for support. Had Rose Ella McCoy just complimented her?

The little woman drew a breath. "You know we're

hosting this summer's hymn-singing? Well, I need as many as I can get to come to practice. I want First Baptist to take the lead. We'll meet every Wednesday night at six. I sure do hope you can be here. You have a lovely voice."

Annabelle had no idea the woman had ever heard her sing. How could she hear one voice above all the others, the way she banged the keys on that piano? "I'm flattered, Rose—Rose Ella. But I don't know that I can get here early of a Wednesday evening. I don't drive. I'm dependent on the goodness of others."

"Oh, that's all right. Miz Connie has already expressed her intentions to join. You can ride in with her."

Annabelle turned her gaze on Connie, who was talking to Judith and Preston. Connie joined the choir? She'd be about to give birth by then. Annabelle mentally ticked off the months. Well, maybe not, but she'd be right large. July and August tended to be so dreadfully hot.

Pressing in, Rose Ella touched Annabelle's wrist. "What do you say? Will you at least think about it? Though, I don't know why you'd need to, with a fine voice like yours. Dear Mr. Tom went on about it the other day. 'Miss Annabelle has a fine voice,' he said. That's high praise in my book. Mr. Tom is an honorable man. Well, you think about it and let me know." She pressed her hands together as if she was about to pray. "Better yet, show up at practice Wednesday night." With a quick nod, she moved past Annabelle and headed toward the rear sanctuary door.

"What was that?"

Lillian's voice startled Annabelle. She turned to look at her friend. "Miss Rose *Ella* wants me to join the choir."

"Well, you ought to. I hear tell our church is planning to host the hymn-singing this summer. Churches coming from all around. You're a shoo-in for a solo part, the way you love to sing. I hope you told her you'd be here."

"I told her I don't drive. I'm dependent on others."

"That won't be a problem. Connie's planning to join."

"I heard that, but I wasn't sure it was true."

"Why not? She's feeling fine. Baby's not due 'til late August. We can all have an early supper on Wednesdays, then Alton can bring y'all to town."

"Huh. Seems like it's all decided for me."

"Don't get your feathers ruffled. It could be God is making room for your talent."

She loved to sing, had always been good at it, according to her friends and family, so why was she so irritated? Was it because it wasn't her idea? What if it was God's plan and she was balking like a silly mule?

Annabelle glanced around, hoping to find Judith and Preston, but they had already gone. A few minutes ago, she'd been on top of the world. Now she was battling a petulant spirit. It didn't seem right. She had a sneaking suspicion it had something to do with Miss Rose Ella McCoy.

"I didn't see Tom at church yesterday." Alton finished stacking the cord of new wood along Annabelle's fence line.

Annabelle gazed toward the house next door. "I reckon he was busy."

"Yep. I heard he's planning on moving soon." He removed his gloves and stuffed them in his back pocket. Then he brushed his hands together. "You'll have a near neighbor. I feel better about that."

Annabelle smiled into his twinkling eyes. Alton was always up to something. "I didn't realize you were concerned about it."

He grinned and wrapped an arm around her shoulders as he led the way toward her front porch. "I'm always looking out for you. Reckon he can shoot the occasional fox that threatens your chickens?"

Annabelle shook her head. "I believe he's more of a fisherman than a hunter."

"I think you're right. So, I'll still have a job looking out for your livestock." He paused near the base of the steps, allowing Annabelle to go before him.

She stood on the porch. "Would you like a glass of tea or something to eat?"

"No, I need to stop by the store, so I thought I could bring us back a bologna sandwich. You need anything?" He whistled for Samson.

"I wouldn't say no to that sandwich." She thought a moment. "And I'm a mite low on sugar."

"Been baking too many cookies, I reckon."

She giggled. "I have at that."

"I'll be back shortly." He strode to the truck, opened the door, then stood aside for Samson to jump in.

Annabelle stood on the porch until the truck disappeared around the bend, headed toward the cotton gin and *Wade Brothers' Grocery*, barely a mile or so up the road. Their small store had been serving the area for nigh on forty years. The Wade family opened it as a company store for those who worked at the gin, lived in their tenant houses, or sold them cotton. Folks could buy groceries on a tab that was paid off with the cotton profits or their work hours.

Annabelle remembered her momma buying groceries on a tab. She was always careful not to overspend and cut too deeply into the year's profits.

"One never knows what will come of the cotton crop," Granny used to say. Annabelle reckoned the woman had seen her share of bad years. Could be boll weevils, too much rain, or not enough. She squinted into the distance, where a dust trail followed a box truck, which turned onto her road. She figured it was probably a delivery to the store, but it stopped in front of her house. The driver called out, "Excuse me, miss." He waved toward Tom's. "Is that Mr. Tom Franklin's residence?"

Annabelle shaded her eyes as she stepped off the porch. "Yes, it is."

He got out and stepped around the front of the truck, a clipboard in his hand. "Can you open the door for me? I have a delivery."

"I reckon so." Tom hadn't given her a word of warning. "I'll meet you up there." She supposed there were times when a telephone would be of some use. What if she'd not been home? The driver would have been obliged to return without making the delivery.

She was walking up Tom's drive when Alton's truck pulled in.

"I plumb forgot to tell you Tom called this morning. He said there'd be some furniture delivered today. He asked me to let you know. Sorry about that, Annabelle."

"No harm done."

The delivery man wrestled a large box onto a dolly.

"Looks like he may need a hand." Alton stepped quickly toward the house.

Annabelle unlocked the door and propped it open.

Alton and the driver unloaded several large boxes marked "home furnishings."

She wouldn't mind getting a look inside those, but it wouldn't be proper. "None of your business, Annabelle." She turned aside, wandered to the fence row where a wild rose bloomed. Nothing like the smell of a wild rose to clear one's mind. She was still standing there when the truck pulled out of the drive, headed back down the road toward town.

Alton didn't bother to move his vehicle. Toting a brown bag, he joined Annabelle at the fence. "I believe your grandmother planted those. Mother said she loved those wild roses."

"They always remind me of her." When she turned, he followed.

Inside the house, he set the bag down and began to unload it.

She set a couple of plates on the table and then prepared two glasses of tea.

"Do you ever get lonely here, Annabelle?"

His unexpected question puzzled her some. She thought about it as she sliced each sandwich into two halves. "Not as much as I used to." She glanced up at him.

"I noticed you put away your pictures." He took a bite of his sandwich.

She nodded. "I figured it was time I learned to live without them, hard as it is."

"I think that's commendable. It's good you're going to join the choir. It can't hurt to get out amongst your friends more."

Everyone was ganging up on her. That silly accident had started all of this. Why hadn't she left that crate where it sat in the bedroom?

Chapter Fifteen

May 16, 1957

Soft morning light bathed Annabelle's face in warmth, sending a glow of joy and peace to her heart. She always liked a few minutes of sunlight before she covered her head.

After donning her bonnet, she opened the crate on the back porch and removed her gardening tools. It was time to transplant the last of the tomato plants she'd carefully sprouted and raised in the kitchen window.

She propped the tools beside the gate. Then she stepped to the chicken coop. This time of year, she loved to take one or two of the hens to the garden with her. They were the best bug killers unless you had a duck or two. Especially when the June bugs came. Ducks loved June bugs.

She chose a red hen, letting her loose inside the garden fence. Then Annabelle returned for the tools.

She'd left the tomato plants outside to harden up and grow accustomed to outdoors. Now, she set the tray beside the row she meant to fill.

The hen clucked contentedly as it scratched in the dirt and devoured grubs.

Annabelle sank to her knees beside the first row. What should she sing this morning? She paused her digging. "Wonder what hymn the choir will choose for the gospel singing?"

Rose Ella's "chorale." Annabelle shook her head at Rose Ella's term for what the locals called "the singin'." Rose Ella had taken a quick offense at such common terminology, but if she called it a chorale, no one around here would know what she meant.

A tiny trill of anxiety wormed its way into Annabelle's heart. Would she be given a solo? She dug deeper in the soil making room for the first plant.

"Halloo, Miss Annabelle! That you?"

Annabelle folded back the brim of her bonnet so she could see Miss Lucy. "Yes, it's me. What're you doing over this way?"

Miss Lucy carried a tow sack that looked heavy. She set it down near the fence. "Totin' some of my soup over to Miss Parmenter. She's been poorly again."

"Oh, I'm sorry to hear that. Maybe I'll walk over there in a day or two."

"She'd love the visit. Be sure to announce yourself first, 'cause her sight's done gone." She gave the garden an admiring glance that ended with a chuckle. "I see you got yourself a helper today."

At first, Annabelle didn't realize what she meant. Then she caught sight of the hen in the upper corner. "She's my exterminator."

Miss Lucy clapped her hands. "I've seen it all, now. It's a right good idea, though, until they get to eatin' your vegetables."

"By the time my tomatoes start to produce, I'll quit having a helper." She grinned at the woman.

"I reckon they good for fertilizer, too."

Annabelle laughed. "You're right about that. This one seems to like digging for grubs. I'm hoping her efforts will give us a few less June bugs."

"That's always a good thing." She took hold of the top of the fence and leaned forward. "I stopped by to see if maybe you've seen Hero in the last day or so?"

Annabelle shook her head. "No, I don't believe I have. Not that I know of, anyway."

"Well. He come up missing."

"Missing?"

Miss Lucy nodded. "School was out for the summer on Friday. He didn't come home afterward. Liv's been beside herself with worry."

"Oh, my. I reckon so."

"I tole her most likely, he hiding out somewhere. Seems he don't want to go to the big city. Some of his school friends prolly talked fear into his ears."

"Probably." Annabelle tried to remember when she'd last seen him. Maybe over at Sutter's, one day last week?

Miss Lucy sighed. "Pray for him, Miss Annabelle. Seem like to me, they's a whole lot more to fear right here if the wrong sorts get wind of him being on his own. They may take it into their minds he'd be a good way to exact justice on Lester." She shrugged her shoulders, as though to ward off a tremor. "I don't need to be talkin' 'bout that, I reckon."

"You're speaking what you know, Miss Lucy. Past experience has given you plenty of reason to fear."

"Yes'm, it's like we been judged for a crime we didn't do but forced to live out our lives paying for. We reapin' for somebody else's bad."

Annabelle didn't really know how to answer that, but maybe she didn't need to respond. "Did you let Mr. Alton know about Hero?"

"I stopped by there late yesterday. They're keepin' a lookout. I shore hope he comes to no harm."

"When was he supposed to leave for Detroit?"

"Goin' by bus on Monday next."

"Well, I'll sure pray. You let Livia know I'm praying for her, too. Sometimes we worry more about our children than we ought."

"Hard not to, ain't it? Even knowing you have the Lord and you can trust in Him, them bad thoughts of what can happen sets your mind to running." She stooped to pick up the tow sack. "I best be on my way and let you get back to your work. You have a blessed day, Miss Annabelle."

"Thank you. Come by any time, now."

Miss Lucy trudged on, carrying her load. Annabelle scanned the field and the woods beyond. Had that boy hidden somewhere nearby? It made sense he'd come out here, where he was most familiar. He'd run about these fields, chopped and picked cotton beside his mama. He must know all the good hiding places. "Lord, keep that boy sheltered from harm."

She went back to work as the words of a favorite hymn spilled from her heart.

"Oh, come to the Savior, He patiently waits
To save by his power divine;
Come, anchor your soul in the "Haven of Rest,"
And say, "My Beloved is mine."

I've anchored my soul in the "Haven of Rest,"

I'll sail the wide seas no more;
The tempest may sweep over wild, stormy deep,
In Jesus, I'm safe evermore."

A whippoorwill called as Annabelle shut up the chickens for the night. Next door, warm light glowed from the big picture window. Through the glass, she could see Riley wielding a paintbrush. It looked like he was talking as he worked. She chuckled at the sight. Riley was a talker.

Near the corner of the house, she was enveloped in the sweet scent of four o'clocks in bloom. What a wonderful smell. She breathed their scent while taking in the brilliance of the sunset.

She chanced to glance across the fields toward the distant line of trees. Something flickered in their midst, like a light, or was it a campfire? Another whippoorwill cried, pulling her attention back to the present. She'd better get inside before it became too dark to see.

"That you, Annabelle?"

She jumped at the sound, though Tom had spoken softly.

He reached to steady her. "Sorry, I didn't mean to scare you."

"I … I thought you were inside." She couldn't keep from smiling. "I saw Riley talking to somebody."

Tom chuckled. "He's got J.W. with him tonight." He walked beside her, toward the front porch. "I hope you don't mind me stopping by."

"Not at all. Can I offer you something to drink? I think I have some lemonade left."

"No, thank you. I just wanted to … say hello." His boyish grin brought back memories of grade school, but his words warmed her heart.

She stepped onto the porch, uncertain where to go from here. Probably shouldn't invite him inside.

He took her hand. "Annabelle, I had a good time the other night."

"So did I. Thank you again, for taking me."

"I was hoping maybe we could go out again sometime soon, just the two of us. Dinner, maybe." He stood on the bottom step, his eyes level with hers, waiting for her response.

Annabelle's heart thumped wildly, hindering her ability to breathe freely. She gave a nod, but could he see the slight movement in this low light? The glow from the kitchen window lit his face, but she stood in darkness. "That would be nice."

He took a deep breath and eased it out, almost as if he'd expected her refusal.

Maybe she'd said yes too quickly. But she wanted to go, more than anything.

"I read in the paper; they've opened a new Italian restaurant in downtown Jackson. It's supposed to be really good."

Huh. Sounded kind of fancy. This time, she really would need to buy a new dress. Maybe even a new pair of shoes. She could get Connie to go shopping with her. Connie would like that, if she felt up to it.

He interrupted her train of thought. "So, what do you think?"

She gazed into his eyes. "I'd like that."

His answering smile sent shivers down her spine. Her knees lost their strength.

"How about next Friday night?"

Could she find a dress in time? She gave a slow nod. "All right."

He leaned close to give her a soft kiss. "I'll pick you up at six?"

A sudden attack of nerves choked off any possibility of an answer, so she nodded instead, not caring whether he saw this one. A broad smile lit his countenance as he released her hand and backed away. "Goodnight, Annabelle."

"Goodnight, Tom." Why were there tears in her eyes? She blinked them back and went inside the house, missing him already.

Tom returned to his house but hesitated before he entered. He didn't really want to go inside and spoil this feeling and the memory of her kiss. He stood on the back steps a moment.

She'd said yes. This time, they'd be alone. He would finally be free to speak to her without others overhearing. Without interruption.

But, what should he say? Was it too soon to repeat his proposal? Would she be ready to hear it now? Ready to give him the answer he longed for?

He gritted his teeth as anxiety twisted his nerves into a tangled mess. She certainly seemed more inclined toward him. She was going out with him, allowing him to hold her hand and kiss her. Not the way he'd like to kiss her, of course. Slow and easy, like he was training a skittish animal.

Riley laughed inside the house, reminding Tom he was supposed to be in there with them, finishing the trim in the den. He was about to turn toward the door when a light caught his eye. A light in a place where it shouldn't be—right in the middle of Sutters' woods. Someone must be camping down there. Maybe Alton and Chase? Sometimes, they did that in the summer. Alton was training Chase to enjoy normal pursuits. Things he hadn't learned in his young life of boarding schools and academic summer camps.

Satisfied with that explanation, Tom turned to go inside.

"Uncle Tom, Pa said you and Aunt Annabelle were sparking, but I didn't see none." J.W. knelt on the floor, carefully painting the trim.

Riley's shoulders shook, but he didn't turn around.

Tom tousled the boy's hair. "Your Pa is pulling your leg, J.W."

Riley turned to grin at Tom. "No sparks, huh? Nary a one?"

"None of your business, Riley."

"She's family, Tom. Of course, it's my business." He pursed his lips like he always did right before he gave that goofy laugh of his.

"That goes both ways, you know." Tom sent a pointed glance toward the boy. "Wouldn't want little ears to hear certain things about his Pa, would you?"

Riley snickered and rubbed his nose with the back of his hand. "Ain't a pair of little ears in this room. That kid's well-endowed in the ear department."

J.W. frowned and scratched his head. "What's that mean, Pa?"

Tom sighed. Poor kid, he was probably teased all the time for the size of those ears. Tom laid his hand on his little cousin's shoulder. "That means you hear really well, J.W."

J.W. looked from one to the other, then went back to painting trim. "I know y'all are talking about girls, all right. I ain't interested. P-yoo!"

Riley almost doubled over, he laughed so hard.

Tom shook his head. J.W. must've been spurned by some young lady. Either that, or he was sweet on one, and didn't want anyone to know. Tom stepped to the sink to wash his hands. Teasing over a girl could be far worse than joking about the size of one's ears.

Taking up his brush, Riley went back to work, but not for long. "Did you hear about Hero?"

"What about him?"

"J.W. told me the boy ran off. They can't find him anywhere."

Tom dried his hands, staring out the window toward the flickering light in the woods. "Are they right sure he ran off, didn't get picked up by someone?"

J.W. sat back on his heels. "He said he wasn't going to Detroit, no way, no how."

"Huh." Tom picked up a clean brush and fanned the bristles against his palm. What if that campfire belongs to Hero? What if he's hiding out down there?

Tom made a mental note to call Alton first thing in the morning. Someone needed to check that out before the wrong people noticed the firelight and figured it out first.

Chapter Sixteen
May 23, 1957

"No polka dots!" Annabelle shook her head. "I look like Walt's mouse."

Connie giggled. "It's made really cute, though, Momma. That style looks great on you." She took a backward step to get a better view. "You've trimmed down quite a bit. Maybe too much." She folded her arms over her chest. "I hope you're eating enough."

"Of course, I am. I can take care of myself." She looked at her reflection in the mirror. "You're right about the style, though. Let's see if they have one in a solid color."

They hadn't gone to Jackson. Annabelle had no desire to empty her pocketbook in one of those expensive department stores. She wanted a decent dress to wear to dinner, that's all. But they weren't having much luck in the little dress shop on the square in

Betty Thomason Owens

Trenton.

"Here's one, and it's a good color for you." Connie held up a pale aqua dress in a similar style—fitted bodice with a gathered skirt.

Annabelle frowned as she fingered the neckline. "Might be cut a little low in front. But I'll try it on."

She admired herself in the mirror before calling Connie back in. It did look nice. The color complimented her complexion and hair. A strand of pearls may detract from the slightly low neckline. She bent toward the mirror, making sure she wouldn't be embarrassed in front of Tom. Then she parted the curtains, so Connie could see.

Connie's eyes widened. "Oh, Momma. This is the one." She smiled and clasped her hands. "Tom's going to love it!"

"Shh! Someone might hear you. It's such a small town."

Connie planted a kiss on her cheek. "So what if Tom hears about it? By now, everyone knows he's sweet on you." She helped Momma out of the dress. "I'll take care of this while you get ready. Then we'll go next door and look at shoes."

"Okay, but don't you pay for it. I've got money put back. It's in my pocketbook."

Connie shook her head. "You can buy the shoes."

Dressed in her slip, Annabelle propped a hand on her hip. "I'm paying for both."

Her lips contorting, Connie folded the dress over her arm. "Get dressed, Momma. You can call it an early birthday present." She whisked through the curtains before Annabelle could protest.

Annabelle rushed to dress, muttering all the while. "That girl! She doesn't need to be spending her money on me." Smoothing her skirt in front of the mirror, she took a moment to catch her breath. But honestly, Connie was probably following orders from Alton. He would do that and often did. He was so thoughtful. A good son to both Lillian and Annabelle.

By the time she joined Connie, Annabelle's nerves had settled. She didn't even object when she noticed the box in the girl's arms and the self-satisfied smirk on her face.

"Let's find some shoes."

The shoe store was busy, as usual. Annabelle skimmed through the wall displays, looking for flats. She preferred them to high heels, which tended to hurt her feet. She needed a nice brown pair or maybe black patent leather. Something she could wear year-round. Sensible shoes.

Connie held up a cute little yellow number with a chunky, two-inch heel.

Annabelle frowned and shook her head. They were cute, but not what she had in mind.

"Oh, Momma, you're no fun at all. At least try them on. See how they look. You don't have to buy them. Shop—have fun."

"Oh, all right. Hold on to it." Annabelle picked up a black, patent-leather pump. Sensible.

Connie looked at it but didn't say anything. She picked up a couple more, both cute, but frivolous.

Annabelle sat in a chair to wait for a clerk. She looked askance at Connie's approach. "Are you trying those on?"

Connie sat beside her, several shoes tucked in her arms. "I might."

"They better be for you, because I'm buying sensible shoes that I can wear all year, for several years. Not just tomorrow night."

Connie opened her mouth, but a young man came to stand in front of them. Perfect timing. "Hello, ladies, my name's Ben. I see you've picked out several styles. He picked up a Brannock device, to measure the shoe size. "Which of you is buying?"

After trying all the others first, Annabelle pivoted her foot in front of the mirror. This was harder than she'd planned. Of course, Ben had taken Connie's side. It was two against one.

"They were made for you," he said.

"They're darling, Momma."

Ben smiled and nodded. "They're on sale."

Annabelle grimaced. He'd said the magic word. She turned her foot again, admiring the yellow shoes. The cute little bow on top made her want to smile. They fit perfectly. No pinching, no rubbing. Comfortable, silly shoes, with two-inch heels. Okay, Annabelle, for once in your life, let go and have fun. She could see herself wearing yellow shoes. Until she remembered her purse wouldn't match. Maybe she wouldn't carry a purse.

Connie appeared at her back, holding up a yellow pocketbook. "They have a matching purse, Momma, also on sale. You have to."

Annabelle eyed the cute fold-over purse. Well, since she hadn't had to buy the dress, she had the money to buy shoes and a purse. They were on sale. Annabelle breathed in the smell of new leather—the heady fragrance caught hold and wouldn't let go. She struggled against a smile. The smile won. "All right. I'll do it."

"Can you stay a bit?" Annabelle and Connie set the

bags and boxes on the bed to put away later. For some reason, she dreaded being alone.

"No, I've got to get the truck back home in case Alton needs it. But be ready to go at nine-thirty in the morning. I made us an appointment at ten o'clock."

Annabelle frowned. "What kind of appointment?"

"Your hair, for one thing. You need a professional do, not one of my butcher jobs."

Annabelle touched her hair. "I don't think you've done badly."

"Maybe you don't, but I want you to look your best." She wiggled her fingers in front of Annabelle's face. "We're both getting a manicure. I can't wait. So, be ready."

"Well, I thank you for making the appointment. I never would have on my own."

"No, you wouldn't have, but you need this, Momma." Connie took Annabelle's hand and examined her fingernails. "All work and no play makes for pretty sad nails. Remember when we used to go every other week? You always paid for me and Emily. Then we'd stop for ice cream on the way home. It was like a mini vacation. Emily and I loved it."

"I was happy to do it for you. I loved you both so much."

"Well, I'm happy to do this for you."

Annabelle hugged Connie and kissed her cheek. "I'm more thankful than I can say."

"Tomorrow, then."

Her cozy little house was too quiet after Connie left. Annabelle reached down to pet Ginger. "Come on, girl. You're probably hungry. I didn't see you this morning." After filling the cat's dish with a few scraps and a little bit of milk, she headed back to the bedroom to put away her new things. "I sure do miss the noise of a family."

Her boys used to run up and down the stairs, getting ready for school or a game. She hadn't thought about that in so long. Memories tended to pop up at the most unexpected times, leaving an empty ache in her heart, deeper even than the one left by Ray.

Maybe it's because the boys were part of her. She'd given birth to them, watched them grow. A lump choked her throat.

"Stop it, Annabelle." To get her mind on other things, she opened her packages and tucked the new shoes into her chifforobe. When she pulled out the purse, she had to sit down on the bed to look at it. Had she ever owned such a pretty purse? Oh, it was a frivolous thing for sure, but sometimes, a woman needed a little frivolity. She set it on her dresser.

Would Rose Ella approve? Would she pronounce

it fitting for a date with Tom Franklin? Annabelle giggled. She'd gotten to know Rose Ella a little better by going to choir practice. The woman fluttered about, but she knew her stuff when it came to music. However, when she proposed they sing "What a Day That Will Be," Annabelle started praying. Though it was a beautiful song, full of meaning, it cut too deep for Annabelle's comfort. In fact, she decided if they chose to sing it, she was going to have to drop out. Most anyone would understand why.

When the decision came, she breathed a sigh of relief. "Great is Thy Faithfulness" won by two votes. Rose Ella was disappointed, but she promised to put forth her best efforts, regardless.

"But there'll be no solo parts," she stated. "No grandstanding. This is going to be a joint effort, all the way."

Annabelle had no qualms with that. She sighed and pushed up from the bed. The last box held the aqua dress. She smoothed the dress before hanging it up. It needed pressing, to remove wrinkles. Other than that, it was ready for wearing tomorrow night.

That familiar fluttering sensation started in her tummy when she anticipated her date with Tom. She crossed her hands over her midsection. Better a nervous stomach than mournful tears. Her lips relaxed into a smile. The Lord replaces mourning with dancing. Instead of tears, He gives joy and thanksgiving.

The smell of ammonia smacked Annabelle in the face as she followed Connie into *Deedee's Salon*. The brightly painted room buzzed with activity. Annabelle recognized several ladies from church. Two sat beneath hair dryers, thumbing through magazines. The third one, the daughter of Annabelle's Sunday school teacher, sat at the manicure table. She stood as they entered. "Miss Connie, I'm ready for you as soon as you get settled. Miss Annabelle, you can sit in that chair by the window. Laura Lynn's going to do your hair."

Laura Lynn? Annabelle had never met the woman, but she'd heard several of her friends talk about her in respectful tones. She was supposed to be really talented.

A slender, young woman brisked in through a curtained doorway. She was not what Annabelle would term attractive, but when she smiled, her eyes lit with an inner glow that could not be imitated. It was the joy of the Lord.

The woman set the bottles on the front desk for the receptionist to put away. Then she turned toward

Annabelle. "You must be Mrs. Cross. I'm Laura Lynn Daley."

Annabelle answered with a nod. "Pleased to meet you."

Laura Lynn led Annabelle to a chair. "Now, what are we doing today? A cut and style?" She fingered Annabelle's hair. "Looks like you have beautiful natural color. Most ladies would envy you that."

Annabelle smiled. "Just a cut and style."

"Let's do it, then. I hope you're having a blessed day."

An hour later, with her hair in tight curlers, Annabelle sat beneath a hair dryer. Laura Lynn had given her a magazine to look at, but she found people-watching much more entertaining. She couldn't hear what they were talking about, but one of their church friends was bending Connie's ear with great enthusiasm.

Connie glanced at Annabelle, then back at the woman.

Annabelle chuckled to herself. The beauty shop was a great place to hear all the latest gossip. She'd warned Connie about it before they arrived, which is probably why Connie eyed her in such a way. That particular friend was almost as skilled at gossip as their neighbor, Mrs. Byrd.

Her hair still in curlers, Annabelle moved to the manicure table. After that, Laura Lynn finished styling her hair.

"I wish I could see you tonight, all dressed and ready for your date," she whispered with a smile.

Annabelle eyed the woman, then relaxed. At least she'd spoken quietly. No doubt, Connie had told her the reason for the new hairdo when she made the appointment. "I wish you could, too. If it was a prom, we'd take a photograph and I could bring it by."

Laura Lynn laughed. "Well, it's possible they take photos at that restaurant. If they do, I'd love for you to bring it in. I hope you'll return anyway, Miss Annabelle. I'd consider it a privilege, and a blessing, to do your hair anytime."

Annabelle blinked. Most likely, Laura Lynn was trying to secure a new patron, but her words struck Annabelle as being sincere. "Thank you kindly, Laura Lynn. I might take you up on that."

Annabelle removed her hand-washables from the clothesline and went back inside. With so much to do, she'd not had time to be nervous. That is until she noticed the hour. She still needed to see to the chickens.

For the second day in a row, the hens had shorted her some eggs. She'd fed them a little more and hoped for the best. Any extra eggs she had went with Alton to Wade's grocery, but this week, there'd be no extra. No pennies to apply to her grocery tab.

Good thing her garden was doing well. Eking a living out of the ground could be difficult when nature didn't cooperate. She hoped to put up a good amount of vegetables to see her through the winter.

The words to *Great is Thy Faithfulness* automatically rolled off her tongue as she made her way back to the house. God had been good to her, that was certain.

She felt His grace as she dressed in her new clothes. Professionally coiffed hair, manicured nails, new shoes, and a matching purse—these were all things she'd once taken for granted.

As she gazed at her reflection in the mirror, guilt pricked her heart. Was it vain to be so proud of the way she looked, all dolled up?

The one photograph she'd left out beckoned to her. She picked it up as her heart swelled with a mixture of love and regret. "I'm sorry we didn't get to spend the rest of our lives together. Didn't we have a good time, though?" She set the photo down, then kissed her fingertips and pressed them to the glass. "I'll always love you."

She jumped when a knock sounded at the door. With a smile, she picked up her yellow purse and went to answer it.

Betty Thomason Owens

Chapter Seventeen

May 24, 1957

Surely, he'd arrived at the wrong house. Tom's mind went completely blank as he stared at the vision in front of him. Had he ever seen Annabelle so glamorous? Not lately.

Dressed in a pale blue-green colored dress, she stood there with a shy smile on her face, which made her even more fetching. He swallowed—twice—before trusting himself to speak. "Evening, Annabelle. You look … amazing."

Amazing, really? Was that all he could come up with? He cleared his throat. "I mean to say … uh … beautiful, Annabelle. You look beautiful."

Her smile dazzled. She closed the door and stepped forward. "Thank you, Tom. Don't you look handsome?"

He fiddled with his tie. "Thank you. Just

something I threw together."

She laughed, setting him at ease. He led her down the steps to the freshly washed pickup truck. He'd paid Fred to wash it earlier in the day. As he assisted Annabelle into the seat, he couldn't help noticing the cute little yellow shoes she wore. They perfectly matched the purse she carried. Somehow, seeing her all dressed up for their date sent a thrill straight to his heart. He was falling more deeply in love by the minute.

That thought scared him a little bit.

Highland Avenue held few cars this time of the evening. Most of downtown had closed for the day and probably for the weekend, which made parking an easier task. *Little Italia's* windows emitted a warm glow and a tantalizing aroma.

He hoped it proved to be a good choice. He held the door for Annabelle, struck again by the change in her. Why she looked good enough to rival any of the best families of Trenton. Not that it mattered to him. He'd never been swayed by class or money. But he'd certainly never mind attending civic functions with her on his arm.

Her eyes sparkled in the candlelight inside the foyer.

After greeting them, a dark-haired young man led

them to a corner table across the crowded dining room. When Tom had called for a reservation, he'd requested a quiet table. He intended to get the most out of this evening, conversation-wise.

The young man offered a wine list, but Tom shook his head. "We prefer tea, thank you." He looked at Annabelle. "I hope that's all right."

She nodded. "Yes, I'd like a glass of tea."

The menu wasn't complicated. They offered simple meals of either meat or pasta. They even had pizza.

"Oh, they have lasagna."

Tom looked at Annabelle. "I've never had that. Is it good?"

"It's delicious. Tomatoes, meat, and cheeses layered between wide strips of pasta. It says they make their own pasta, too."

"Huh. Well, maybe I should stick with something I know, like spaghetti."

"Judging by the smells coming from that kitchen, I'd guess whatever we order is going to be good."

He nodded. "I hope so. I really want you to enjoy our evening, Annabelle."

"Oh, I'm already enjoying it, Tom. Since the moment you arrived at my door."

Did she guess how much that thrilled him, to hear

her say so? She'd been married a lot of years. Could be, she knew all about how to preen a man's feathers and make him feel good.

He didn't like to think about her being with Ray or any other man. He'd seen it often enough in high school, though. She was popular. All the guys liked her, but mostly in a friendly kind of way. She was like that. Open and friendly, like a sister. Except to him. He'd loved her since early on. He hadn't been at all surprised when she attracted a guy like Ray Cross. Handsome in his uniform, he'd swept her off her feet and out of Tom's life, he'd reckoned forever. Until now.

He smiled into her eyes. Did she have any idea how much he loved her?

This evening was turning out to be one of the best of Annabelle's life so far, almost like a dream come true. Not only was the restaurant top drawer, but the man seated across from her dazzled. She'd always thought him handsome, even in high school. Back then, he'd seemed more like an older brother. Wise and safe, a best friend. Now, he was so much more.

She allowed her gaze to sweep over this handsome man in a stylish black suit. He wore a crisp, white shirt, burgundy tie, and gold cuff links. At ease, and very much the gentleman. His mother and dad would be so proud to see him now.

After they'd ordered, she sat back in the comfortable dining chair, trying her best to relax and pay attention. Men liked when you paid attention to what they had to say. Tom always listened to her with interest, as though she was the most important person in the world. She supposed that was one reason she liked him so.

He took her hand. "What are you thinking about?"

Should she say? She bit down on her lip, uncertain. "I was thinking how proud your parents would be if they could see you now."

His brow furrowed. "You mean here, with you?"

"No, I meant … the way you look, so handsome, so self-assured."

"Ah, well, I'm good at pretending. I'm not at all self-assured. Not sure about the handsome part, either."

Their waiter reappeared with a salad and a basket of bread. "Is there anything else you require at the moment?"

Tom shook his head. "No, thank you." After the waiter left, he turned his eyes on her. "Mind if I ask a blessing?"

"Not at all." She bowed her head. After a quiet

prayer, the meal continued, along with the conversation.

"Do you really think that?"

She met his eyes. She couldn't resist teasing him. "That your parents would be proud, or that I think you're handsome?"

He chuckled as a flush of color rose in his cheeks. "Now, you're teasing me."

"I am." She took a bite of salad, savoring the fresh olive oil and garlic. "Oh, my, this is delicious."

He agreed. "I'm glad we're both having this garlic feast. Otherwise, the trip home might be uncomfortable."

He had relaxed enough to make jokes. That was a good sign. While they waited for the main course, a young woman with a camera asked if they'd like their picture taken.

"It's only fifty cents. We'll mail you the photograph."

Annabelle gripped Tom's hand. "Let's do it."

He smiled at her. Pulling a dollar from his wallet, he gave it to the young woman. "Keep the change."

After a couple of flashes, the woman took their information, then moved on to the next table.

Tom still held her hand. She had no desire to let go. "I'm glad they do that. We'll have a way to remember tonight."

He gave her a smoldering glance. "I'm not going to forget tonight."

After the main course arrived, they talked of everyday life. He asked about her garden, she asked about his workday. How wonderfully ordinary it all seemed.

"I'm not sure I can handle dessert," he told her, as the waiter removed their empty plates.

The waiter looked at Annabelle.

"I agree. No dessert. Maybe next time." She glanced at Tom.

Alone again, Tom took her hand. "I'm glad you feel there'll be a next time."

"Was that too presumptuous?"

He shook his head. "No, ma'am. Not at all. I hope they're successful and stay open for a long time, so we can visit on our anniversaries."

Annabelle caught her breath. "Anniversaries?"

"Too presumptuous?" He smiled into her eyes.

She shook her head. "Not at all."

He took a deep breath, as if he meant to say more, then exhaled as the waiter returned with the check. Was he disappointed by the interruption?

As he examined the check, she took the opportunity to excuse herself. "I have to powder my nose."

When Annabelle exited the ladies' room, she heard a familiar voice, speaking in a not-so-friendly manner.

"I told you to keep your distance." Was that Jensen Wade?

A man whose voice she didn't recognize answered, "I had to do something. You wouldn't return my calls or acknowledge my requests for a meeting. That makes me wonder if what I heard is true."

Annabelle paused, uncertain whether she should turn the corner and reveal her presence.

Jensen's answer froze her to the spot. "You do anything that reflects badly on me or my family, I will not hesitate to take whatever steps are necessary."

Annabelle covered her mouth. What did he mean by that?

A moment later, a red-faced Stuart Fox rounded the corner, nearly slamming into her.

Now she knew who owned the other voice, but the knowledge didn't settle her nerves. Scuttlebutt was, he now headed the area Klan activities. After he'd passed without even asking her pardon, she straightened her shoulders and stepped forward to find herself face-to-face with Jensen.

As recognition dawned in his eyes, he glanced past Annabelle to the place where Fox had disappeared, and then back to her face.

"Annabelle, what a surprise."

Steeling herself, she answered, "Jensen."

"What're you doing in Jackson this time of night?"

"I … uh … I'm here with Tom."

Pulling back, he gave her an appreciative look. "Dinner date, huh? Well, this is a nice place for it. I plan to return soon with Marla. She'll love it. Now, if you don't mind," he nodded toward the men's room.

She stepped aside. "Oh, I'm sorry, I'm blocking your way. Have a good evening, Jensen."

"And you, Annabelle. I'll talk to you soon, all right? We need to catch up."

She stood still a moment. Catch up, what had he meant by that? She willed her feet to move. He probably wanted to find out whether she'd overheard anything incriminating. Same old Jensen.

Though she tried her best to disguise her unease, Tom picked up on it right away.

"Everything all right?"

She put on her best smile. "Yes, I'm fine. You'll never guess who I ran into—Jensen."

"Jensen, really?" He glanced around. "Must be a

business dinner. I don't see Marla anywhere."

"Yes, he mentioned he plans to bring her here sometime."

Tom leaned forward. "Are you sure you're all right? He didn't say anything to upset you, did he?"

"Oh, no, I'm fine. Really. I was surprised, is all." She fiddled with her napkin but kept a smile directed at him. Was he fooled? She hoped so. He'd been so sweet before she left. She really hated to break the mood. Could they get back to it?

Tom held Annabelle's hand as they strolled to the truck. He didn't want the night to end but had no idea what else they could do. As he opened the door, she turned to face him.

"What a wonderful dinner. Thank you, Tom. I haven't enjoyed myself this much in such a long time."

If they weren't standing on the street, he'd take her in his arms and kiss her. "It was wonderful. I meant what I said. I hope to repeat this, often." He handed her up into the seat.

As he rounded the front of the vehicle, he noticed Jensen leaving the restaurant. He almost called out, but something about the man's demeanor gave him pause.

He climbed in and started the engine.

Annabelle touched his hand. "Was that Jensen?"

"Yes, it was." Before he backed out of the parking space, he looked at her. "Are you right sure you're okay?"

She kept her gaze on something outside the window, rather than turning to him. "Tom, I overheard something."

He cut the engine. "What was it?"

"He sort of made a threat to someone." She faced him, her eyes troubled. "It was Stuart Fox. Afterward, he came around the corner and almost knocked me down."

"Stu Fox? What did Jensen say to him?"

She shook her head, as though she didn't want to say.

"Annabelle, what did he say?"

"Jensen said, 'You do anything that reflects badly on me or my family, I will not hesitate to take whatever steps are necessary.'"

Tom sat back, staring straight ahead. "That could be taken several ways. Stu Fox is a little unpredictable. Kind of like dry kindling. Anything could set him off. Now that he's involved in politics, Jensen doesn't need someone like that casting a bad light on him." Especially in times like these.

"I know. You're right, that's probably all it was."

Tom looked more closely at her. She still seemed upset, like something troubled her. He touched her chin and angled her face toward him. "Annabelle, what is it?"

She gave a short laugh. "When Jensen saw me there, he told me we need to talk. Sometime. Catch up on things."

Tom leaned toward her, pressing a gentle kiss against her brow. He hoped to calm her nerves. "Maybe it's nothing, Annabelle. He wants to talk. He may be wondering if you overheard and wants to make sure you know it was nothing. Regardless of what he's done in the past, I really feel he's trying to do right. He's probably trying to keep a distance between himself and … those men."

Annabelle nodded. "I want to believe that. I really do." She sat back and looked at him. "I'm surprised to hear you talk about him in such a positive way."

"I've forgiven him, Annabelle."

"You're a good man, Tom."

"I try to be." He started the engine again and backed out of the space.

On the way home, he kept the conversation light, hoping to regain the earlier mood. He had her laughing by the time he pulled into her drive.

She dabbed at her eyes with a handkerchief. "Oh, Tom, I don't know when I've had such a good time. Have I already said that?"

"It doesn't matter. I love to hear it." He turned off the engine. Moments passed as he hesitated. He wanted the evening to continue, but he did have work in the morning. When he helped her out of the truck, she moved into his arms, as though it was the most natural thing in the world. His heart overflowed. How he longed for her, and for the time when they wouldn't have to say goodbye.

She lifted her eyes to his. "Thank you, Tom. I don't know why, but I really needed a good, strong hug."

He bent to kiss her, then held her again. "I'm happy to oblige, anytime."

She gave a contented sigh as they moved apart, then preceded him up the steps.

He drew a deep breath and slowly released it, wishing time would slow. "I love you, Annabelle."

For a moment, he wondered whether she was going to respond at all. She didn't seem surprised or hesitant, just calm. She touched his arm and then took his hand, intertwining her fingers with his. "I know I've made you wait a long time, Tom." She raised her eyes to his. "You've been a perfect gentleman, patient, and kind. I do love you, I know that now."

He couldn't keep from grinning. "I've finally worn you down, then."

Her gentle laughter reassured him. She leaned against him and lifted her lips to his.

Chapter Eighteen

June 8, 1957

Dressed in a long-sleeved shirt, baggy dungarees, boots, and a wide-brimmed straw hat, Annabelle headed to the back pasture to pick blackberries. She hoped to find enough for a cobbler to take to Tom's housewarming. Everyone loved her blackberry cobblers. Tom always told her it tasted like summertime.

She opened the gate and stepped through. Thank goodness, Thelma had limited the guest list to the Franklins and Alton, Connie, and Lillian. Alton had offered to grill some burgers for supper.

Annabelle had responded to Thelma's news with an arched brow. She would have given Tom time to settle in before throwing a party. But that was Thelma. She probably wanted to celebrate the fact she'd have her husband back, after so long working on the house.

Thelma had also mentioned Tom and Riley meant to go on a fishing trip soon. She said it was Tom's way of thanking Riley for his help.

Annabelle fastened the gate and paused a moment, gazing across the dew-laden grass, shimmering in the early morning light. Almost three years had passed since Ray and the boys went on a fishing trip and never returned. She pushed the memory from her mind.

A stick in one hand, a bucket in the other, she skirted the tall grass of the back pasture. It wouldn't be long before Alton would have to mow the field for hay. The year was flying by.

Deep-throated tree frogs competed with crickets and other singing insects, filling the warm morning air with sounds pleasing to Annabelle's ears. With careful steps, she moved closer to a clump of luscious berries. Why did the best ones always end up out of reach? She tossed a handful into her pail. The harvest was plentiful this year. Her mouth watered, anticipating the taste of the pie she'd make.

As the sun rose, it warmed her back. Her fingers flew through the task, filling the pail, which she emptied into the larger bucket. Then she made her way back into the thicket. All the while, she kept a sharp lookout for snakes. They often hid in the berry-laden brambles, waiting for birds.

She'd emptied two more pails full of berries when she heard the putt-putt of a tractor. She raised her eyes to the wagon road that connected her property to Sutter's. When the tractor cleared the tree line, she waved to Willie. He lifted his hat to her and smiled a greeting before turning the tractor toward Tom's house.

She set the pail down and removed her gloves. He must be taking firewood and supplies over for the cookout. Her heart skipped at the thought. By evening, she'd have a full-time neighbor. A right handsome one, too.

Thoughts of Tom had weaved in and out of her mind since waking. She'd already relived their date a dozen times. He'd treated her like a princess. She could get used to that, especially after the last couple of years. She'd felt a little like a princess, too, with her new outfit, the hair-do, the manicured nails. She looked at her hands now stained by berry juice. She had to chuckle. What a different picture she'd make today, dressed as she was. With her slight figure hidden beneath too-generous dungarees, her hairstyle wilted under a wide-brimmed straw hat.

What would Tom think of her now? Would his gaze still burn her soul like glowing embers?

"Ouch!" She pricked her finger on a thorn, drawing blood. "Serves you right. Better pay attention to what you're doing, Annabelle."

After mopping her brow, she sipped from her water jar. Looking around, she checked for the best direction to take. The blackberry thickets continued all the way into the woods on Sutter's property. She'd always found the biggest berries on the vines near the woods, so she picked up the bucket and stick and headed that way.

When a faint scent of wood smoke greeted her near a narrow path that led into the woods, her thoughts continued in a different direction. The other night, she'd seen the light of a campfire. That was the same day Miss Lucy told her about Hero's disappearance. Maybe the boy hid out in the woods overnight. She hadn't heard another word about it. Oh, how she hoped he'd been found.

She shrugged away the strain in her shoulders and took a step back as something moved among the twisted briers. She reached for the stick, in case she needed to stave off a snake. This one kept out of her way, so she went back to picking. One more pail should do it.

When she came level with the path, she noticed footprints in the damp earth. Maybe someone else had been curious about the campfire. She looked closer. A lot of someones. A chill raced up her spine at a noise, the crack of a branch. She squinted into the deep shade of the woods.

"Who's there?"

No one answered. Other than birdsong and insects, she heard only the distant bark of a neighbor's dog. She sent one last glance around the perimeter. It was probably a limb falling, or even a rabbit in the woods.

She emptied the last berries into the bucket, then grabbed her stick and her water. May as well call it a day. But she couldn't seem to shake the feeling she was being watched.

Annabelle rinsed the berries at the kitchen sink, then put the cobbler together. She placed it in the oven. While it baked, she finished the deviled eggs Thelma had asked her to make and set those in the icebox to chill.

Already, the house smelled delicious. She left the heat of the kitchen to go bathe. Maybe the activity would help rein in her growing excitement.

Like most everyone else, this would be her first opportunity to see the finished interior of the home. Oh, she could've gone in at any time, since she had a key, but it didn't seem right. It irked her a little that Rose

Ella had gotten the first look. The woman had admitted as much after choir practice last week.

"No one was home, but I found the back door unlocked, so I went on in. I'm sure it was all right since Tom hadn't properly moved in yet. But, oh my stars, I have to confess to being vastly disappointed, Annabelle." She closed her eyes and shook her head. "That man hadn't taken one of my suggestions—not one!" She huffed. "I left some flowers on the kitchen counter, to remind him how nice a woman's touch could be. But he never even said a word about it. Can you imagine?" She'd dusted her hands together as if to brush off the memory.

Annabelle could fully imagine it. Most men wouldn't pay attention to flowers. Tom probably figured Thelma sent them with Riley. But that conversation kicked Annabelle's curiosity into high gear. Tom hadn't taken Rose Ella's advice about the colors.

He had probably gone ahead and painted all the walls white like he'd wanted to in the first place. Except the kitchen, which would be yellow. Of that, she was certain.

Annabelle lined a basket with a kitchen towel before setting the freshly baked cobbler inside. She set her hands on her hips. "Looks like I'll have to make two trips."

A car horn blared. She quick-stepped to the screen door and peeked out. She smiled and waved as Judith strode toward the house, carrying her pocketbook, along with an overnight bag.

"I hope you don't mind if I stay the weekend."

"Not a bit." Annabelle held the door wide. "It'll be wonderful to have company. You're here in time for the housewarming next door."

Judith set her things down and then hugged Annabelle. "Is that today? I'm so glad I didn't miss it." She paused to sniff the air. "Blackberry cobbler? Yum."

Annabelle returned to the basket. "I'm packing it up right now. You'll save me having to make two trips."

Judith crossed to the kitchen window and looked out. "Is anyone over there yet?"

"No, I planned to be first." She gave Judith a conspiratorial grin. "I'm eager to get a look at the house."

"Me too. How can I help?"

Judith covered the cobbler while Annabelle retrieved the deviled eggs and a jug of tea. With the key safely tucked in her apron pocket, she led the way across the yard.

"Looks like you've already worn a path in the lawn." Judith giggled. "Hey, how was your dinner the other night?"

Annabelle glanced at Judith. How had she heard about that?

"You know Ma told me all about it when I talked to her the other day."

"When did you talk to her?" Thelma didn't have a phone and seldom made a trip anywhere.

"Oh, she calls me once a week from the pay phone at the cafe. You didn't know about that?" Judith grinned. "She likes to keep tabs on her eldest daughter, you know."

"And keep her daughter abreast of all the local news, seems like." Try as she might, Annabelle couldn't keep from smiling. She loved her cousin Thelma, but you couldn't tell that woman anything you didn't want reported all over town. Thelma was like Trenton's version of the evening news.

Sunshine illuminated the soft colors of the inside walls of Tom's house. Though Rose Ella had done her best to obliterate all Annabelle's choices, he had somehow figured them out. Annabelle wanted to shout for joy as she and Judith entered the butter-yellow kitchen.

Judith set the basket on the counter. "What a bright, happy place, Aunt Annabelle. I can see you cooking on that fancy new range." She peeked in a couple of the cabinets. "Filling the cupboards with flowery dishes and pretty glasses." The girl's mischievous grin assured Annabelle she was teasing.

"You better behave yourself, young lady."

After stowing the perishables in the refrigerator, Annabelle stepped outside to empty the sad remains of Rose Ella's bouquet.

Judith turned from looking out the window. "Let's go see the rest of the house before everyone else gets here."

Most of the rooms lacked curtains or any sort of window treatments. Maybe Rose Ella was right about one thing—the place did need a woman's touch. Annabelle's fingers itched to sew some pretty curtains. Wonder if Tom would allow her ... Judith's voice broke the spell.

"Isn't this nice? I do like white tile. It looks so shiny and clean." She ran her fingers over the smooth surface of the pretty white tile in the bathroom.

Annabelle agreed, but she couldn't help remembering Rose Ella's disdain. It was all a matter of taste. Some folks were as different as night from day.

Judith joined Annabelle in the front bedroom. "What a nice-sized room. I can sleep in here when I visit."

Annabelle opened her mouth to comment but paused at the sound of voices.

Judith looked out the window. "It's Ma." She bustled to the front door as J.W. and Stevie approached the steps, each carrying a cardboard box. Annabelle waited in the kitchen. She stepped aside as the boys entered.

"Morning, Aunt Annabelle," J.W. said, echoed by Stevie, who lowered his box to the floor before taking off down the hall.

Raydeen appeared next, followed closely by Thelma. "Look at you, Annabelle, already making yourself at home."

Annabelle chose to ignore Thelma's implication and took one of the grocery bags she carried. "Riley not coming in?"

"No, he's heading back to town. Drew had to work this morning, but he wanted to help with the move, so Riley's going to pick him up." She poked J.W.'s shoulder. "You'd best get. Pa's a-waiting."

Thelma set the other bag on the kitchen counter, along with her purse. Then, she glanced around. "My, my. What a good job they did. I'm right proud of our men."

Raydeen and Stevie passed through the kitchen, headed out the back door.

Thelma called after them, "Y'all don't run off, now. Stay close." She hugged Judith and kissed her cheek. "It's so good to see you, sugar. I'm so glad you could make it for the housewarming. It'll make your Uncle Tom happy, too."

"What can I do to help?"

"There's a dust mop in that closet yonder. Why don't you run it over the floors while we clean the kitchen cabinets?"

Thelma commenced unloading boxes. "How was dinner at that fancy I-talian restaurant y'all went to?"

"The food was delicious."

She eyed Annabelle. "Land sakes, Annabelle, loosen up." She grinned. "Remember how we used to tell each other everything? I do. I remember when you were dating Rudie Buckson, …"

Annabelle held up her hand. "All right. My goodness, no need to bring up ancient history." She unwrapped water glasses and set them in the cupboard. "The place is sort of fancy, with plush red chairs and white linen tablecloths, and music playing in the background. A nice young woman came around with a camera, so we had our picture made."

Thelma opened the refrigerator door to stow a couple of dishes she'd brought. "What did you eat? Something not so ordinary, I hope."

"I had lasagna."

"I read about that in a women's magazine. Just reading about it made my mouth water." She rinsed her hands at the sink and dried them. "I hope Tom tried something different."

"Spaghetti."

"Of course, he did. He's so predictable." She opened the icebox again, to place a jug of tea inside. "Oh, don't those eggs look scrumptious?" She turned to face Annabelle. "So, y'all had a photograph made? Tom must truly love you. He hates having his picture made."

Annabelle smiled but gave no response.

Judith leaned through the kitchen door. "Guess what, y'all? Uncle Tom has two bathrooms. Two! What's a man living all alone going to do with two bathrooms?"

This was news to Annabelle. How had she missed that?

Thelma swept past. "It's a powder room, I'll bet. No bath to it. Come on, Annabelle, I've got to see that before the men get here."

Annabelle trailed at a distance as the two women entered the last room on the right, the largest of the three bedrooms. Tom's bedroom. A place Annabelle had never been. Even now, she hesitated outside the door.

Thelma's voice bounced off the barren walls of the empty room. "Come look, Annabelle. Did you know about this?"

Annabelle forced her feet to move, till she stood inside the bedroom door. "I sure didn't." She had assumed that second opening in the side wall was another clothes closet. It didn't seem much bigger than a good-sized closet. Painted to match the bedroom, it held a pedestal sink and a toilet. The black-and-white floor tiles were the same as in the main bathroom. "Well, it's right handy if you have to get up in the night."

Judith cackled. "Aunt Annabelle!"

Thelma's raucous laughter echoed through the house.

Annabelle shook her head. It didn't take much to entertain these two. On the way out, she scanned the room. Four windows gave it a bright, airy feeling. Nice as it was, her discomfort increased by the second. What if Tom walked in? She did not want him to catch her ogling his bedroom.

Thelma toed the floor. "Riley showed me this tile after they bought it. Won't it be cold in winter, though?"

Was that a car door slamming? Annabelle threw up her hands and skittered out as the front door opened and there he was. Her steps faltered. The look he gave her sent her heart into palpitations.

Chapter Nineteen

Tom opened the front door and stepped inside as Annabelle entered from the hallway. He started to smile but paused at the expression on her face. Embarrassment? Was he reading that correctly? "Everything all right?"

She nodded, though all the signs said no. "Yes. All right. Everything is." Color crept into her face. "Fine." She smoothed her hair before looking away.

He wanted to laugh out loud but held back. That might embarrass her further, or make her mad, though he wasn't sure why. Was she thinking about how they'd last parted, after that mind-searing kiss? He tore his eyes from her face as Thelma bustled in.

"It's about time. What took you fellas so long?"

She was followed closely by Judith. "Congratulations on finishing the house, Uncle Tom. It sure is nice."

"Thank you, Judith. I didn't know you were making the trip over."

She grinned. "It's not far. Just Jackson."

Thelma looked out the door. "Where're the others?"

Tom still watched Annabelle, who had taken off toward the kitchen. What was going on with her? He focused on Thelma. "They went up to the store to get colas. Riley promised the boys. They'll be right back."

Thelma shook her head. "They're supposed to be helping you unload. Anything we can do? The house is all clean and ready for you."

"That's a whole lot, right there. You don't need to worry about anything else." He took a step closer and lowered his voice. "Is Annabelle feeling all right?"

Thelma's eyes darted toward the kitchen door and back to his face. "Oh, yes. We were admiring that fancy powder room of yours." She covered her mouth and giggled.

Huh. Why would that make her act all embarrassed? Maybe she hadn't liked it.

Riley pulled his car into the drive, wresting Thelma's attention from Tom.

She and Judith headed outside, leaving Tom free to find Annabelle. But he couldn't ask her if she was all right again since he'd already done that. Instead, he stood in the kitchen doorway where he could see her, working at the sink. Like a man dying of thirst, he drank in the scene. She looked so right, as though she belonged there. Well, maybe not at his kitchen sink, but in his house, taking care of things. Taking care of him.

He jumped when someone touched his arm.

"Uncle Tom?" Twelve-year-old J.W. stood next to him, holding a table lamp.

Out of the corner of his eye, Tom saw Annabelle turn to look at them.

"Where's this go?" J.W. asked.

Tom cast a quick smile at Annabelle. "In the living room, J.W. I'm right behind you." After one more long, sweet exchange of glances with the woman of his dreams, he spurred his feet into action as Riley's voice filled the rooms. "Let's get this done. I'm a hungry man."

Tom had trouble concentrating with all the activity and folks asking where things went. After the Wades arrived, Alton and Willie got a fire going. The ladies began loading the tables with food.

Judith strode through carrying bed linens. "Pa and

Drew got your bed up, Uncle Tom. I'll get it made for you."

Tom dogged her steps down the hall. "You don't have to do that."

"You'll be tired later, and glad it's all done." She gave him a bright smile that reminded him so much of a younger Thelma. It was easy to see why that preacher had latched onto her.

"Well, thank you, Judith. I appreciate it."

Tom wandered back to the front of the house, his mind filled with Annabelle. Every time he entered the door, his eyes automatically sought her out. When she went outside to help set up the table, he found himself standing in front of the picture window, gazing out at her.

After too long standing there, he shook himself to clear his thoughts. He secured Drew's help repositioning the living room furniture. Riley joined in as they set up the dining room table.

When that was finished, Riley plopped down and declared himself done. He mopped his neck and forehead with a handkerchief and sat back.

As if she'd read his mind, Thelma appeared with a tall glass of iced water. "Here, Riley. Cool yourself off." She looked at Tom. "Food's almost ready."

"Thank you, Thelma. I'll be right out." Tom strode

to what Thelma had called his "powder room," washed his hands and rinsed his face. He smiled to see towels already neatly arranged on the towel bar, ready for use. Those women were mighty handy to have around.

He stood inside the back door a moment, taking in the scene as his family assembled for a meal at his house. He hoped it was the first of many.

Alton caught sight of him and waved. "Hey, Tom, come on out here. We're ready to ask a blessing over the food."

Tom stood at the head of the table they'd put together with planks and sawhorses. He held up his hands. "First of all, let me give thanks to all of you who helped make this day happen. I'm forever in your debt."

Riley cleared his throat. "You might not ought to say that."

This was greeted by laughter, all around the table.

Tom chuckled. "You're right, but I won't take it back. I mean it. Now, let me ask a blessing over this delicious food so we can eat."

"Amen to that," Riley said.

Thelma slapped his arm.

Tom gave them a moment to settle before sending up a heartfelt thanks to God.

After the meal, Tom, Alton, and Riley sat looking toward the back of the property. It wasn't long before Riley dozed off.

Alton sat forward, resting his elbows on his knees. "Thanks for calling me the other morning."

Tom gave a slight nod to acknowledge his thanks. "Did you find the boy?"

"Right where you saw the firelight." He drew back a bit, his brow furrowed. "And none too soon."

"What happened?"

"Willie and I found him hiding in the woods. It took some doing, but we talked him out and took him to my house. We got him cleaned up. He slept at Sutter's in that back room where Annabelle stayed after her accident."

"Oh, yes. I visited her there."

"Uh-huh. That same night, Samson went to barking. When I got up to check on it, I saw lights shining in the woods." He aimed a piercing glance at Tom. "Lots of lights. Four or five vehicles were parked along the old wagon road with their headlights pointed into the woods."

"You think it was—"

Alton gave a slow nod. "I know it was. I stayed

put, not wanting to draw any attention to the house. I prayed they'd move on when they didn't find the boy." He sat back. "They did finally, after about an hour searching those woods."

Tom couldn't help thinking of Annabelle, who lived so short a distance away. Thank the Lord they didn't come over this way. He looked at Alton. "Where's Hero now?"

"Marla picked him up the next day. She drove him and his mother all the way to Paducah, where she put them on the train. They called her yesterday evening to say they were in Detroit."

"All the way to Paducah? Was she thinking somebody would be watching—looking for the boy?"

Alton ran his fingers through his hair before replacing his hat. "She didn't want to take any chances. That new fella's a powder keg."

He didn't have to mention the name. Tom knew exactly who he was talking about. The altercation between Stuart and Jensen at the restaurant had been in and out of his mind ever since. "I've heard that. I'm glad Hero's safe, and they're both away from here."

Alton agreed. "Yes, sir. I sure hope Lester stays out of trouble."

"Times are changing."

"I know, and up north, it's some better for the

black man, I hear."

Tom sat forward. "I've heard that, too." He couldn't help but wonder if things would ever improve for them here, or in all the south, for that matter.

Riley gave a loud snore.

Alton glanced at Tom and chuckled. "I guess I'd better get my family home. Got evening chores to do." He pushed up from the chair.

Tom stood with him. "Well, I'm mighty obliged to you and Willie for making those fine burgers."

"We enjoyed it. I hope it's the first of many meals between our families." He started to turn away but paused to lay his arm over Tom's shoulders. "Come to think of it, there's no between to it. We are family." He removed his arm and held out his hand.

Tom gripped it. "Thank you, Alton. That means a lot to me. Sometimes life takes unexpected turns." Warmth enveloped him as they ambled to the patio where the women sat.

Alton's eyes were on Connie. "Boy, doesn't it though?"

Connie looked up at their approach. "Is it time to go?"

Alton helped her rise. "Yes, it is."

Tom hadn't paid much attention to Connie lately, but couldn't help noticing now, she was blossoming, as his mother used to say.

With a warm smile toward Tom, she smoothed the front of her maternity blouse. "What a wonderful place you have here. This backyard is pure relaxation. You get such a nice breeze on this hilltop."

"Thank you, Connie. I hope you'll visit often."

She cut a quick glance toward Annabelle. "I will. We all will."

Miss Lillian stood, holding an empty dish. "You've got enough leftover food in your kitchen to keep you a few days, Tom. Along with a couple of surprises from Regina."

"Well, you tell Regina I'm obliged. I can't wait to see what she sent."

At their car, Alton nudged Tom's arm. "You going to church in the morning?"

Tom nodded, wondering why he was asking. "I reckon so."

His voice low, Alton said, "Judith's here tomorrow, but we usually pick up Annabelle in time for Sunday school. I wanted to make sure you hadn't planned on bringing her in town with you."

Tom hadn't thought about it. Not yet. Not Sunday school. He gripped the back of his neck. "Not sure about that."

Alton gave him a reassuring smile. "I'm not going

to pressure you. It's your decision. But my class meets outside in good weather. We're a little less rigid than some. You're welcome to visit."

He was almost tempted, especially when he thought about spending more time with his beloved. But was he ready to go public? They'd be on display for sure, sitting on that up-front pew she preferred. He shrugged. "Maybe after the fishing trip."

Alton opened his door and got in. "All right then. Let us know if you need anything, you hear?"

"Will do." He waved to all of them, noticing for the first time that Chase had been in the group. The boy sat in the back seat with Miss Lillian and Joseph. How had he missed that? If he was going to be part of the family, he'd need to be more observant.

Annabelle stood on the back porch with Judith, watching the sunset as Tom rounded the corner of the house. He paused when he saw them. An odd feeling swept through her. Did he wonder why they were still there? She touched Judith's arm. "We better get going, hon. I'm sure Tom's looking forward to relaxing in his new home."

He took a step nearer. "Actually, I was wondering

if you two would like to join me in a piece of Regina's lemon meringue pie." He gave them a welcoming smile.

Judith looked at Annabelle. "I'd love a slice, wouldn't you? Regina makes the best lemon pie."

They sat at the kitchen table, drinking the last of the tea, and enjoying the wonderful dessert. Judith's presence lent a family atmosphere as she and Tom shared favorite memories of years and events that Annabelle had missed. Sometimes, she deeply regretted missing so much of their lives, but it was a path she'd chosen. One she didn't regret, though the road had taken a tragic, unexpected twist.

Tom touched her hand. "Are we boring you, Annabelle?"

"Oh, no, I love hearing about those days. I've got some of the photographs Thelma sent me over the years, so your stories kind of fill in the blanks for me."

Judith took their empty plates to the sink. "I used to love getting mail all the way from California, Aunt Annabelle. We looked at your pictures and wondered about the palm trees and the ocean. It seemed like a faraway land. Daddy used to talk about someday visiting, but we never did."

When Annabelle stood, Tom stood too, reaching to slide her chair beneath the table. She smiled into his eyes. "It's been a wonderful day, Tom. I know you're going to love it here."

Judith was rinsing the last of the dishes.

While the girl's back was turned, Tom gave Annabelle that look she'd seen more often of late—the one that burned right through her. He had definitely found a way to set his hook in her heart. She didn't mind, except it made her weak in the knees.

"We'd best get home, Judith. I need to shut the chickens up for the night."

Judith dried her hands on a towel and smoothed it out on the countertop. She stood on tiptoes to plant a kiss on Tom's cheek. "Good night, Uncle Tom. I reckon we'll see you tomorrow."

Tom walked with them until Annabelle turned toward the hen house. She lifted her hand to him. "Good night, Tom."

A moment later, Judith caught up to her. "My stars, Aunt Annabelle, I thought the very air was gonna melt between you two."

Annabelle frowned in her direction. "What are you talking about? How would the air melt?"

Judith snorted. "He's so in love with you, it brings joy to my heart."

It brought joy to her heart too, but Annabelle wasn't ready to discuss it, even with Judith. Instead, she gave her attention to the task at hand. The chickens were already roosting, so she fastened the gate before walking to the house with Judith. The girl hadn't said another word.

Inside the house, she pulled the string to turn on the light in the kitchen, then stepped to the sink to wash her hands. When she returned to the front room, she found Judith seated on the sofa with Ginger curled up on her lap.

Annabelle lowered herself into the adjacent chair and laid her hand on Judith's knee. "I hope I didn't hurt your feelings, sugar. I'm not ready to talk lightly about my feelings for your Uncle Tom."

Judith looked up. "What? Oh, no, I'm not … my feelings aren't hurt. I'm sorry I teased you, though. I didn't mean to make light of such a serious situation." A spark of mischief in the girl's eyes kindled a small smile.

Annabelle returned the smile. She started to rise, intending to go get ready for bed, but something in Judith's demeanor held her in place. "Is everything all right, dear?"

Judith took a deep breath and exhaled before raising her eyes to Annabelle's. "I have something to tell you, Aunt Annabelle."

Chapter Twenty

Annabelle searched Judith's face. "It's good news, I hope?"

Judith chewed one side of her lip as she peered at Annabelle. "Preston has asked me to marry him."

"Ah."

Judith gave her a pleading look. "Don't say anything to Ma, please? Not yet."

"I won't, but I'm not sure why not. She loves Preston."

"I know she does. But she'll tell everyone. She can't help herself." Judith went back to stroking the cat. "I'm not ready for that, Aunt Annabelle. You understand, I'm sure."

"Indeed, I do." Sitting back, she rested her hands in her lap and watched the girl, waiting for her to continue. When she didn't speak, Annabelle ventured a question, "So, have you given him an answer?"

Her eyes on the cat, Judith nodded. "I have accepted."

Annabelle watched, unable to keep from smiling as roses bloomed in Judith's cheeks. Oh, to be young again and so sure of yourself. "Are you ready to be a pastor's wife?"

The girl gave a full-on grin, complete with brimming eyes. "He's in my heart, Aunt Annabelle. I'd go to the ends of the earth, as long as I can be with Preston."

Annabelle leaned forward to pat Judith's knee. "That sounds a little bit like love."

The girl's gaze took on a dreamy cast. "Oh, it is love." She heaved a sigh. "I knew you'd understand. Thanks so much for being here for me. For listening, and not giving your opinion."

"Oh, ho." Annabelle chuckled. "The truth comes out. Now I understand why you're waiting to make it public."

"You know Ma better than anyone. Well, almost anyone. She'll rake me over the coals, interrogate me till I want to scream. Then when she's satisfied I've made up my mind, she'll act like it was all her idea. Something she'd known was going to happen, all along." She hid a giggle behind her hand.

Yes, that was Thelma, all right. Annabelle had to laugh. This pretty, little redheaded girl of hers was set on doing things her own way, just like her mama. "Are you still planning on graduating?"

"Oh, yes. I'll finish at the same time as Preston. Then we can get married. Maybe have a little time before we're sent someplace. I hope it's not too far from home."

"Well, if it is, you'll be fine. You make friends easily, and so does Preston. He'll be with you, and so will Father God."

Judith took Annabelle's hand. "We're never alone, are we, Aunt Annabelle? You've shown me—no, all of us—that through it all the Lord is with us like He promised. He will never leave or forsake us. I can't say whether I'd do as well as you through the deep troubles that should have overwhelmed you. But I aspire to know the same kind of faith. A faith that will never be shaken."

Annabelle sat still, unable to utter a single word at Judith's proclamation. She could not take credit for it. The way she'd muddled through the last few years, licking her wounds. But no one saw that. No one knew her innermost thoughts. None but God, and He wasn't telling. She tried to swallow, but her mouth had gone dry. All the wetness had risen to her eyes. Fearing she might cry, Annabelle forced a smile, but words were not necessary. She dabbed at a couple of runaway tears while waiting for Judith to speak again.

"I know I can do whatever needs doing, as long as it's His will." She smiled at Annabelle. "I'm ninety-nine percent sure it is."

"That's wonderful, sugar. I'm so happy for you." She sat back. Why couldn't she be as certain of her own decision?

Pastor Nathan had barely uttered his final amen when Rose Ella called out, "I need to see the choir members for a moment before you leave."

Annabelle internalized a groan. She'd hoped to get out fast enough to maybe catch Tom. He'd been there today, had actually stayed for the benediction. It had been wrong of her, but she had not resisted the temptation. She'd sneaked a peek at him during the prayer.

"The choir fest is only two months away. That means we need to add on some extra practice time."

Most everyone groaned, including Annabelle.

A deep bass voice rang out. "I thought we sounded pretty good last practice."

"Pretty good is not nearly good enough! So, we can meet on Saturday mornings, or an hour before service on Sunday evenings."

Annabelle looked at the folks around her. Most of them were farmers. They had little time to spare.

The bass singer held up big, work-worn hands. "My stomach is rumbling for its dinner, so let's settle this right quick. Let's meet Sundays since most of us are already coming in town for evening service."

His suggestion was followed by the fastest exodus Annabelle had ever observed in church. She darted between two pews to avoid being trampled. After everyone else had gone, she walked with Connie toward the door.

Rose Ella caught up to them. "I'm beginning to regret not electing a soloist. I heard through the grapevine; Windy City has a pinch-hitter. One of their college-age girls, home for the summer. She attends Vanderbilt and is widely known for her arias."

Annabelle wasn't sure what an aria was, but she recognized the panic in Rose Ella's eyes. "Breathe, Rose Ella, it'll be all right. Let's vow to do our best to glorify God."

Rose Ella glared as if Annabelle had suggested she play piano in her underwear. "It's a competition, Annabelle. You're supposed to try to win it." She swung her arms in the air, almost whacked Annabelle with her purse. "That's ... that's the whole point—to win."

Alton stepped inside the door. "Are you ladies ready to go?"

Connie quick-stepped to his side.

Annabelle was right behind her.

Hot on their trail, Rose Ella sputtered. "I'll think of something, but you'd both better practice at home. We want to be at our absolute best."

Outside, Annabelle searched the parking lot in vain. Tom had gone. Even knowing he lived next door and she'd see him most every day did little to relieve her disappointment.

Alton opened the car door. "Judith is having dinner with her family, I guess?"

"Yes. She's heading back to Jackson this afternoon. She has to work tomorrow."

In the back seat, Lillian touched her arm. "Tom waited, hoping to speak to you. He had to go finish something at the pharmacy. I asked him to dinner, but he said he needed to get home, to settle in a bit before the work week starts back up."

Annabelle huffed. Rose Ella! Bless her heart. The one time Tom waited.

Joseph peeked over the back of the seat. "Granny

coming too?"

"Yes, I'm coming with you, Joseph." She glanced around. "Are we waiting for Chase?"

Alton eyed her in the mirror. "He's having dinner at home today. He'll come back after evening service."

Connie helped Joseph climb into the backseat before addressing Alton. "We have to be here an hour early."

He started the engine and backed the car around. "Why is that?"

"Rose Ella's worried about the singing."

Lillian put an arm around Joseph. "Seems to me Rose Ella's always worried about something."

Annabelle sighed. "You are right about that."

Tom's short to-do list at the store had taken twice the time it should have. How long could he continue to work through such distraction?

He'd waited outside the church, but when Miss Lillian told him the choir was meeting with Rose Ella, he saw little point in staying longer.

Back home, the house brought him some satisfaction. He liked the way things were shaping up. He'd already stowed most of his belongings, so the refusal of Miss Lillian's invitation was mostly unfounded. But, how long had it been since he had a place of his own? Or, been able to enjoy things he'd once taken for granted—like peace and quiet, being able to do whatever he wanted, whenever he wanted.

He warmed up a few leftovers from the cookout. When he sat at his kitchen table, he thought of Annabelle. "A lonely supper," she had once called it. How many lonely meals had she endured these past couple of years since Connie and Alton married? Too many to count, he reckoned. Leaning forward, he turned on the radio. A body could have too much quiet.

The dishes washed and put away, he stood gazing out the back window. One more week, maybe two. Fourteen days at the most? He closed his eyes and prayed, "Dear Lord, please let it be so."

Crossing the room to his desk, he opened a side drawer. He took out a small velvet box. He flipped open the lid to admire the ring nestled inside. He'd bought it a year or so ago. He'd held onto it, waiting for the perfect time. But he'd let time get away. This week, these few days, seemed to come around so fast. This was the one time of year he needed to avoid. He couldn't ask Annabelle to marry him on, or even close to the anniversary of her greatest tragedy.

It was also bad timing that Riley scheduled a

fishing trip the weekend after the fourth. Tom was pretty sure it would cause problems, at least in Annabelle's mind. So, he'd put off telling her about it. Oh, she knew, but not because he'd said anything. Riley wasn't the sensitive type. He wasn't unkind on purpose. He never gave a thought about how others might react. He'd bragged long and loud about the upcoming excursion at the housewarming. Tom had winced at his words. He'd sought Annabelle's eyes, but she was looking away.

No one else seemed concerned about it. Maybe they all assumed the past was forgotten, but Tom knew Annabelle. He removed the ring from the box, held it between his thumb and forefinger, let the stone sparkle in the sunlight. He imagined her wearing it, something he hadn't been able to do in the past. Her confession, that she loved him, had given him confidence.

He replaced the ring and then put the box in the drawer. After the fishing trip, before too many days had passed, he'd repeat the question he'd asked months ago. Then, he'd put the ring on her finger. If she accepted his proposal.

Annabelle fastened the chicken house gate. This

had surely been the longest Sunday in all of history. Because of the add-on choir practice, she'd stayed at Sutter's all day, when all she'd wanted was to come home.

In case Tom chanced to visit. She glanced toward the house next door, then hurried toward her back porch, hoping he wasn't looking out his window. She wouldn't want him to get the wrong idea and think she was watching his house like a nosy neighbor.

She washed her hands at the kitchen sink and made it halfway to the refrigerator when footsteps sounded on the porch.

"Knock, knock! Annabelle, you home?"

Tom. Her heart sputtered like an overfilled coffee pot. "I'll be right out." She stopped to check her hair in the mirror. It wasn't perfect, but nothing could be done about it. She opened the screen and stepped out. "Hello, Tom."

Light spilled out through the screen door, lighting his face as he held up a couple of bottles of pop. "I thought you might like to sit a while and drink a soda with me."

She accepted one before moving toward the swing where they could sit side-by-side. "That was thoughtful of you."

He sat next to her. "Well, no, it was selfish of me."

He smiled into her eyes. "I wanted to see you."

"I wouldn't consider that selfish, since you're here right now, keeping me company." Yes, she could get used to this.

He tipped his bottle toward her. "I like that answer." They drank in silence for several minutes. "Did you ever hear any more from Jensen?"

She shook her head. "No. I haven't seen him, except at church this morning."

"Maybe it'll all die down."

"I hope so. Alton said Livia and Hero are in Detroit. I was glad to hear it."

"He told me yesterday. That boy's bound for something special, I think."

Miss Lucy's story popped into her mind. "You could be right."

They sat in silence for several minutes, sipping their colas.

The call of a whippoorwill reminded Annabelle it was getting late. She didn't want the evening to end. It had taken too long to get here.

"How I've missed that sound," Tom said, almost whispering.

"It is right pleasant until you're trying to go to sleep."

He chuckled. "I suppose that's true."

Why did she get the feeling he was holding back something? She sent a furtive glance his way, then smiled when he caught her looking.

"What?"

She retrieved a hankie from her pocket and touched it to her lips. "Nothing. Nothing important, anyway. Are you all settled in?"

"Pretty much. Enough for now. I reckon it's an ongoing process."

"I know that's true. If you need any help, let me know."

He tipped his bottle toward her. "I'll do that."

Once again, silence reigned, but it was not uncomfortable. As dusk descended, peaceful, country sounds enveloped them. Annabelle imagined a time when they'd be like this every evening in sweet companionship. She drank the last of the pop and held the bottle on her lap, waiting.

He cleared his throat. "Well, we both have to get up early, so I'd best head that way." He leaned forward but didn't rise.

She tilted her head. Was he waiting for her to stand first?

When he reached for her empty pop bottle, their fingers touched. He kissed her brow. "Goodnight, Annabelle." The swing rose as his weight left it.

Annabelle released the breath she'd held, expecting a different kind of kiss. "Goodnight." Her hand on the chain, she stood but waited as he stepped away. She missed him already. "Have a good day tomorrow."

He nodded and smiled. "I'll do my best." He hadn't gone far when he turned back. "If you ever need anything, I'm right next door now. All you have to do is ask."

"Thank you, Tom. I will." Would she? As he walked away, tears burned her eyes. She could never ask for the one thing she needed most right now.

Annabelle turned and stepped inside, surrounded by a quiet that was no longer peaceful. Every fiber of her being wanted to follow him next door.

Betty Thomason Owens

Chapter Twenty-One

July 6, 1957

Stop staring. Annabelle shook herself. What was wrong with her? Why was she still so upset? Well, she wasn't going to mope. She'd make herself busy. She'd … go see if Connie needed her help with anything.

On a mission now, she marched into the kitchen and hung up her apron. After running a comb through her hair, she headed out the back door.

The weather was fine. The sky, one big expanse of blue. Though it was early, voices sounded from the cotton fields. The workers were in for a long, hot day of chopping the weeds out of the cotton.

Annabelle padded along the dry ruts of the old wagon road, alongside the newly mowed hayfield, where grass lay drying in straight rows, awaiting the hay bailer.

Near a stand of tall oak trees, wild roses twined

among the honeysuckle vines on an old wrought-iron fence. Her steps faltered. She shouldn't stop. Unable to resist, she crept in among the old gravestones, trying not to tread directly on a grave. It was cool and quiet, except for a constant chirp of insects. She found an old stone bench and sat.

"No point in moping." She flinched inwardly at the strength of the emotions coursing through her mind. She bowed her head beneath the weight of it. Three years had passed. By now, her mourning should be over.

But it wasn't. The pain dug in, clawed at her insides, and wouldn't give up till it had wrenched sobs from deep within her breast. *Why, God?*

Why now, when she'd been so happy?

She forced a deep breath. How could he take off like that, on the anniversary of the tragedy that had stolen her husband and sons? What if he didn't come back, either? What if … she bent forward, allowing the sobs to wrack her body. Taking up a corner of her skirt, she staunched her tears, because she'd gone off without a hankie.

Breathe, Annabelle. Let God calm your heart and soul. Trust in Him.

Positive thoughts swirled around her like an eddy in a pond, stirring the water, but doing no real good.

They were only words, after all. Until she was ready to let go of her feelings, she'd be bound to this sorrow.

She smoothed her hair before pushing up from the bench. Laying her hand on the cool granite of a gravestone jerked her back to reason. Rooted her, somehow.

Her husband and sons had been laid to rest in San Diego. She hadn't been back there. Couldn't go back. On occasion, she'd come to this small family plot seeking solace. Sometimes it helped, but not today. Surrounded by the monuments of Sutters and Sterlings, the pain didn't let up, it increased.

Looking out beyond the covering of the trees, heat waves wrinkled the air. She clasped her hands and stood still as her mind traveled back to quite a different place. Where bougainvillea bloomed along the white walls surrounding a memory garden. Palm trees towered outside the wall, like silent sentinels.

Three gaping holes stood ready to receive three identical caskets. Folks dressed in black surrounded them, hovering, wearing masks of sorrow. His voice low and rumbling, Brother Matthews read the words of the twenty-third Psalm. Bittersweet.

Stalwart soldiers folded the flags. One for her. One for Connie. One for Emily. Emily broke into loud sobs as men lowered the caskets, one by one. She could still remember the sound of the hand-full of dirt striking the wood.

A hawk cried, slowly drawing Annabelle out of her dreamlike stance.

"Why do you seek the living among the dead?" It seemed as if the words had come from someone else's lips. She had spoken them. They'd come unbidden, without thought. Was God speaking?

If so, He was telling her to get over it. Her husband and sons were long dead.

Tom's words returned to her, "If you ever need anything … all you have to do is ask." The memory brought comfort and warmth.

God had given her a gift, a second chance at love.

Pushing forward, she fast walked toward the dry creek bed, hoping to put distance between herself and the deep, dark sorrow of her memories.

Joseph's laughter rang out as she crossed the rocky creek. Samson barked and then ran to greet her, sniffing around her feet, his tail all a-wag.

Joseph called out. "Granny!"

The warmth in her heart intensified. She was a blessed woman.

"You must've read my mind," Connie called from her resting place in the shade. "I was wishing you'd come."

Annabelle picked up Joseph and kissed his sun-warmed cheeks.

His little arms encircled her neck in a toddler-sized hug.

When she set him down, he commenced to dance around, flinging his hands in the air. "What are you doing?"

"I'm dancing, Granny."

Connie giggled and patted the chair next to her. "Come sit, Momma."

Annabelle examined her daughter-in-law's face. "Are you all right?"

"Oh, yes, I'm just tired is all. It's so hot."

"Where is everyone?"

"Alton drove Mother over to her sister's. I'm afraid she's taken a bad turn."

"Oh, no." Annabelle looked around the yard. "Did Chase go, too?"

"He's at the barn, helping Willie groom the horses. He's a hard worker, that boy." She shifted in her chair. "So, how are you doing this morning? Not too sad, I hope?"

Annabelle patted her knee. "You know me so

well."

"I'm guessing you didn't manage to talk Tom out of going fishing?"

"I didn't try. It wouldn't be fair." She didn't tell Connie how she'd clammed up, sulked like a three-year-old, and then turned her back on Tom as he was leaving. She'd almost slammed the door.

Connie sighed and fanned herself. "I'd like to be relaxing at the lake right now. Can you believe it's so hot already?"

Annabelle pushed up from the chair. "I'll go get you something cold to drink."

The kitchen was steamy hot but smelled wonderful. Such a mixture of aromas wafted through the open doorway.

Regina had a tray in progress. "I seen ya comin' Miss Annabelle. Got fresh lemonade. Miss Connie tell ya about sister?"

"Yes. How bad is it?"

"Bad. Mr. Alton called. He's staying a while. Said Miss Susan may not make it through the day."

"Oh, no. Well, I'll stay a while, if you need to get on home."

"Thank ya kindly. That's right thoughtful. I'm nearly done with Sunday's meal." She finished the tray with a plate of sugar cookies. "There you go."

Annabelle set the tray on a table beneath the tree, within Connie's reach. "Regina said Alton called. He's going to be a while longer, so I'll stay here with you." She seated Joseph on the ground between them before handing him a cup and a cookie.

Connie sipped her lemonade. "Thank you, Momma. I appreciate it. Poor Aunt Susan. She's had such a tough time of it." She sniffed the air. "Why do you smell like ham?"

"Hah! Regina's cooking up a storm."

"She's a godsend. Funny how easy it is to let someone else do all the work."

Annabelle patted her hand. "You need someone to do it right now, so you can take it easy."

Connie looked at her. "Thank you, Momma. But I bet you didn't have anyone to help you."

"I never did. Neither did you, the first time. Remember how hard you had it? Picking cotton until your fingers swelled up? I felt so sorry for you, yet I had no idea you were carrying Joseph. How on earth did I miss that?"

"Grief, Momma. You were deep in the throes of grief. I could've brought an elephant in the house and you wouldn't have noticed."

"Oh, I think I would've noticed an elephant." She swirled the lemonade in her glass.

"Where's a elephant?" Joseph asked. "I don't see a elephant."

Annabelle laughed so hard, she had to wipe her eyes. "Oh, it feels so good to laugh."

Joseph climbed in her lap. "Why you crying, Granny?"

Annabelle gave him a hug. "I'm laughing, Joseph, because you say the funniest things."

He leaned against her, gazing into the tree branches. "I no see a elephant." After a big yawn, he promptly fell asleep.

Annabelle shook her head. "Takes after his father." She smoothed his hair. "My Joe used to play until he dropped. He'd fall asleep wherever he was."

Connie yawned. "He never stopped doing that." She smiled at her little boy, snoozing on Annabelle's lap. "It's amazing, isn't it? How much he looks like your Joseph, yet when he smiles and laughs, he reminds me so much of Alton."

"I agree. Must be ..." Annabelle didn't bother to continue since Connie was also drifting off. Instead, she finished the thought inwardly. She'd noticed the same thing about Joseph. It wasn't really a mystery since the boy spent so much time with Alton. He mimicked the only father he knew.

"Tom."

Tom looked up.

Riley chuckled. "Been talking to you, or at least trying to. You been staring at that ugly hat for ten minutes." He slapped his knee and sat forward. "You got it bad, man. Real bad."

Tom tugged at the brim of his favorite fishing hat. "What are you talking about?"

"You're lovesick, cousin. Plumb discombobulated."

Tom wanted to deny it, but he couldn't. She was all he could think about lately. He even had to double-check his prescriptions before handing them out.

He donned the hat and gazed across the peaceful water, hoping an unlucky fish would bite on Riley's hook and take the attention off Tom's love life.

Riley gave another goofy chuckle. "Discombobulated. Thing is, you're doing it all wrong."

Huffing out a breath, Tom leveled his gaze at Riley's face. "Doing what all wrong? What're you talking about?"

"Dragging your feet when you ought to march right on over there and put a ring on her finger."

Tom lowered his head to stare at his boots. "She knows how I feel."

"You sure about that? Why ain't she living in your house then? Seems to me y'all ought to have things settled by now."

"She needed time to recover."

"You been saying that for months. She's over it. Can't you see that? She watches the church door every Sunday is what Thelma says. Watching for you, cousin. Waiting for the day you're going to march right in there and sit down next to her."

Tom raised his eyes to Riley's face. "Now, you're talking church? I told you I wasn't going to play that card. I'm going, whenever I can."

"Slinking in and sitting on the back row, then sneaking out before the service is over ain't real church-going, Tom."

Tom removed his hat and tossed it down. He set his palm on his thigh and leaned toward Riley. "Are you really talking to me about going to church, holiday Christian?" Tom wanted to jerk those last words back as soon as they left his lips. Why had he said that? Riley sure could get under his skin sometimes.

Riley stared. After the initial shock wore off, he laughed and shook his head. "I know, man. But, hey, it works for me. Thelma don't jaw about it as much as she used to."

Tom shrugged. "I shouldn't have said that. I know you do what you can." He picked up his hat and dusted it off. "I'll have more time now the house is finished." Now that he'd given Riley this fishing weekend. He didn't dare add that. Riley would be offended for sure. After all, the man had given up a good deal more to help Tom build his house. Tom swiped at a drop of sweat trickling down his cheek. "I can start thinking about other things now."

"I hope Annabelle is one of them other things." Riley sat up straight. "Got a bite. Come on, take it." The line went slack. "Fiddle faddle." He scratched his head. "Probably got my bait. Maybe time to get out the bologna sandwiches."

"What? You're gonna bait your hook with bologna?" Tom grinned.

"Hey now, that's an idea." He set his pole aside and grabbed the ice chest. "You hungry yet?"

Tom glanced at his watch. "You know it's only nine o'clock, right?"

"Time to eat. It's been three hours since breakfast."

"I do believe you get sillier with age." He watched Riley bite into a sandwich. Maybe he'd have a few moments of peace.

After his snack, Riley lay back and dozed off. Tom shook his head as he sent another cast into a shady spot of water. That man could sleep anywhere, anytime.

Free to think his own thoughts, Tom relaxed. It had been tough, leaving Annabelle. Was it only yesterday? It seemed much longer. The look on her face still haunted him. She didn't argue, didn't try to talk him out of going, but a wall went up between them. It was almost like she'd regressed a little. That worried him. They'd been so close lately. She had even admitted she was in love with him.

Maybe if he'd taken her to church, like Alton suggested? Something tightened in his chest at the thought of all their friends, watching him walk down the aisle with her. They'd be whispering and tittering. There'd always be talk, but he hoped to put it off a while. He was kidding himself. They were probably already onto him. Mrs. Byrd, Annabelle's neighbor across the way, was one of the biggest gossips in town. Maybe in all of Gibson County. Right up there with Thelma.

He reached for his thermos and took a big gulp of cool water. A gentle breeze blew, rippling the surface of the lake, troubling the boat. He glanced at Riley, hoping he didn't wake. Not yet.

Annabelle's attitude bothered him. She'd been all

warm and tender, then cold as ice. Is this how it would be, up one day, down the next?

Elbows on his knees, he lowered his head to his hands and sent up a silent prayer. He'd need a good dose of patience to get through the next few days. When he lifted his eyes to gaze across the water, something had changed inside. His heart felt lighter.

It was a beautiful Sunday morning. He reckoned this was as good as any church service he'd ever attended. One could commune with God anywhere. He missed the music and seeing Annabelle, but he reckoned he could save that for later. That is if she'd see him.

A prickling sensation in his ankle alerted Tom that he'd sat too long in one position. He shifted to relieve the pressure.

Riley yawned and sat up as his pole jumped. He grabbed it. This time, the fish didn't get away. Riley made his first catch.

Annabelle sat on her porch waiting for her ride to church when Tom sauntered across the lawn. Her pulse quickened at his approach.

"Afternoon, Annabelle. I brought you a present."

"If it's a fish, it better be cleaned. I don't clean fish."

He gave her a sideways grin. "That's what I heard. No, it's not a fish. I sent those home with Riley."

"So, you did catch some?"

He held out a small brown bag. "We caught a good mess."

Annabelle took the bag and looked inside. "Chocolate drops."

Tom laughed. "A little birdie told me you love those. So, I picked some up."

"Thank you, Tom." Or, should she thank Riley? She folded the bag and stowed it in her pocketbook.

"I thought I might need a peace offering."

"A peace offering, huh? Well, there's no need, Tom. I'm sorry for the way I acted. It was silly of me."

"No, Annabelle, it was not silly. I knew what day it was."

She raised her eyes to his and found empathy, rather than the judgment she'd expected. "It's been three years, but sometimes … it's still hard to breathe."

"There's no time limit on grief, Annabelle. The loss you suffered—it's outside my imagination." His brow furrowed. He shook his head. "I can't fathom it. But I intend to be here for you as long as it takes."

Annabelle rose from her chair and almost fell into

his arms. How did she deserve a man like Tom?

Alton's truck rumbled into the drive.

Annabelle took a step back. "I have to go to church." She reached for her purse.

Tom led her down the steps. "If I wasn't so tired, I'd go with you."

She glanced up. "Would you, Tom?"

"I absolutely would. You can tell Alton, next week, you've got a ride to church."

Annabelle didn't care that her family sat in the truck watching. Laying her hand on his forearm to steady herself, she raised up on her toes and gave Tom a kiss on the cheek. "Thank you, Tom."

He grinned. "My pleasure."

Betty Thomason Owens

Chapter Twenty-Two

July 9, 1957

Annabelle left the hen house with four brown eggs cradled in her apron. The hens didn't like this hot weather any more than she did. Her morning chores completed, she picked up a bushel basket and headed to the garden. The pole beans were plump and ready for picking. Early tomorrow morning, she'd head over to Sutter's to join in the canning.

Sutter's still had a big, outdoor kitchen that dated back to when slaves did all the cooking. Lillian's mother once told Annabelle their people had even created the red bricks used to build it. Annabelle loved the rich history of the old place. She could almost feel the presence of the folks who used to work there. These days, the big open kitchen was the perfect spot to put up produce.

She had picked about halfway down one row when

Miss Lucy's rich voice came to her, singing, "What a Friend We Have in Jesus." The little woman made her way across the cotton field, singing all the while.

Annabelle smiled as she picked a few more beans and dropped them into her basket.

"Mornin' Miss Annabelle!"

Annabelle looked up to where Miss Lucy stood alongside the fence. "Good morning. How are you this fine day?"

"Singin' a happy tune, and feelin' spry." A walking stick in hand, she made her way around to the gate. "Just left Sutter's. Miss Connie's doing well. Looks more like mid-August though, in my opinion. Maybe sooner."

Annabelle adjusted her hat. "I thought so, too. She seems farther along."

"Uh-huh, she does. It's different this time. I'd venture a guess, she's carryin' a girl child."

"Oh, I'd love that. A pretty little girl." Annabelle pulled a few more beans from the vines.

Miss Lucy dug in the dirt with her stick. "You going over to the cannin' tomorrow?"

"I am. I look forward to it every year."

"So do I. It's looking like a bumper crop this year. Regina's already got a few acorn squash."

"Has she? Well, it has been mighty hot, but we've

had a good amount of rain, too."

Miss Lucy propped her stick against the fence and commenced picking beans. "Did you attend the funeral for Miss Lillian's sista?"

Annabelle nodded. "I did. It seemed more like a reunion than a funeral."

"Praise the Lord. That's the way it ort to be—a celebration. Miz Susan Whitman lived a good, long life. We ort'a be happy she's entered her rest. I hope folks will do the same when my time comes."

Annabelle suspected Miss Lucy's passing would bring a lot of tears, but she held her tongue.

Miss Lucy eyed her with an expression that reminded Annabelle of a wise, old owl. "It's different, ain't it, when they go before their time?"

Her words sent a shock wave through Annabelle. Tears stung her eyes. She blinked to clear her vision. "Yes, it is."

Miss Lucy didn't speak, she watched, as though she understood Annabelle's deepest need.

Annabelle fingered a bean blossom. "If I had known I was never going to see them again … I'd have hugged them longer … kissed them—" Her voice broke. She closed her eyes and forced a deep breath, trying to gain control of her emotions. "I don't remember if I told them I loved them."

Miss Lucy touched Annabelle's arm. "They knew."

"I do know that, but it's not enough, is it?"

"You'll always find regrets lurking in the shadows. Believe me, I know all about regrets."

Annabelle looked at the little woman. She had lived a long time, experienced so much. Of course, she knew. She'd been through that terrible time after her boy died when she'd wanted to die along with him.

Miss Lucy rubbed Annabelle's back. "It's still better to love. You know that. Take the risk, sista. Let yourself be happy. God has offered you a gift. It's up to you to grab hold of it."

Annabelle met the woman's eyes. Was she talking about Tom now? She drew another deep breath and expelled it with a sigh. "Thank you for that, Miss Lucy."

The old woman went back to picking beans. "I've outlived two fine men, Miss Annabelle. The losing was hard but being loved by them was worth all the pain."

Annabelle hadn't realized Miss Lucy had been married more than once. She reckoned there was bound to be a lot she didn't know about the wise, old woman. A lot she could learn, too. The expression on Tom's face after she'd kissed his cheek the night before told her all she needed to know. He loved her. "You are right about that."

Miss Lucy worked alongside Annabelle until all the beans were picked. "I'll see you in the morning, Miss Annabelle." She took up her stick and strode off.

Moments later, Annabelle heard her singing, "What a friend we have in Jesus," as she traversed the near waist-high cotton.

Annabelle hummed the tune as she picked a few ripe tomatoes, then burst into song as she left the garden. It did put the spry in one's step.

Tom opened a carton of headache powders and inspected the contents, trying to ignore the grunt from the regular customer at the end of the counter. He didn't even want to ask what Bo was upset about.

Shaking his head, Bo folded his newspaper. "Humph."

Fred had no such qualms. He paused as he stacked the dishes from the last customer. "What's got you groaning, Bo? More bad news?"

"More and more every day. The government telling us what we can and cannot do." He shook his head.

"What have they done now?"

Poor Fred. Didn't he realize he was opening Pandora's box?

Tom's new intern, Jim, had already learned to leave well enough alone where Bo was concerned. He was a quick learner, that one. Tom handed the carton to Jim, who raised his brows before turning his back to arrange them on the shelf. They were both trying not to look at Bo. A look might encourage him.

"Forcing desegregation. It ain't just the schools, either. They've taken aim on businesses, too. Folks are talking about arming themselves." He thumped the counter.

Tom picked up empty boxes and crossed to the back of the store. He left them in a stack for Fred to deal with later. When he returned to the front, Bo rounded on him.

"What'll you do if those people show up here, sit down at your soda fountain, and insist on being served?"

Tom looked at Bo, then returned to his desk. He really didn't want to have to answer that question. He didn't like being put on the spot, for one thing. No matter how he answered, he could be in hot water over it.

Why did he suddenly think of Connie? Maybe because the girl had lofty ideas about how things should be. She shared the hopes and dreams of that preacher who was speaking all over the place these days. Though Tom admired his message, he wondered whether it would ever bring about the desired effect.

Even though it had been almost a hundred years, many southern whites were still licking their wounds over losing the civil war. They chafed at the government telling them how to live.

He pulled in a long breath and exhaled, hoping the phone would ring, or a customer would come in and spare him the need to answer. Coward. He straightened his shoulders before turning back to Bo.

"I reckon I'd try to do what's right."

Bo slapped the counter. "What's right! That'd be calling the sheriff. Getting them hauled out of here."

"That's what they want, though." Jim's voice brought everyone's attention. Color rose in his cheeks. He glanced at Tom and then cleared his throat. "I read it in a magazine article. It's the attention they want. It gets them on the evening news."

Bo stared into his cup. "It's wrong. They don't belong where they don't belong."

Fred stood still, watching Tom.

Tom caught the younger man's eye, then strolled toward the door. He knew Fred was waiting for him to agree with Bo. Or not. Fred was young. His nature was still pliable. He tended to agree with whatever opinion seemed strongest among his peers. Though he'd taken up for Hero, he tended to shy away from volatile attitudes that could get him in trouble with the wrong folks. That was Fred. An all-American fence-sitter, who tried to keep everybody happy.

Tom ran a finger under his collar to loosen it. He couldn't blame the boy. He wanted to shy away, too. Right now, he contemplated opening the front door and running out so he wouldn't have to answer. *Coward.* "If I had to call the law in to protect my customers, Bo, I would. But it goes both ways. I'd want to protect those other folks, too."

Bo sputtered. "Protect them? It'd be their own fault, whatever come of it."

Tom suppressed a groan. How on earth should he answer that?

The door opened. Pastor Nathan stepped inside. "Woo-wee! Does it ever feel good in here." He crossed to the counter and took a seat. "I'll have the biggest chocolate shake you've got, Fred." He nodded at Bo. "How are you, Bo?" He turned to catch Jim's eye. "Jim, good day to you."

Jim nodded.

Bo lifted his cup. "Pastor."

Tom prayed Bo would hold his tongue.

Pastor leaned his elbows on the counter, his attention on Tom. "Installing air conditioning is one of your best business moves, Tom. I'm surprised folks aren't flocking in here today."

Tom wished they had been, but he supposed Bo would express himself anyway and maybe drive those customers back out into the heat. "It is nice until I have to go home."

"Ha! I reckon so. I'd be tempted to keep a cot in the storeroom."

Tom grinned. "That's actually a good idea."

Pastor Nathan gave him a thumb's up as Fred set a large, frosty glass on the counter.

"Here you go, Pastor. Drink up."

Bo fiddled with his paper. He opened his mouth.

Tom cringed. "What's your day been like, Pastor?" He glanced from Bo to Fred.

Fred nodded and poured more coffee in Bo's cup.

Pastor wiped his lips with a folded napkin. "This heat got me thinking about the fiery furnace. Got my sermon written in record time." He toasted Tom with his glass and took another sip.

The bell jingled as the door opened and a customer walked in.

Tom sighed under his breath as he made his way back to the prescription counter. Bo tried his patience on the best days, but today, when his heart brimmed over with thoughts of his beloved, he wanted peace and quiet. Time to think and plan.

The bell jingled again, announcing more customers. These made a beeline for the soda fountain. Pastor was right. Folks were looking for relief from the heat. He was happy to provide a safe environment for them. As he rang up a purchase, he prayed he'd never have to turn anyone away.

Tom locked the front door and turned off the "open" sign before heading to the back where Fred and Jim were breaking up boxes.

"You did a fine job today, Jim. I appreciate you handling the phone while I was dealing with customers."

Jim smiled. "I was happy to do it, sir."

Fred broke down the last box and added it to the pile. "What would we do if something happened, like what Bo asked about?"

Tom rolled up his sleeves and grabbed a couple of the boxes. "I hope we never have to find out. Things are changing, but change has never been easy for some." He was skirting the issue. He really wanted to be honest with Fred, but a careless word in the wrong ear could bring down trouble on everyone involved. He didn't want trouble, nor did he want to cause someone else hurt. He pushed the door open.

Fred gathered up the remaining boxes and followed Tom out to the back. "I reckon it has to come. What with the government getting involved and all." He glanced over his shoulder. "Jim said it's done happened on campus, where he goes to school."

Jim helped stack the flattened boxes beside the trash can. "It was strange at first. But folks are getting used to it. Some are reacting badly, but I think it's the way things are headed."

Tom nodded. "Be careful, son. I think it'll be a long road yet. And there's some that will fight. I've seen pictures of the violence. I'm sure you have, too. I hope we never see anything like that in our town."

Eyes wide, Fred agreed. "I heard Mr. Jensen Wade say he was gonna put a stop to it. The violence, I mean."

Tom looked around. "You heard him say that?"

Fred nodded. "Yes, sir, I did, with my own ears."

As he drove home, Tom tried to free his thoughts, but something had taken hold of him. He had a bad feeling, but he wasn't sure what it was about. Maybe what Fred said was true. Maybe that was why Stu Fox had accosted Jensen in a public place. Tom hoped

Jensen could do some good. It would certainly be against his old nature, but it would go a long way toward winning back trust.

As he drove around the final turn and headed up the road toward Annabelle's house, an alarm went off in his brain. Jensen Wade's car sat in Annabelle's driveway.

Chapter Twenty-Three

July 9, 1957

Annabelle hadn't heard anyone pull up when a rap came at the door. She dried her hands on her apron as she stepped through to the front room. Though he stood in the deep shade of the porch, she recognized that silhouette.

"Jensen."

"Can we talk, Annabelle? I've got something to say to you."

After a quick intake of breath, Annabelle stepped out. She gestured to a rocker. "Won't you sit down?"

Hat in hand, he waited until she sat, then he perched on the edge of the chair beside her. He dropped the hat on the floor beside his chair.

She folded her hands in her lap, hoping that would steady her nerves. "Can I get you anything?"

He shook his head. "No, Annabelle, I'm fine. I

wanted to clear the air between us. Make sure you understood what happened the other night at the restaurant."

"I … I'm not real sure what I heard, Jensen."

He gave a nod. "That's what I thought. I didn't want you to be alarmed in case … well, in case anything comes of it."

She examined his expression. He seemed sincere. So, what would come of it? Before she could ask, he continued.

"Stuart Fox is a troublemaker. Unfortunately, he has aligned himself with a large group of troublemakers. I thought they'd fizzle, but it's not happening. Not soon enough. So, there could be difficulty ahead."

He rubbed the back of his neck, reminding her of Alton. They were brothers, after all.

He stood to pace away from her. "I'm staying out of it. My future as a politician depends on me steering clear of rabble." He faced her again, a half smile replacing the usual haughtiness. "You know my past. I wasn't exactly Mr. Nice Guy." He picked up his hat and held it, watching her.

Annabelle pressed her lips together. Mr. Nice Guy. She arched her brow. When he started to step away, she rose. "Stay a minute longer, Jensen. I have something to say to you as well."

He tilted his head to the side. "I'm listening."

"I've been rather harsh toward you ever since … well, ever since we talked in your office."

The half-smile faded. "Uh-huh, after your arrival."

"Yes. I held that against you. I'm sorry."

He looked at his hands as though examining his fingernails. "I'm the one ought to apologize, Annabelle. I made an unkind assumption. You've proved me wrong several times over. You and Connie both." His head pivoted as he examined the front of the house. "I never expected you to make a go of living out here, but you've settled in, haven't you? It looks right nice." He shrugged. "Well, I have a meeting to get to. I hope we're in accord?"

Tom drove by and honked his horn. Annabelle waved and then gave her attention back to Jensen. "I believe we are, Jensen, maybe for the first time ever."

Jensen set his hat on his head. "Good." He started down the steps. "I'll see you in church."

Annabelle watched him drive away. When she turned back, she noticed Tom headed across the yard. She waited for him on the steps. "That may possibly be the most unusual conversation I've ever had."

Tom stopped in front of her, his expression taut. "What did he say?"

Annabelle told him everything.

"Sounds a little odd, don't you think?" A frown creased his brow.

She nodded. "I do. But I'm not sure, Tom, it almost seemed he was clearing the air. I'm kind of worried about him."

Tom gazed at her a moment, then relaxed. "There you go mothering again. Don't take on more trouble, Annabelle."

She nodded toward the porch. "Won't you sit a minute?"

He straightened his shoulders. "No, I'd best get home. I wanted to check on you, make sure you were all right."

Annabelle took a breath, hoping to mask her disappointment. "I hope you had a good day at work."

He stuck his hands in his pockets. "A very good day. Busy, but good."

"How's Jim doing?"

"He's doing well. A big help when traffic gets heavy. He's also adept at taking calls."

She nodded, then stepped aside, giving him the opportunity to leave.

He smiled into her eyes. "You know we're being watched?"

Annabelle inched her gaze toward the house across

the road. It was too far away for anyone to overhear them, but Mrs. Byrd could most certainly see them. "Poor thing, she's lonesome these days. Her son and his family finally moved out. I heard he got work at that new warehouse Mr. McCoy is building."

"Oh, good. I'm glad to know they're using local talent." He took a couple of backward steps. "Well, I'll talk to you later, Annabelle. If not today, then tomorrow."

She hoped today.

He winked. "We have unfinished business."

She could almost feel a kiss in the air between them as he walked away. That was surely what he'd meant by "unfinished business." He certainly knew how to hold her interest.

Giggling, she turned to wave at Mrs. Byrd. May as well let the woman know they could see her.

Annabelle carried another bushel basket in from the back porch at Sutter's. As she wedged herself and the basket through the door, she bumped into Lillian.

"Too many cooks in the kitchen!" Lillian laughed out loud, her face reflecting pure joy. She loved these "canning bees," as she called them.

Regina mopped sweat from her brow as she manned the hot stove where four pots held jars of green beans.

Miss Lucy and her daughters washed newly snapped beans in a big sink, preparing them for canning.

Connie sat on a stool beside them, filling jars.

Annabelle kept a sharp watch on Connie, for signs of fatigue or heat stroke. She made sure the girl drank enough water to replace the almost constant perspiration. Even though they were outdoors, the place was a steam bath.

It was only ten o'clock in the morning, but they'd been at it since dawn, trying to finish before the hottest part of the day when the thermometer would rise to intolerable. By then, they all hoped to be sitting on the porch in front of a big fan, sipping ice cold lemonade, their reward for a good day's work.

It was close to noon by the time they finished. Lillian made the last marks in her notebook. "Two hundred and forty quarts of beans altogether. Not bad for a day's work."

All the women clapped and cheered.

Annabelle looked at the rows of jars, cooling on the counter. Some held shellie beans, others had been left whole, but most were snapped. She mopped her brow with a damp rag. "That's a lot of beans."

Lillian stood with her hands on her hips. "That's a lot of work. We'll be glad of it, come winter."

Annabelle nodded. Lillian always said that. It was true. Of course, she never mentioned how many of those jars were given away, along with bushels of corn, potatoes, turnips, squash, and several varieties of dried peas. The Wades were praised for their generosity, but they never bragged about it. Except Jensen. He had inherited his ego from Charles, Senior. But, where Jensen may have mellowed a bit, his grandfather never had. The elder Charles had been her grandfather, too, though he had never claimed her. She was a Sterling. Wades didn't mix with Sterlings.

He had forbidden the marriage between his eldest son and her mother. Annabelle figured her daddy must have been as stubborn as his father. The two butted heads. John defied his father's wishes when he and her mother eloped. Four years later, John Wade died somewhere in Germany during the Great War. Charles, Senior had promptly turned Annabelle's mother, along with three-year-old Annabelle, out of his house. He had never spoken to Ma or mentioned her again. And he had never sought out his granddaughter. John hadn't left a will, so there'd been no money.

Annabelle mopped her brow. Ma had moved back

home with her parents, in the old Sterling house, where Annabelle now lived. Funny how life sometimes turned out. Funny, indeed.

Lillian patted her back. "Wake up, dear Annabelle. Where's Connie?"

Annabelle turned. Had she missed something? "She went inside for a nap a while back."

"Good for her. It's too hot out here for our little momma." She linked arms with Annabelle. "Let's go sit down and put our feet up. You look as tired as I feel."

Cold lemonade and sandwiches waited for them on the porch. After helping herself, Annabelle sank into the nearest chair. Alton had placed a fan on a small table in the corner. It not only cooled them but also helped keep the flies away.

Lillian settled in, her feet propped on a hassock. "It feels so good to sit down."

Annabelle swallowed a bite of egg salad sandwich before answering. "Yes, it does." She glanced at the group of women relaxing in the cool shade of a big maple tree on the front lawn. Regina sat with Miss Lucy, and two of Miss Lucy's daughters. The little granddaughter Miss Lucy called, "Sis," sat on the ground beside her. The women seemed content in each other's company.

The screen door swung open as Connie stepped out. "I don't know when I've been so hungry."

Lillian laughed. "This morning at breakfast, dear heart, I believe you said those exact words."

Connie's laughter rang out. "You're probably right, Mother."

Annabelle got up to fix her a plate. "You sit down, Pumpkin. I'll get your food."

"Have you heard from the menfolk?" Lillian asked Connie.

"They were in a while ago. Ate their lunch, then headed back out to the barn. Alton said Joseph has been a big help, can you imagine?" She accepted a filled plate from Annabelle. "Oh, my this looks good."

Annabelle set a glass of lemonade beside her. "How are you feeling?"

"Some better now, since my nap and a couple bites of this sandwich. Oh, and Marla called. She said they've enrolled Hero in school. He's been accepted into some special program for young men of color. They're going to prepare him for college. Isn't that exciting?"

Lillian set aside her empty plate. "Yes, it is. How about that?"

Annabelle sat forward. "Did you tell Miss Lucy yet?"

"I did, while they were setting up our lunch. She almost danced a jig right there in Mother's kitchen."

Lillian cackled. "I would love to have seen that."

"Me too." Annabelle sought Miss Lucy, who reclined on the quilt probably catching a quick nap. "What was meant for evil, God has turned to good."

Tom stomped on his brakes in front of the Wade mansion. He blinked his eyes to clear his vision. Surely, it couldn't be. But it was.

A charred cross stood on the front lawn. The grass around it was burned, as well. Tom raised his eyes to the drive, where the sheriff's car sat. What had happened? He hoped no one was hurt.

Annabelle's words returned to him, "...it almost seemed he was clearing the air. I'm kind of worried about him."

For good reason, it seemed. Tom took his foot off the brake and eased toward the corner, where he turned on 4th Street. He had a delivery to make before work. Otherwise, he would never have passed the Wade mansion. It was not his usual morning route.

If Annabelle had a phone, he'd call and let her know. He steered the truck to the curb and parked.

After the delivery, he went straight to the store, hoping someone knew what had happened at the Wade's.

Arnie was already behind the counter, whistling a tune as he scrubbed. "Morning, boss, coffee's almost ready."

"Thanks." He was still changing into his coat when Jim entered the back door. "Morning, Jim."

"Morning, sir." Jim shrugged into his coat and followed Tom to the front.

Arnie leaned on the counter. "You hear what happened?"

Tom didn't usually condone gossip, but if Arnie had information, he wanted to hear it. "What happened?"

Arnie glanced toward the door before answering. "Stu Fox got arrested."

"What for?"

"I don't have all the details, but it's pretty shocking."

"Does it have to do with a cross-burning?"

Arnie's eyes widened. "You know about it?"

"I saw it on the way in."

Arnie set three cups on the counter and filled them with coffee.

Jim stirred in cream and sugar. "I heard a lot of

sirens last night. I thought maybe it was a house fire."

Arnie sipped his coffee. "I reckon Bo'll be in soon. I bet he knows all about it."

Before he finished speaking, the door opened. Bo stepped inside and hobbled toward his stool. "Y'all hear the news?"

Tom moved to his desk. He could hear Bo just fine from there.

"Cross-burning at the Wade mansion, of all places. Stu Fox got arrested for harassment."

Arnie leaned on the counter. "Did they catch him in the act? Cross-burning, I mean?"

Bo shook his head. "No, sir. Not for burning. He knocked on the door and commenced to yelling for Miz Wade." He looked at Tom. "Called her a few not-so-nice names. Jensen was at some meeting, they said. When he heard about it, he had Stu arrested. It was after that, Stu's cohorts set that blaze."

Jim spoke up. "Was it the Klan?"

Bo shook his head. "No, sir. Sheriff said it wasn't. He called them hoodlums trying to place blame on the Klan. Said they were incensed over Stu's arrest."

Tom spoke up. "You talk to the sheriff?" He had to wonder how much truth was in the man's words.

Bo scratched his bald head. "Not personally, no. I heard it on the radio this morning. Roy Bishop, he's a reporter, he talked to the sheriff."

Tom stared at the prescriptions on the desk, not really seeing them. How long could they keep Stuart locked up?

"You think it's over?" Bo asked Tom.

Tom took a breath and released it slowly, thinking all the while. "I hope so. I really do, but I'm afraid they may have stirred up a hornet's nest."

Jim looked worried. "You think there'll be more trouble?"

Tom opened his drawer and pulled out a clipboard. "Oh, I imagine the Wades will take precautions."

Bo stirred his coffee. "Jensen's gonna need some muscle sure enough. I reckon Miz Wade's on the hot seat, too. Maybe a good time for her to take a trip somewheres."

Tom rubbed his forehead. Why would anyone go after Marla Wade?

Tom planned to stop at Annabelle's on the way home. He knew she'd want to hear about the trouble, especially since she'd had that feeling about Jensen. Tom had seen the sheriff in front of the courthouse, so he'd stopped to say hello, hoping to get a firsthand account.

Sheriff wouldn't say much, but he did confirm that Stu was in jail, and someone had burned a cross in front of the Wade residence. He'd been quick to point out that the Klan was not involved. Made Tom wonder if the sheriff had connections to the KKK. Why else would he keep telling everyone they were not involved?

Annabelle stood on the porch, her arms crossed over her chest, looking like she might cry. He wanted to take her in his arms, but most likely, eagle-eye Byrd was watching from her kitchen window. He longed for the day when he could make Annabelle his wife so he could hold her and kiss her anytime he wanted. Well, almost any time.

He bent to look her in the eye, hoping to reassure her. "Sheriff thinks this is the end of the matter. He doesn't think those guys will do anything to get themselves in more trouble. They'll probably lay low a while until it all blows over."

She nodded. "I hope you're right."

He shifted his weight from one foot to the other. "I can't understand why Stu would attack Marla like that. Verbally, I mean. Unless he did it to get back at Jensen. It doesn't make sense."

Something in her expression made him wonder.

Maybe she knew something he didn't. Maybe there was a reason for Stu's attack. But whatever it was, Annabelle wasn't telling.

"I'll see you later, Annabelle. Maybe after supper, you'd like to take a walk?"

She gave him a tentative smile. "I would, thank you." She relaxed her arms and took a step toward him. "Thank you for stopping to tell me. I'll be praying for everyone concerned."

Her words followed him as he drove the short distance between their houses. Annabelle knew how to deal with trouble. She took it all to the Lord in prayer. And she was his woman. Well, almost.

Chapter Twenty-Four

July 14, 1957

Most of the men in Alton's Sunday school class were some years younger than Tom, but no one seemed to object to his presence. They sat in a circle of metal chairs beneath a tall maple tree beside the church. Today's topic was "Who is Your Neighbor?"

It turned out to be quite a lively discussion as the men shared their ideas. The time sped past, ending sooner than Tom liked. He still dreaded walking that aisle and sitting down front. So much so, he hung back until all the other men had headed toward church, each carrying his folded chair.

"I know what you're doing." Alton folded his chair and stood looking at Tom. "We can go in from the front of the sanctuary. You won't have to pass all those pews."

Tom nodded. "I hadn't thought of that. I guess you

think I'm a coward." Tom looked away. Alton would be right. It was certainly true in this case.

Alton led the way toward the side door. "No, brother. The town gossips are formidable. I do not blame you one bit." They entered the door, stowed the chairs and walked along the side corridor toward Pastor Nathan's office.

Pastor stopped and stared. "Tom, is that really you?"

Tom paused to shake his hand. "I don't need you teasing me, or making any sort of announcements from the pulpit, Brother Nathan."

Their ongoing friendship over the years hadn't suffered from Tom's long estrangement. He was glad of that. They'd enjoyed lunch together most Wednesdays since the Nathans moved here.

Pastor crossed to the choir door. "I won't embarrass you, Tom, but don't keep me waiting too long, you hear?"

Before Tom could answer, Pastor disappeared behind the door. Tom turned to find Alton looking at him, a definite question in his eyes. Tom cleared his throat. "He's always kidding me about something."

Alton gave a soft chuckle. "I can see that. Still, I hope it won't be long, Tom." He removed his hat, then turned and continued toward the sanctuary door.

"I have the same hope," Tom whispered as they entered. Annabelle sat near the end of the second pew, so he sat beside her. She was wearing that pale green dress. The one she'd worn on their dinner date. Boy, did she look a picture. Within seconds, the music started. The congregation stood.

Tom eased out a breath. *Thank you, Lord.* Now, what would he do when the service ended? Could he leave the same way he'd come in? When he looked at Annabelle, all his doubts melted away. His arms itched to hold her.

Realizing he still held his hat, he eased it down onto the pew, then turned to take the hymnal she offered. Better get it together, Tom. Folks are watching, sure as the sun is shining overhead. If he appeared agitated or nervous, there'd be even more to talk about.

Annabelle allowed Tom to lead her from the church. It was no easy task. They were stopped at least a dozen times, as folks greeted them and gave her the once-over. Now, they'd all be wondering. Tom and Annabelle would dominate the grapevine for a few days unless something more noteworthy happened in the interim.

A good half hour had passed by the time they finally stepped outside. Tom headed straight for his truck. "Let's make a break while we can."

Annabelle giggled as she trotted beside him, trying to keep up with his long legs.

He helped her into the truck, then walked around to the driver's side and got in. "I hope you don't mind if I stop by the store for a moment. I need to check on a couple things, then we can head home. Alton invited me to dinner." He grinned. "I wouldn't want to be late."

She smiled into his eyes. "I believe Chase will be there, as well, so you do want to be on time. That boy has developed quite an appetite."

Annabelle waited in the truck while Tom went in the drugstore. It was nice to have a little time to herself to think about this morning. The moment she'd waited for, hoped and prayed for. When Tom walked through that door and sat beside her, she feared her heart might burst. The way he looked at her—the memory sent shivers down her spine.

She glanced away when he came back out, hoping to calm her racing heart.

He got in and started the engine. When he turned to back out of the parking space, he paused. "What?"

She shook her head. "I'm happy to be here, Tom."

He reached to squeeze her hand. "I'm happy

you're here, too."

Dinner held the same dreamlike quality as the drive. Maybe the entire morning. It was certainly a day for a journal if she kept one. Maybe it would last longer if she took the time to write it.

She watched Tom interact with her family, let the joy spill over in her heart. This would most likely be her life going forward. She'd passed through the hard times, now the fields of her life seemed ripe and ready to harvest. Soon it would be time to enjoy what she'd toiled so long for. It all seemed too good to be true.

Connie touched her arm. "Where are you, Momma?"

Annabelle laughed. "I'm sitting beside you on the swing."

"I had the feeling you were far away."

Tom looked up and smiled at her.

Annabelle forced her attention back to Connie. "No, I'm right here."

Connie touched her swollen belly. "I asked you if you'd like to watch Joseph on Tuesday morning, while Alton and I go to the doctor?"

"I'd love that."

"I thought you might. Alton will bring him by. If you need anything, let him know. We'll pick it up for you while we're in town."

"I'll check the pantry when I get home."

Tom didn't go to the evening service. Annabelle figured the day had been a bit much for him. He waved goodbye as he pulled out of the drive at Sutter's, but he'd promised to drop by her place later in the evening. She'd gotten used to his nightly visits. He'd walk over to say goodnight. Sometimes, he helped her shut up the chickens. They'd spend a few minutes sitting in the swing, talking about their day. Then, he'd head home, leaving her to wonder, how much longer would he wait? Would he ever repeat his proposal?

Annabelle pushed the screen door open as Alton's truck pulled into the drive. Joseph had fallen asleep on the sofa, so she walked out to meet Alton.

He opened the truck's door but didn't get out. "That's fine. Connie thought he might be napping. I'm on my way to the store, you want anything?"

"There's nothing I really need."

He grinned. "I didn't ask if you needed anything, I asked if you wanted anything."

She crossed her arms at her waist and smiled back. "That's right, you did. Still can't think of anything." She waved away a fly. "How's Connie doing?"

"Doctor said she's progressing well. He agrees with Miss Lucy about her being farther along, though."

"That's a good thing, right?"

"She's just fine with it. I think she's tired of being tired." He shut off the engine.

"I remember that feeling. Is there any more news from Marla?"

"Well, they picked up a couple of the men involved in the cross-burning. Jensen said they were all pretty drunk. Their stories are all over the place, though. No one seemed to agree on anything, except the fact they don't want to go to jail."

"Jensen is a powerful man to cross."

"Yes, he is. Like he said, they were all drunk."

"What on earth got them so riled up about that boy?"

"Being thwarted, I believe. They wanted to make Lester pay for bad-mouthing one of their friends."

She propped a fist on her hip. "And house-burning wasn't enough to satisfy them? Thank goodness Livia and Hero made it out alive."

Alton nodded. "I know. The good Lord was watching over them."

"Well, I hope it's over now."

He pulled the door closed, resting his arm in the open window. "I believe it is."

"How long is Stuart in for?"

"He'll be held until his trial, is what I heard. No bail." He started the engine. "I'll be back in a bit. Why don't you get ready and come to supper with us?"

She nodded. "I might do that." Of course, she'd have to leave a note on the screen door, let Tom know she'd be back soon. She didn't want to miss one of his evening visits.

Saturday morning's sky held fluffy white clouds piled up to the south. Annabelle hoped the weather held off for a couple of days, though the almanac had predicted more rainfall for July.

When she opened the gate, Ginger ran ahead of her into the garden.

"Oh, look! The hollyhocks are blooming!" Of course, Ginger had no comment but made a beeline for the catnip.

Annabelle laughed at the cat's silly antics.

The hollyhocks stood almost as tall as Annabelle. Dark red blooms had opened on one stalk. Another held yellow buds.

Annabelle gleaned the plants for ripe vegetables, and then snipped a few zinnias and snapdragons for her kitchen table. Before returning to the house, she looked in on the last of the brooding hens. She didn't need any more chicks, but Alton told her he could sell them.

The kitchen seemed dull in comparison to outside, so Annabelle sat on the front porch to pick through the produce from the garden. She'd made a good haul. Her mouth watered at the thought of summer squash and tomatoes on her dinner table.

She sang as she worked, practicing the song for the gospel singing. With two more weeks until the event, Rose Ella insisted everyone "practice, practice, practice!" That poor woman would never settle for second place.

Inside, the clock chimed the quarter hour. Must be after ten by now. She had in mind to bake a pie for Tom. He worked a half day on Saturday, so she planned to have it ready to deliver around two or so.

She set the basket near the icebox, then headed to the pantry and parted the curtains. She'd put up several jars of blackberries for pie. It wasn't quite as good as fresh, but she didn't think Tom would care.

She set a jar on the table, tied her apron on, and stepped to the Hoosier cabinet. She could never look at that cabinet without thinking of Lillian. Once a centerpiece in the original kitchen at Sutter's, it had not been a gift, but a loan. Lillian wanted the cabinet used and cared for, so she'd sent it over after Annabelle and Connie moved in.

In fact, most all their furniture had been provided by friends and family. What a wonderful time that was. It had seemed as though the entire community welcomed her home.

She sifted enough self-rising flour for the cobbler and mixed the sugar in, singing all the while.

The cobbler baking in the oven, Annabelle took her Bible to the front porch. She spent time reading through her Sunday school lesson. This week, they'd talk about the thirteenth chapter of first Corinthians. How many times had she read this passage of scripture? Yet each time, she found new meaning.

Today, she couldn't help thinking of her struggle with Rose Ella. Annabelle had to admit she'd been jealous. So, she'd made a point to concentrate on the good parts of the woman's nature, rather than those grating elements of fast-talking and bossiness. Close friendship with Rose Ella might be out of the question, but Annabelle could now tolerate her through most of choir practice.

"Love bears all things," she whispered. Rose Ella had accomplished an amazing feat. The choir was quite good. When accompanied by her expert piano-playing, they sounded almost professional.

The luscious aroma wafting from the kitchen alerted Annabelle that the cobbler was ready. She got up and went inside.

She set the pie on the table and spread a towel over it to keep the flies away. After turning off the oven, she checked to make sure all the messes had been cleaned. Funny how long the day seemed when no one was around. She found herself looking for ways to fill it.

Before heading to the bathroom to freshen up, she paused to look out the window and allowed herself to dream of the day when she'd bake her pies in the beautiful new kitchen next door. How sweet to think she'd be waiting there with dinner on the table when Tom arrived home from a hard day's work.

She laid a hand at the base of her throat. Sweet dreams, indeed.

Annabelle waited until Tom had been home for about an hour. Her heart beat faster as she gathered the pie in her arms and backed through the screen door, headed down the steps. She fast walked along the well-worn path toward the house next door.

The afternoon sun had burned off most of the clouds. Now it was a sweltering heat, compounded by humidity. Annabelle bit back a smile, imagining herself showing up at Tom's door drenched in sweat. How unladylike would that be?

She paused at the rose-covered fencepost, balanced the pan on her hip, to unhook the gate. On the other side, she paused. A car sat in Tom's drive—a familiar one. She stood still a moment, holding the pan in front of her. Slowly, she stepped forward until the front of the house came into full view. At that moment, the door swung open. Rose Ella stepped out, followed by Tom.

Annabelle stopped again. Her feet would go no farther. She shook her head to clear her mind. Perhaps Rose Ella's brother was there with them? Another moment passed and the two headed for Rose Ella's car.

Tom opened the door and held it as Rose Ella got in, jabbering all the while. No one else was around.

Just Tom and Rose Ella.

Tom looked up.

Her face on fire, Annabelle turned and darted away so fast, she almost lost her grip on the pie.

Had he seen her?

Chapter Twenty-Five

July 20, 1957

Annabelle didn't want Tom to see her. He'd know she'd caught him with Rose Ella. She rushed to the gate, fumbled with the latch, nearly dropping the pie again.

Rose Ella honked her horn as she drove by.

Annabelle's heart beat so hard, so fast, she could barely catch a breath. Blurred vision marred her hurried retreat across the yard toward the house and the solitude of her kitchen. Once inside, she set the pie on the table with a loud clunk.

The nerve of that woman! And Tom! How could he? He wouldn't even let Annabelle in the house without someone else around. Maybe now she knew why he hadn't repeated his proposal.

An inner voice warned her she was wrong. The voice of reason, perhaps. But she was too far gone to listen to reason. What her eyes had seen—that's what she had to believe.

A sob clogged her throat as she fought for breath. She didn't want to cry. She wanted to scream, but no more crying! She had enough of crying.

At the sound of the screen door's opening, she glanced over her shoulder. No. She shook her head at him. She couldn't talk right now. Especially not to Tom, looking all stricken, like she was to blame.

"Annabelle, I—"

She held up her hand. "No, Tom. Don't say it." She turned her back on him, but the view out the window ripped her raw. His house. Moments ago, she'd stood here dreaming it could be her house, too. Foolishness.

Fresh tears ran down her cheeks. She grabbed the dish towel, the only thing within easy reach, and tried to staunch the flow.

"Annabelle."

Was he still here?

She shook her head. "All I ever wanted in life was to be a wife and a mother. That was torn from me." Another deep sob broke loose. An arm at her waist, she bent double. When she'd managed to get her breath, she continued, "I don't know why—what did I do to deserve that?" Still not looking at him, she drew a shaky breath. "I can't do this, Tom. I still hurt. So much. I can't … I can't …"

She hadn't heard his approach. With gentle hands, he gripped her arms, pulling her toward him. He held her against his chest. His lips brushed her brow.

She wanted to break away. Hadn't he just been with Rose Ella? Entertaining her in his house, unattended? "I can't!"

"You can't what, Annabelle? What is it? Are you mad because Rose Ella was at the house? It wasn't a social visit."

She drew back. "I don't care. I can't do any of this. I'm miserable, Tom. Can't you see that? I'll make you miserable."

"But why, Annabelle? Why are you so miserable? Help me understand."

Good question. Did she know the answer? "I can't lose somebody else. I can't live like this, always afraid." Was that really it? She was afraid of losing him. To another woman—or even worse—like she'd lost Ray and her boys.

"You're afraid of losing me? Afraid I'll die, too?" Before she could step away, he drew her back into his arms and held her. "I'm not going anywhere, Annabelle. Not on purpose. Not without you."

She closed her eyes and fought to gain control of her roiling emotions.

After a long moment, he gave a soft chuckle.

Was he laughing at her now?

He spoke in a quiet voice, "If you're afraid of losing me, does that mean you still care for me a little, Annabelle?"

She shook her head. "No, Tom. I don't care for you a little. I care deeply. I love you. So much, it hurts. That's why ... I hurt so bad. Maybe it's not meant to be."

He kissed the top of her head. "Oh, Annabelle, we're two lonely people, who've been friends most of our lives. To me, it seems like providence."

She squeezed her eyes shut. Providence. God providing for her. No, for them. Tom was lonely, too. He'd told her that, many times. She'd broken his heart time and again. Dashed his hopes, yet, he was still here. Right now. How could she ever have doubted his love?

"You might be right." She drew in a shaky breath. "I want to be happy again, Tom, I really do."

"Then be happy, sweetheart. Don't be running afraid at every little thing. You're going to have to learn to trust me."

When she dared to glance up into his eyes, the love she found there sent a shock wave through her.

He kissed her deeply, passionately, leaving her weak and clinging to him. All the doubts, the fear, the anxiety, scurried away in the wake of that kiss. She laid her head against his chest, breathed in the scent of him. If only they could be married right now before her mind and emotions played their usual tricks. She'd have to be strong when those thoughts came knocking again.

Tom had made up his mind, he was going to end this right here, right now. He was tired of dancing around, walking on eggshells, or whatever it was you called this crazy thing. He was done. It was all or nothing. He'd held onto Annabelle, even when she'd tried to break free. When she'd finally relaxed in his arms, then met his gaze, he knew what he had to do next. Kiss her like she'd never been kissed. Until her knees went weak, and she gasped for air.

Feeling pretty good about it all, he loosened his grip on her. She didn't move. Progress.

"Don't make me wait, Annabelle."

She blinked up at him. "What?"

"We're too old for long engagements. Let's get married right away. Today. Tomorrow. Soon."

"Oh, Tom, we're not old. You're not even six months older than me. We're not fifty yet."

He smiled into her eyes. "You know what I mean.

I want to marry you soon, Annabelle. I don't want to wait any longer." He kissed her again, hoping to convince her.

She breathed out a sigh as she relaxed against his chest. "I never had a church wedding, Tom. I really would like to be married in church."

He held her away from him, so he could look into her eyes again. "Are you saying yes, Annabelle?"

Her lips curved into a shy smile. She nodded. "I guess I am."

He looked up toward the ceiling. "Glory hallelujah!" He gave her a quick kiss. "I love you, Annabelle. We can get married in church if you want. We'll just need to talk to Pastor Nathan and see what's available."

Pure joy shone from her eyes. "I don't want anything fancy. Family and close friends, that's all."

He nodded. "Whatever you want." Wait. He turned her loose. "I'll be right back." He paused at the door to look her in the eye. "Right back, Annabelle. I promise."

He almost ran to the house. Inside, he bolted toward the desk and found the velvet box.

She stood on the porch when he jogged into her yard. Her eyes brightened at his approach.

He climbed the steps and stood for a moment, looking down at her. And breathing. Golly, how long had it been since he'd run anywhere?

For a moment, he lost himself in her gaze. She was so beautiful, and she loved him. She'd said yes! What a blessed man he was. He opened the box, presented the ring.

Her hand shook as she lifted it to cover her lips. "Oh, Tom. It's gorgeous."

He removed the ring, held it between his thumb and forefinger. "I hope it fits." He slid it on her finger. It was a tad loose, but they could get that fixed.

She put her arms around his neck and leaned against him. "Oh, Tom. I'm so happy right now, I could bust."

He chuckled. "I know what you mean. I feel exactly the same way."

The sound of childish laughter startled Annabelle. She stepped away from Tom, not wanting anyone to catch them embracing.

Little Joseph's voice rang out. "Granny?"

She grinned at Tom. "I'm right here, darling."

A moment later, the boy rounded the front of the house at full speed. "Whatcha doin'?"

She bent to his level. "I'm talking to Uncle Tom.

What are you doing? Where's your momma?"

He stomped onto the porch. "Slowpoke."

Tom caught the boy in his arms and swung him around.

Joseph squealed. Then he belly-laughed. "Do it again, Gom-pa!"

Tom's surprised gaze met Annabelle's. "Did he say, grandpa?"

Joseph sobered. He rested a fist on Tom's chest and looked him in the eye. "Gom-pa?"

Tom set Joseph down, his eyes on Annabelle. "That's right. He should call me grandpa because I'm planning to marry his granny."

Joseph's little brow furrowed. "Where kitty-cat?"

Annabelle giggled. She shook her head at Tom. "He's already lost interest." At that moment, she caught sight of Connie, strolling along the drive.

Connie gave a tired wave.

Annabelle went out to meet her. "Come sit down. I'll fix you a glass of iced water." She glanced at Tom. "And we have blackberry cobbler, freshly baked this morning."

Connie huffed out a breath. "Yum. Sounds so good. But sitting down sounds even better. I believe I will."

A worried look on his face, Tom hurried over to

help her climb the steps. "Are you sure you should take on a long walk like that?"

"Oh, yes, I'm fine. Doc says I need exercise." She sank into a chair with a loud sigh.

Annabelle left to get the refreshments as Tom replied, "I'm not sure he meant for you to run a marathon."

Connie laughed out loud. "Oh, that's a good one, Tom."

Joseph pulled the screen door open and scurried across the floor to the table, where he climbed onto a chair to see what Annabelle was doing.

When he tried to stick his finger in the pie, she caught it and kissed his hand.

He giggled. "Joe is hungry, Granny."

"Well, you have to wait until we're out on the porch. Would you like some milk with your pie?"

He gave an exaggerated nod.

She filled three glasses with water, a smaller one with milk. After returning the milk pitcher to the refrigerator, she picked up the tray and headed for the door. Joseph ran ahead of her and held the door open.

"What a gentleman you are."

He gave her a wide grin before marching over to the steps to sit down. "I ready for my pie, Granny."

Connie sent a pointed glance his way. "What do

you say?"

He pursed his lips. "Pweeze?"

Annabelle could not say no to that face. When she handed him a plate, Connie caught her breath.

"Is that a ring sparkling on your finger, Momma?" Her eyes wide, she turned to Tom. "Tom?"

Tom grinned. "Yes, ma'am. That just so happens to be my ring on your momma's finger."

Connie covered her open mouth. Her eyes brimmed.

Annabelle sat next to her. "Don't you do that. You'll make me cry."

Joseph got up and came to stand beside his mother. He laid his hand on her knee. "Don't cry, Momma."

Connie's laughter freed the tears from their mooring. She swiped them away before she reached for Joseph. "I'm crying happy tears, baby. I'm so happy right now, I could kiss you."

Joseph pulled away. "No. No kisses." He ran back to his place and sat, still shaking his head. "No kisses." He picked up the spoon and dipped into the pie.

After taking his last bite, Tom set his plate on the side table. "Well, I hate to leave good company, but I have a couple errands to run." He stood, but hesitated, his eyes on Annabelle.

She rose and followed him down the steps. "See

you later, Tom."

He smiled into her eyes. "Yes, you will." He turned to Connie. "Is Alton coming for you?"

Connie nodded. "He'll be here in a bit. Like you, he had errands to run." She gave him a warm smile.

Tom tousled Joseph's hair before he strode off.

Annabelle heard him whistling as he walked away. Knowing she'd made him happy warmed her heart, but oh, what a day she'd had.

Annabelle rocked in silence, anticipating Connie's question before it came.

"All right, Momma. He's gone, so, spill it."

Annabelle told her everything, even the part about seeing Rose Ella leaving Tom's house.

"So, did you ask Tom why Rose Ella was there, Momma?"

Annabelle looked away. She hadn't thought about it after all that had happened. Had he distracted her on purpose? Mentally, she replayed their conversation. "No, he'd said it wasn't a social call, but I'm afraid I never gave him the chance to explain further. I was so surprised, and ... overcome."

"I expect you were. When you get a chance,

though, you need to find out. For your peace of mind, Momma. I know how you are. You'll worry over it, even though you're always telling me to turn a thing over to the Lord." She gave Annabelle a wry smile.

"I'll admit it, that's exactly what I do. I'm trying to quit, though." She angled a glance at Connie. "Shame on me for being a worrywart."

"No shame in it, Momma. Especially when you're really trying to improve."

Annabelle patted Connie's knee. "You sound like a teacher."

"That's because I am." She sipped her water. "Did you set a date?"

"Not really. Tom said he wanted it to be soon." She chuckled at the memory. "Said we were too old for a long engagement."

"Hah! Too old. That's a good one. Neither of you seem old to me." She set her glass down. "You know how you were wondering why Marla confided in us?"

Annabelle came to attention. "Yes."

"I think I know why. She came by yesterday evening, asked to speak to me in private. We strolled through the flower garden. She loves it, Momma. She wanted cuttings from several of the plants. Anyway, she thanked me for keeping her confidence. She said she'd never really had a close friendship with a woman, other than her sister, and she had pretty much burned her bridge there. I encouraged her to reach out to Melva."

"Is she going to?"

Connie shrugged. "I'm not sure. She told me what happened the other night when those men came by. Stuart Fox was crazy drunk. He blamed her for all his troubles. He said she should have stayed out of that whole business with the boy. Of course, he meant Hero. He said the whole family would pay for what she had done."

Annabelle tilted her head to look at Connie. "The whole family?"

Connie nodded. "I don't think he meant us, but all of them. He's awaiting trial. Jensen got them to withhold bond, so Stu can't get out yet. She said the others are running scared, thinking they'll be next. Jensen is a powerful man in his way."

"That's pretty much what I told Alton the other day." Annabelle remembered her last conversation with Jensen. "But this time, he's in the right. His family has been threatened."

"Well, I think Marla suspected what was coming, so she wanted to make sure we knew why she'd gone to such great lengths to save Hero. I think she was reaching out, in a roundabout way. She needed someone to understand, and she's come to trust us."

"Well, whatever the reason, I'm glad of it." Annabelle finished her water and set the glass down.

Connie reached for Annabelle's hand. "Let me get a good look at that rock." She examined the ring and then raised her eyes to Annabelle's face. "Think about it, Momma. If you hadn't wanted to come back here, our lives might have been so different. But I can't imagine us happier than we are now, can you?"

"I don't even want to contemplate what might have been, Pumpkin. I'm content to bask in what is."

Connie laid her hands on her swollen belly and closed her eyes. "So am I, Momma."

Chapter Twenty-Six
July 22, 1957

"Joyful, joyful we adore thee." Her mouth filled with clothespins, Annabelle hummed the next bar. As soon as she'd emptied her mouth, she sang more words, "… hearts unfold like flowers before thee …"

The wind whipped around the corner of the house. If that kept up, her laundry would be dry in no time. She worked faster, finishing with the last dish towel.

Monday was always laundry day for Annabelle. Her mother had done the same, and maybe her mother before her. Annabelle squinted at the clouds overhead, scuttling by on the wings of the wind. What a wind. Here it was almost the end of July, but there was a definite chill in the air. Weird, just weird.

She continued to sing as she entered the house to work on the next load. She always washed the towels first, because they took the longest to dry, then her clothes, and after that, the bedsheets. Annabelle loved a routine.

Back in the kitchen, her brand-new engagement ring caught her eye. She'd set it on a saucer on the kitchen table. Somehow, that didn't seem right. She hated taking it off, but it was loose. Since she was doing laundry, her hands in and out of the water, using the wringer, it seemed best to remove it. What if it fell off and got mashed? She'd be heartbroken. Annabelle had never owned an engagement ring. She and Ray only had thin, gold bands.

After a moment's thought, she went to the pantry and took out a spool of string. She cut a length of it and passed it through the ring. Then, she tied the string around her neck. She knotted the thing so tight she'd probably have to cut it off, but that was okay. She gazed at the beautiful diamond, surrounded by a nest of smaller stones, before tucking it into her work dress. It felt good there, as though it was a part of her. A symbol of Tom's love. She closed her eyes and relived his expression as he'd placed it on her finger.

The washer stopped agitating. "Better get busy, Annabelle."

She pinned the last of her laundry to the line. On the way back to the house, she fingered the towels. They were already dry. The wind whistled around the eaves. "Must be a storm coming."

When Ginger rubbed against her ankles, Annabelle looked down. "There you are. I wondered where you'd gotten yourself off to. We better hurry and get the sheets done. Looks like rain is coming."

The sun hid behind the clouds again. Annabelle rubbed her arms. "Strange weather, though."

Tom peered out the front window of the store, not liking what he saw. Angry clouds gathered in the southeast. What was it Bo had read in the paper this morning? Something about a big hurricane in the gulf. He narrowed his eyes as the sun penetrated the clouds. Well, the gulf was only a few hours from here. If that thing headed this way, they could be in for some rough weather.

The back door opened. Tom looked up as Fred waved. "I thought I was going to blow away out there."

Arnie removed his apron. "I'm glad you're here. I'd like to get home before the rain hits."

Tom wandered back to the prescription desk where Jim was adding up yesterday's sales. "Take care, Arnie. Looks like we're in for a gully-washer."

Bo swung around on his stool. "Must be that hurry-cane. They said it was a big-un." He held his cup out to Fred. "You going to make some fresh?"

Fred grinned. "I can." He went to work rinsing the pot. "What's this I hear about you getting engaged, Boss?"

Tom shook his head. News sure got around fast.

Fred leaned against the counter. "Is it true?"

"It is."

"When y'all getting hitched?"

Bo chuckled. "You better make it quick before she gets away again."

"She's not going anywhere." Tom sat two stools down from Bo. "We haven't set a date yet. She's worried about that baby coming."

"Oh, yeah. You can't expect her to make plans when there's a grandchild due any minute." Bo crossed his arms on the counter and leaned forward. "Still, I'd get some kind of a date on the calendar, to keep her attention."

Fred poured fresh coffee into Bo's cup. "Listen to you. I didn't realize you were an expert on marriage, too."

"I told you, boy. I know everything. You ever need to know anything, you ask Bo." He gave a goofy laugh as he stirred sugar into his cup.

Unable to sit still and listen to their banter, Tom

stood and walked to the window again. "Turn on the radio, Fred. Let's keep an eye on things. I don't like the looks of those clouds."

Annabelle folded her laundry into the ironing basket and set it in the corner of the kitchen. Then she traipsed back outside. The way the wind was blowing, the sheets were probably already dry. She felt the pillowcases. They needed time, so she strolled to the back yard. She hadn't seen the chickens scratching about. Where were they? When she reached the pen, she found them tucked beneath the coop.

Chickens knew when a storm was coming. She rubbed her arms. "Looks like it'll be a rainy afternoon."

She paused on her way back toward the house as a flash in the distance drew her attention to the cloud bank—one long, straight line of the blackest clouds she'd ever seen. A niggling sensation started in her belly and worked its way into her chest. She had a bad feeling about that one.

As though her feet had grown a mind of their own, they took her to the clothesline. She began removing the sheets, bundling them into her arms. She stowed the pins in her apron pocket. By the time she'd removed the last pillowcase, the air had stilled.

She paused, looking up. The sky overhead still showed traces of blue, but she could smell the rain. She walked toward the front of the house, carrying the sheets, hoping to make it inside without getting wet.

But when she stepped onto the porch, she nearly dropped everything.

Off in the distance—was that a funnel cloud? She bent her knees a bit to see better. That's when she noticed the green cast to the air. She'd heard about that, a long time ago.

Her heartbeat quickened. She opened the screen door and rushed to unload the sheets onto a kitchen chair. She glanced around, wondering what to take with her. That dank, old storm shelter was a disaster. She dashed to the pantry and found her flashlight. Did she have time to go to the back porch to get a couple of tools? Maybe she'd take the broom.

Lightning struck. Seconds later, thunder boomed, jarring her breastbone. No time!

She scurried out the door then ran back in to grab her slicker.

The rain had started. When she stepped down from the porch, the wind ripped the slicker right out of her hands and pulled it up into the air. The screen door blew open, slamming hard against the side of the house.

Annabelle stood like a rabbit on the road, staring at the giant creature headed in her direction.

No. Straight at her.

Another bolt of lightning got her feet moving. Her heart leapt into her throat, throbbing till it nearly took her breath. Could she make it to the shelter? Should she stay at the house?

One glance at the clouds made up her mind. She ran toward the gate, fumbled with the latch, threw it open and ran toward Tom's drive. That would be the shortest way to get to the storm shelter. Rain pelted her. Wind ripped at her dress. She wasn't going to make it!

Tom couldn't quit thinking about Annabelle. He sat at his desk, his open prescription book in front of him, but his mind was not there. Last night, as they said goodnight, she'd told him, "Thank you for waiting, for not giving up on me. I can honestly say, you have my heart. You've had my devotion for some time now, I couldn't seem to … let go of my past and trust the future. You were right when you said I've let fear guide my life and steal my choices."

He concentrated so hard, his pencil lead broke. He looked around the store. Bo still sat at the counter. Fred was washing dishes. Jim stocked shelves. They had no trouble concentrating.

Lightning struck something close by. A moment later, the lights flickered and fizzled. Tom left the dark corner to cross to the window.

"What's it doing out there?" Bo asked.

Fred walked over and looked outside. "Now that's a bad storm. Hey, boss, looks like the worst of it might be out your way. I hope your new house is all right."

The same thought about the direction of the storm had passed through Tom's mind. But he wasn't worried about the house. Would Annabelle be all right? He thrust his hands in his pockets and frowned as another bolt of lightning struck.

"Phones are out," Jim said.

Tom turned to look at him. Great. Now he wouldn't be able to call Sutter's and find out about Annabelle. He chewed his lip, trying to think what to do next.

Jim joined them at the window. "There won't be anything much going on here. Why not ride out to your place, make sure everything is okay? If it is, you can come back."

Jim's words made sense, but it was difficult for Tom to turn loose of the reins of the place. He stared out the window, jingling the change in his pocket.

"That sounds like good advice, Boss." Fred nodded to Jim. "We'll be here to look after things. Not much can happen with the phones down and electricity off anyway."

Tom gave a slow nod. "I reckon you are right." He walked toward the back door.

Jim followed along behind. "I hope all is well out there."

"So do I." Tom hung up his lab coat and grabbed his hat. "I'll be back if I can. Otherwise, close her up tight, okay?"

"Will do, sir," Jim said. "Just like you showed me."

Bo called out. "Tell Miss Annabelle hello from Bo."

Tom lifted his hand in answer before he opened the door and headed through the deluge to his truck. He was soaked by the time he got there, but he was doing the right thing. That inner voice kept urging him on. This time, Tom was listening.

Chapter Twenty-Seven

Annabelle stumbled and fell on Tom's gravel drive. As she picked herself up, she caught sight of Ginger dashing across the back lot. The cat jumped on the cellar door behind Tom's house.

Tom's cellar! How had she forgotten it? Without a backward glance at the approaching storm, she rushed toward the side of the house, praying the door would be unlocked. Praying she could make it in time. "Please be unlocked!"

Annabelle grabbed the handle. The door opened, but the wind fought her. Ginger dashed in through the narrow opening. Annabelle would need a bit more room. She tugged with all her might and managed to squeeze through. The door shut with a loud bang but kept rattling. Annabelle feared the wind would blow it off its hinges.

The light. Where was that switch? She found it at the base of the steps. With the light on, she could see the slide lock, so she pulled down on the door and slid the lock until it caught. She almost collapsed on the steps but thought better of it. A tornado that big could still rip the door off, lock or no. She made her way down the steps on wobbly legs, her eyes on the bench between the shelves. She sank down on it and leaned back against the cool, concrete wall.

Lightning struck, jarring the ground. The electricity went out, leaving the cellar in total darkness. Before she could get a breath, the air exploded with the loudest thunder Annabelle had ever heard. In the same instant, Ginger jumped on Annabelle's lap and dug in her claws.

Annabelle screamed but managed to hold onto the frightened cat. Trembling hard, she sat back, struggling for breath. Before she'd had a moment to relax, there came a tremendous crash that shook the ground, like something big had dropped down outside. Was that one of her trees? Or was it her house—like in that movie she'd seen so long ago? Did things like that really happen?

She pulled in a ragged breath. "Oh, Lord, keep us safe."

Something rattled the cellar door until she

wondered if someone was trying to get inside. She was about to go check when all the noise suddenly stopped.

Tom pressed the gas pedal against the floor, navigating the mostly empty road like a race-car driver. He dodged limbs and flying debris before arriving at the turnoff. There, he came to a dead stop. The road was blocked by a large tree. He sat looking at it far too long. Then he put the truck in reverse, careful to avoid the mud on either side. It wouldn't do to get stuck out here with no one around. He backed onto the highway and took an alternate route.

When he passed by Miss Lucy's house, he felt hopeful. It looked untouched. Sutter's Landing had a tree down in the backyard, but other than that, it seemed okay. He breathed easier. He'd been worried over nothing. But when he rounded the curve below Annabelle's house and his place, he slowed down to look. Many of the trees in the Byrd's front yard lay on their sides, exposing giant root balls. The barn's roof had been rolled up like the lid of a sardine can.

He drove slowly, praying all the way, but his heart almost stopped when he saw what was left of Annabelle's house.

He stomped on the gas. "Oh, Lord, no. No!" The truck fishtailed when he turned in too fast at the drive. He cut the engine, jumped out and ran to the house.

"Annabelle! Annabelle, are you in there?" She had to be okay. Had to be. God wouldn't do that.

He took a breath and stared at the demolished house. Would He?

Annabelle lifted her head. The storm had only lasted moments, though it seemed like hours. From the noise, she guessed it had torn everything to bits.

Were they okay at Sutter's? Had they made it into the cellar? "Oh, dear Lord, I pray that everyone is safe."

Houses could be rebuilt, but could she stand another loss of family? She'd rather be dead herself. She straightened and set her feet on the floor. A weight in her apron pocket jogged her memory. The flashlight. She pulled it out and switched it on.

Ginger jumped down from her lap and began to prowl around the room, howling.

Annabelle stood and followed the beam of the flashlight to the door, where now a thin beam of light shone through at the base. She slid the bolt aside and turned the knob, but the door wouldn't budge.

"Oh, no." That loud noise she'd heard—something must have fallen against the door. She was out here all alone with no way to get hold of anyone. No one would know where she was.

Ginger rubbed against her leg and gave a loud "meow."

"We're trapped, Ginger." She blew out a breath. Now what?

What time was it? She'd taken her watch off to do the laundry and hadn't thought to put it back on. Her fingers went to the string around her neck, found the ring and held on to it. Thank the Lord she had put it there.

Surely Tom would come home soon. Then another thought struck her. Were the roads passable? Sometimes twisters left a path of destruction a mile wide. It could take days to clear the roads and return to normal. Could she survive in here?

She sent the beam of the flashlight around the room. Tom should outfit this place with a few necessities, in case of a bad storm like this one. Things like a lantern, some water, maybe. Her mouth felt parched.

She searched the shelves, in hopes of finding something of use. Ginger pounced on the shelf in front of her, causing Annabelle to jerk. "Ah! Ginger stop that. Nearly gave me a heart attack, silly cat." Of course, the cat was trying to get Annabelle's attention, but land sakes.

Now her fingers trembled so badly, the flashlight beam faltered. She set it on the shelf. Might as well sit back down. It could be hours before someone found them.

His head swam as Tom gazed at the devastation. The porch was gone. The roof had collapsed into the front room. The kitchen had no roof. A dining chair hung kitty-corner on top of the fence.

Panic rose in his throat. "Annabelle! Annabelle!" He climbed up into the house and began to pull at the nearest debris, tossing it aside. He called her name while his heart cried out, *Please, be all right.*

He stopped and fought for breath. Hands on his knees, he gasped for air. He loved her so much, it hurt. She'd been his fiancée for barely two days. Or was it three? Could she really be gone? Please, God, no.

Tom looked up as another truck sped into the drive and Alton jumped out. He sprinted toward Tom. "Oh, dear Lord! Where's Annabelle?"

"I ... I don't know! I don't know!" His face felt

wet. Tears? He grabbed at a section of metal roofing and tossed it aside. "Annabelle, are you in here?"

Alton grabbed his arm. "It's okay, Tom. We'll find her. She's smart. She's somewhere safe. You'll see."

Tom didn't answer, but kept grabbing and pulling and tossing, trying to make headway. All he could think about was finding Annabelle.

"Maybe …" Alton climbed into what used to be the kitchen. He glanced back at Tom. "The bathtub. They say to get in the tub."

Tom pulled in a breath and waited, not daring to hope.

Alton climbed slowly through the mess, disappeared from Tom's view a moment, then reappeared. "No. Not in there."

Gritting his teeth, Tom turned away until he could gain control. Then he inched toward what was once the front room. He had to kneel to see under the bowed roof. All he could make out was the potbellied stove. The flue pipe hung loose.

"Hello!" Two of the Parmenter boys ran into the yard. "Where's Miss Annabelle? She all right?"

Alton shook his head. "We don't know yet. Is anybody up at the shelter?"

One of the boys gestured in the general direction of the old storm shelter. "We checked it first. Nobody's been in there in years. That twister came so fast, there was no time for anybody to get to it."

Tom looked at his watch. He didn't know why. His stomach muscle tightened. He blew out a breath, but he wanted to shout. Time's a wasting!

"Y'all's place all right?" Alton asked the Parmenters.

The boy nodded. "Daddy sent us over here to check on Miss Annabelle."

Tom took a step forward, stumbling over something. "Help us find her. See if maybe she's in here." He looked around. "Somewhere." He swallowed as panic rose in his throat.

Alton removed his hat and looked around. "Let's think about it first, Tom. Where would she go if she saw the storm coming?"

Tom looked at him. *If she saw the storm coming.* That was key. The Parmenter boy said it came too fast to get to shelter. She might have been working inside and not seen it coming. He crouched down as an ache inside took his breath away.

"What about your cellar, Tom?"

Tom rose, his eyes on Alton. Of course, the cellar. He'd shown it to her. Would she think to go there?

The Parmenter boys glanced at each other, then took off running toward the house next door. Before

Tom and Alton made it halfway, they returned.

"There's a tree on it," one of them said.

"A big one," the other boy said.

Tom frowned. "I don't have any trees."

The boy shrugged and pointed. "I reckon it's the one from Miss Annabelle's yard."

Tom turned to gaze at the big hole in the front yard. He looked at Alton. "You reckon?"

Alton took off at a canter, with Tom close behind. The boys ran alongside. They all reached Tom's backyard at about the same time.

"Oh." Tom drew up short and looked at Alton.

Alton blew out a breath. "That's a big tree."

Tom got as close to the house as possible and crouched down. "Annabelle? You in there?"

They listened. Nothing.

"Annabelle!" After a moment, Tom looked up. "I think I heard something." Had he? Or was it an echo? Someone in the fields, talking. Voices carried around here.

Alton put his hand on the tree's trunk and jumped over it. There was barely room to stand between it and the house. "Annabelle? Momma, you in there?" He gave Tom a thumb's up. "I can hear her. He bent as close to the cellar door as possible. "I can hear you, Momma. We're going to get you out." He put his hands on the tree's trunk and pushed. Nothing happened. "Somehow."

Tom raised his hands as in surrender. "Anybody got a saw?" He had tools in the garage, but his little carpenter's saw wasn't going make a dent in a tree this size.

The Parmenter boys set off at a trot.

Tom hoped they'd come back and bring tools.

"I'll head home, get a saw." Alton jumped back over the tree and jogged toward Annabelle's.

Tom sat on the tree trunk, feeling useless. His gaze swept over what was left of the house next door. Thank God she'd made it to the cellar. He laid a palm against the brick wall of his house and leaned in. "Thank you, Lord." He swiped at tears as his thoughts turned to what Annabelle must've suffered. He kind of understood now, how she'd felt when she'd lost her family.

He'd almost lost Annabelle. She was everything to him. He pulled in a shaky breath. How had she endured that awful emptiness after losing Ray and her boys? He'd experienced it for moments, and it had almost done him in.

"Tom!" Riley jogged across from Annabelle's gate. "I saw Alton leaving. Where's Annabelle? She all right?"

Tom struggled for control. He gave Riley a nod.

"She's trapped though. In the cellar." He pointed to the tree. "My cellar."

Riley took a deep breath. "Thank God." He took a backward step and hollered. "Thelma! She's all right!"

Hearing voices outside brought Annabelle to attention. She'd turned off the flashlight to conserve the batteries. Now she turned it back on again and hurried to the stairwell.

She heard Tom call her name, then Alton. Hope flooded her heart until she heard them talking about needing a saw. Something big must be blocking that door.

Anxiety threatened to squash the fresh hope, amplifying her need to get out. Maybe she was claustrophobic. She sent the beam of light around the room again to reassure herself. The cellar was a good size, but she reckoned it being dark made the walls close in. Well, that and wondering how much longer she'd be trapped inside.

Deep breath, Annabelle. Praise God, I've been found. I'm safe. I'm alive, not blown into the next county. She was right here in what would soon become her cellar, where she'd store jams and jellies and canned goods. Another deep breath settled her mind and calmed her nerves.

A few more minutes passed before she heard more voices. Was that Thelma? What was she doing all the way out here? A new thought rattled her brain. If Thelma was here, then Riley was too. A foreboding filled her breast. The storm must have been a really bad one if folks were driving out this way to check on her.

She sat back down. Ginger climbed on her lap and curled up. Annabelle smoothed the cat's fur. "I sure am thankful to have you here with me."

The cat responded with a contented purr.

The noise outside escalated. More help coming? Then a new sound drowned out all others. Was that a chain saw?

Tom couldn't stand still. He had to find something to do other than watch the saw blade's slow progress. Thelma was in the house sweeping up broken glass. Riley was covering a damaged portion of the roofing with a tarp.

Everyone else was working on the tree. So, Tom helped carry limbs to a pile. When the saw sputtered and stopped, he hurried over.

Willie stood there, shaking his head. "I reckon this tree's too big. Too thick and old for this saw. It's chewing up the blade."

Wasting no time, Alton turned to his truck bed, lifted a heavy chain and handed it to Willie. "Let's see if we can pull the thing far enough away from the house to get that door open." He lifted a second chain.

Tom helped him pass it beneath the tree.

Alton clamped the links together. "We'll have to be careful. Don't want to do more damage to your new house."

Tom didn't care about the house. He only cared about Annabelle.

When they had secured three chains around the base of the trunk, Willie started the tractor's engine. Alton started his truck. Between the two of them, they managed to pull the tree far enough to clear the entrance to the cellar.

Tom tugged at the badly damaged door. Would it even open? It was stuck shut. Maybe the latch was closed inside. Before he could utter a sound, Alton used a crowbar to pry it up. As soon as it came open, something scurried past Tom's leg. He jumped back. What was that?

"Tom!"

Annabelle! She was in his arms, leaning against

him. He held onto her, not wanting to let her go. "Oh, Annabelle. I thought I'd lost you."

Chapter Twenty-Eight

If her heart hadn't been so full of love for all those who had helped her escape from the cellar, Annabelle might have felt worse about the house. But in perspective, it was just a building, and an old one, at that.

Tom stayed close, holding her hand, his eyes on her face.

She gazed at the wreckage. "I suppose it'll all turn out for the best."

He leaned close. "You know you have a home with me, Annabelle. Whenever you're ready."

She caressed his cheek. "I know I do."

Alton walked over to them, his face a picture of weariness. "I shut off the power, just in case. We wouldn't want the rest of it to burn up when they get the lines reconnected." He stuck his hands in his pockets. "Willie and Anthony gathered up what's left of the chickens and carried them to Sutter's."

Annabelle hadn't thought of any of that. Good thing folks were looking out for her. "Thank you, Alton. I appreciate that."

He looked at Tom. "Can you bring her to Sutter's when she's ready?"

Tom nodded. "Sure."

Alton started toward his truck, now parked in the drive at Annabelle's. "And plan on eating supper with us. I invited Riley and Thelma, too, but they had to get back to town."

All her energy left as fast as water down a sink drain. Annabelle leaned against Tom.

He put his arm around her. "Maybe we ought to go on over there now."

"I think it just hit me." She hid her face in his side.

He held onto her, stroking her hair, not saying anything. On the way to the truck, he kept her close by his side, as though he didn't want to leave her, or even have her more than a few inches from him.

"I'll be fine, Tom."

He stopped to look into her eyes. "I thought I'd lost you." His voice broke. After a deep breath, he continued, "I could almost imagine how you must have felt three years ago."

Her eyes moist, Annabelle nodded. "I'm glad you've been spared that."

He helped her into the truck. As they passed the old house, she wanted to look away, but she couldn't. She swiped at tears. "It's really gone." Was she not allowed anything? The enemy seemed bent on stealing all she had.

A scripture filled her heart, a sweet whisper in her mind, "I will lift up mine eyes unto the hills, from whence cometh my help."

Thank the Lord. She breathed out a sigh. How did folks make it through troubling times without the Lord by their side?

After Tom pulled onto the road, he took her hand and kissed it. Then he lifted concerned eyes to hers. "Annabelle, where's your ring?"

Her other hand flew to her neck, seeking the string. She found it and pulled it free of her collar. "Right here, Tom. Safe and sound." She noted the relief in his eyes. He thought she'd lost that, too. "I was doing laundry. I'd left it on the table, but it didn't feel right. So, I tied it on this string."

He kissed her hand again. "I'm so glad. Most likely, we'll find more of your possessions, Annabelle. When we clean up that mess back there."

She settled next to him. "I'm not worried about all

that stuff, Tom. I've got all I need." She leaned her head against his shoulder and closed her eyes.

Sutter's again. Seemed like a repeat performance. Annabelle sat on the side of the bed, looking out the window. Not the same room, though. She was upstairs this time, in the room Connie's dad had slept in when he visited. She could see why Mac had liked it. The double-wide window afforded a view of the cotton fields, lush and green. Thank goodness, the crop had survived that monster storm.

She stood in front of the open window, watching as Chase and Alton traipsed to the barn. Samson danced in front of them, leading the way. What a peaceful start to the new day.

Her gaze moved farther out, taking in the surrounding area. Many of the neighbors had damage of some sort. Mostly barn roofs and downed trees. She chose not to think about that now. Instead, she donned yesterday's dress and prepared to go downstairs.

The electricity was still out. Alton had spoken to one of the workers driving by. The man told him it could be three days to a week. Sutter's by candlelight, even better.

When Annabelle walked into the kitchen, Regina turned to glance at her.

"Mornin' Miss Annabelle. I heard you'd be joining us again. I was so sorry to hear about yo' house." She poured a cup of coffee.

Annabelle accepted the cup. "Thank you, Regina. I'm blessed of the Lord. No one was injured. Not over this way. Not that I've heard."

Regina nodded. "Good thing it happened during the day, is what Willie said. When they strike at night, that's most often when they kill folks."

The breakfast table was well occupied. Annabelle enjoyed the meal so much more, looking around at all her loved ones. No more lonely meals.

Alton buttered a biscuit. "After breakfast, you want to go over and get started on cleanup, Momma?"

"I hate for you to take time out of your busy day, Alton."

"It has to be done. The sooner we get it cleaned up, the sooner you can get on with your life."

Lillian poured more coffee in Annabelle's cup. "Alton thinks we can rebuild on the foundation."

"Is it worth it, though? Won't the cost be prohibitive?"

After a glance at Connie, Alton shook his head. "You don't need to worry about cost right now. But we do need a house on the property. Else, where will your tenants live? The land will be worth more if it's occupied."

Annabelle frowned as she stirred her coffee. "I reckon." But where would she get the money to rebuild? She didn't want to take anything more from Alton and Connie. Tom had spent all his savings building his new house.

Alton took hold of her hand. "Don't worry, Momma. God has everything under control. His timing is perfect."

She nodded, but her heart held back.

"So, when are you and Tom getting married?" Lillian folded her hands in her lap. She'd always been deft at changing the direction of a conversation.

Annabelle eyed her long-time friend. "Well, it's a bit hard to make plans right now." She moved her gaze to Connie. "I wouldn't want the ceremony to be interrupted by ... anything."

Connie smiled. "Like ours almost was? When you had that attack?"

"It wasn't an attack. It was stress, the doctor said."

Chase interrupted by clearing his throat. "Uncle Alton, may I be excused?"

Alton gave him a nod. "Yes, you may."

Joseph raised his arms over his head. "May I

'scused?"

Connie kissed his cheek. "No, you may not."

The heap of rubble grew as Willie and Anthony made one trip after another to offload the wagon.

Annabelle placed her laundry basket, found completely intact, still filled with folded clothes, in the back of Alton's truck. One by one, things were coming out of the house that she'd thought were lost forever.

The discovery of her chest of drawers gladdened her heart. Though sadly broken, its drawers had kept her belongings safe, including the photos she'd placed there earlier in the year. If she hadn't done that, most likely, she'd have no photographs left.

"There's more," Alton told her. He mopped the sweat from his brow and replaced his hat. "But it's nearly noon. Let's go home for dinner."

After the midday meal, Annabelle joined Lillian and Connie on the front porch. Alton was off somewhere with Chase. Little Joseph played with his trucks on a pallet next to Connie.

"What a peaceful afternoon," Lillian said. "After such a ruckus yesterday."

Annabelle opened her mouth to respond but held

her words as a red and white car pulled into the drive. "Oh, dear."

Connie sat forward. "Who is it?"

Lillian rocked slowly. "Rose Ella."

Annabelle got up from the swing. "I'll go see what she wants."

Lillian stood, too. "Most likely she's heard about your loss. Wants to see firsthand. I'll come with you."

Shielding her eyes from the sun, Rose Ella stood next to her car, looking toward Annabelle's house. "Oh, my goodness gracious." She faced Annabelle and Lillian. "It's worse than what I heard. I'm so, so sorry. Oh, my dear, you've lost so much already, and now this. Sometimes I wonder."

Annabelle waited for Rose Ella to breathe, then dove in. "My loved ones are safe, and I'm alive. I'm thankful to the Lord for that."

Rose Ella propped a fist on her hip. "Well, you are a better person than I am, Annabelle Cross. I'd be pitching a fit right now." She cupped her hands. "But that's not why I've come. I'm hoping you'll still be able to join us at the singing. I sneaked over to Windy City last night and heard a little of their practice session. That girl is a sensation." She leaned close. "We've got to step up."

Annabelle aimed a sideways glance at the woman.

"Step up?"

Rose Ella gave an exaggerated nod. "I know I said no showcasing, but we have to compete, Annabelle. So, I want you to sing the last verse."

"What?"

"The last verse." She gazed heavenward and waved her hands in the air. "It'll be powerful. The choir will stop and let you do your thing. They'll come back in on the chorus. We'll end with a flourish. Can't you just hear it?"

Lillian patted Annabelle on the back. "I can. Annabelle's got a beautiful voice."

Rose Ella nodded. "That's right." She pressed her hands together again, apparently ready to beg. "Please say yes, Annabelle."

After several moments to mull it over, and a slow intake of breath, Annabelle gazed at the sky.

Rose Ella shifted her weight from one foot to the other, clearly impatient.

Annabelle smiled. "All right, I'll do it."

The woman almost bounced on her little feet. "Oh, I'm so glad! We are back in the running. I can't wait for the next practice. The choir's been bugging me all along to let you do a solo."

Annabelle glanced at Lillian, who gave her a quiet, little smile, but said nothing.

Rose Ella stood a bit taller now. She leaned in again. "So, have you and Mr. Tom set a date yet? I heard y'all got engaged. Let me see that ring."

Oh, dear. Annabelle extended her hand.

Rose Ella clutched it. "Well, that's not bad. Not bad at all. I have to tell you; I had hoped to turn his head. But that was before I knew him better. Anyway, he never saw me at all, only you. That poor man. You'll have your hands full with him. He doesn't even know the difference between a glass and a crystal vase. Why, when I asked him to return my vase—you know the one I took over there that day, filled with buttercups and lilacs? He couldn't even tell me where it was. So, I stopped by there the other evening, intent on leaving with it. He still couldn't find it. He stood at the front door while I went in the kitchen and where do you think I found it? In the cupboard with the drinking glasses. Oh, my stars." She shook her head.

Lillian turned away rather suddenly.

Annabelle bit her lip.

Rose Ella clapped. "Oh, I almost forgot! I brought you a little something since I heard you lost most everything." She reached inside her open car window to retrieve a flat, white box. She cocked her head and jutted her chin as she passed it to Annabelle.

Heat flooded Annabelle's cheeks. "Oh … well …

you shouldn't have."

Rose Ella waved her hand. "Oh, just open it, Annabelle."

Lillian stepped closer as Annabelle removed the lid and folded back white tissue paper to reveal an exquisite silk scarf. "Oh. I love it, Rose Ella, thank you."

Rose Ella aimed a smile at no one in particular. "Well, I figured you could wear turquoise, with your hair and creamy complexion." She glanced at her watch. "Look at the time. I'd better get home. I'll see you two ladies on Sunday. And practice that last verse, Annabelle." She opened her door and got inside in one fluid motion.

As Rose Ella backed around and drove down the drive, Annabelle turned to look at Lillian, whose face sent Annabelle into peals of laughter.

Lillian almost doubled over, laughing.

They held onto each other's arms, gasping for air.

Annabelle had almost recovered when Lillian giggled again. "A crystal vaaaws! Oh, dear me, but that woman puts on airs."

Betty Thomason Owens

Chapter Twenty-Nine

August 3, 1957
Sutter's Landing

"Today's the day," Annabelle told her reflection in the bathroom mirror. The day of the singing. Annabelle's debut as a soloist, in Trenton at least. She'd often sang in her San Diego church.

The day started off like any other Saturday. Regina stayed busy in the kitchen, cooking up a storm so she could take Sunday off.

Connie stayed longer in bed. Alton and Chase did their best to whittle down a massive pile of biscuits. Joseph jabbered away about a bird outside the window while Lillian fed him scrambled eggs and gravy.

Annabelle soaked it all in. Her heart swelled with love for these beautiful souls. God had turned a bad thing into a sweet blessing for her.

"Momma?" Connie's voice echoed from the

stairwell. Annabelle got up and crossed to the hall. "Yes, Pumpkin? You want me to bring you a plate?"

"Could you come up here first?"

Annabelle headed up the stairs. Connie most likely felt poorly and didn't want to come down. Annabelle wouldn't be at all surprised if the girl couldn't make it to the singing.

One look at Connie's face confirmed Annabelle's suspicions. "You should stay in bed, darling. No need for you to be up and about. Do you want me to bring you a plate?"

Connie drew a prolonged breath. "No, Momma. I'm not a bit hungry. I don't think I'll make it to church tonight. I wanted to let you know early, so you wouldn't be disappointed."

Annabelle sat down next to Connie on the beautifully carved four-poster bed. "I figured you wouldn't be able to. Don't you worry about anything. You rest."

"Tom can drive us in." At the sound of Lillian's voice, Annabelle looked up as Lillian strode into the room and laid her palm on Connie's brow. "You rest, sweet girl. We'll take Joseph with us, too. He'll love it. That way, you won't have to be concerned about anything."

Connie gave a soft sigh. "Thank you. What would

I do without you both?"

Lillian winked at Annabelle. "I hope it's a long time before you have to find out."

Annabelle watched Connie's face, giving special attention to her eyes. Maybe she'd take a walk over to Miss Lucy's and give her a forewarning. The baby wasn't officially due until mid-August, but Annabelle suspected they didn't have that long to wait.

"A deep breath will settle your nerves." Tom smiled into Annabelle's eyes before returning to his seat in the packed sanctuary.

Annabelle waited with the other choir members, ready to enter the choir loft. As the host church, they were the last ones to perform. The waiting gave her nerves a workout. On top of that, she had to not think about Connie and what may or may not be happening at home.

Seven churches had entered the gospel singing. Rose Ella said seven was a perfect number. Since they performed last, that made them number seven. So, of course, they'd be perfect. Annabelle hoped she was right. She mouthed the words to the final verse several times for good measure.

All the other choirs had done well. Most had sung traditional hymns, except Windy City. They showcased their young opera star with "His Eye is on the Sparrow." What a voice that girl had.

"Time to go." Rose Ella led the way. Once everyone was in place, she took her seat at the piano.

From the first words of the opening stanza, Annabelle stood in the center of a supernatural presence. What a wondrous thing. The choir blended so well, it seemed they were one voice.

As she sang the final verse, Annabelle never missed a beat.

"Pardon for sin and a peace that endureth,
Thine own dear presence to cheer and to guide,
Strength for today and bright hope for tomorrow
Blessings all mine with ten thousand beside!"

The choir joined in on the final refrain, "Great is Thy faithfulness ..."

They finished with surprising passion. That last chorus brought the entire congregation to their feet. All this from a staid bunch of traditional Baptists.

Tears dampened Annabelle's cheeks. She wasn't sure what had happened, but her heart sang on as the applause continued. There was no doubt in her mind that a miracle had occurred. She wasn't quite sure why, or who needed it. Until she noticed Tom's expression.

When their eyes met and locked for a moment, Annabelle held her breath. More than anything, she wanted to speak to him right now, to know what he was thinking. But that would have to wait.

Pastor Nathan invited the other pastors to join him at the front. "We cannot let this moment pass without giving an opportunity for anyone who needs prayer to come down front. If your heart is burning, sir or madam, you may need to come to Jesus and accept Him as your personal Savior."

One by one, folks filtered toward the front, seeking the prayers of their pastor. Annabelle dabbed at her eyes. God surely had done a mighty work in this place tonight.

After the prayer time, Pastor Nathan stepped aside for Windy City's pastor. "We had hoped to carry home the trophy this year but judging by the thunderous applause afforded the home church, I believe we'll have to leave it right here." This brought another round of applause.

The closing prayer seemed to go on for a long time. Annabelle kept peeking at Tom, wondering about that look on his face. But her path to his side led to one roadblock after another. Several of the other choir members embraced her. And then Rose Ella stopped her.

The little woman shook her head. "I am in awe, Annabelle. In awe."

Annabelle waited for the onslaught of words that didn't come. Well, that was a first. "Thank you, Rose Ella, but I can't take the praise for that. It was the Lord's anointing."

Rose Ella took a backward step. "Whatever it was, I am in awe. Now, we have that handsome trophy. I only wish I could be here next year to try again."

"You're leaving?"

Rose Ella shrugged. "I always meant to leave once Lincoln was settled in. I'm returning to North Carolina sometime this fall. I will hate leaving my new friends, but I will not miss this hot weather—not one bit." She took hold of Annabelle's forearm. "Have you seen the tea light exhibition at the high school? Oh, my stars. I was breathless looking at all those beauties. Before I leave town, I want to take you there. Then we'll have lunch, how about that?"

Tom waited for Annabelle at the door. He had no desire to interrupt her or speak with Rose Ella. Besides, he needed time to process what had happened. He had never experienced anything quite like that. What a woman God had sent him.

As Annabelle headed his way, he cleared his mind.

She stood in front of him, a question in her eyes. One she didn't put words to right off. Good. He'd no wish to discuss what had happened in front of others.

He tipped his head toward the door. "Shall we go?"

She walked ahead of him, smiling and greeting others as she made her way out of the church and down the front steps.

Lillian waited near the truck with Joseph. "There you are. Did you have to sign autographs?"

Annabelle laughed. "You're so funny." She allowed Tom to help her into the truck.

He helped Lillian also and then boosted Joseph into Lillian's lap.

If only they were alone, but Tom guessed it was best this way. He'd have time to think this through. He needed to be sure of what to say when she asked. He was certain she would ask.

Lillian held Joseph, who leaned against her. He'd probably be asleep before they pulled out of the parking lot.

With Annabelle so close to him, Tom had a time paying attention to the road.

"Wonder how Connie's doing." Lillian's statement didn't really sound like a question.

Annabelle folded her arms. "I hope she's resting."

"You did right to ask Miss Lucy to come by. Chances are, we'll have another little one in the house before the week is out."

When he pulled into the drive at Sutter's, Tom didn't really know what to expect. He'd take it a moment at a time. He walked around the outside of the truck, looking to the Lord for guidance. Before he could open their door, Alton called from the porch.

"Baby's on the way!"

Tom drew in a long breath and exhaled. He'd take that as God's answer. He'd no intention of crowding Annabelle's mind and heart with more concerns at the moment.

Annabelle opened her eyes as a touch of pink in the east preceded a full burst of glorious apricot and lavender. She sat forward, blinking. It took a moment to clear her weary mind and realize where she was. She'd fallen asleep in a chair beside Connie's bed.

She massaged a stiff ache in her neck and hunched her shoulders. What a night they'd had. Slowly rising, she crept closer to the bassinet. The baby yawned, sending a tiny fist upward before drifting back into an exhausted sleep.

Annabelle touched the sweet cheek. "Thank you, Lord, for such a beautiful gift."

Connie stirred. "Good morning, Momma."

Annabelle sat on the bed beside her. "I didn't mean to wake you."

"You didn't. I had my eyes closed. Has Alton gone out to feed the animals?"

"He has."

Connie rose up on one elbow to look at the baby. "Isn't she beautiful, Momma?"

"I was thinking the same thing."

With a sigh, Connie relaxed onto her pillows. She fastened her eyes on Annabelle. "Well, Momma, now, you and Tom can set a date. If you can wait two more weeks, I daresay this sweet little somebody will be ready to make her debut."

"Most folks wait a month before taking the baby out."

"I figured you'd say that. It's a bit old-fashioned, in my opinion. Poor Tom has waited so long. Think about it, Momma. Anyway, I'll bet Miss Lucy would be happy to take care of the baby for a couple of hours so I could attend a ceremony."

Annabelle recognized the mischievous twinkle in the girl's eyes. She patted Connie's knee. "We'll see, sugar." Rising from the bed, she tiptoed toward the door. "How about I go see what I can stir up for breakfast?"

Connie nodded. "Yes, please. I'm starving."

Tom sat in the truck for several minutes, wondering what to do. Most likely, Annabelle and the rest of the family would miss church this morning. He'd received the call from Alton around six o'clock. "It's a girl!"

They'd all be tired from the night of waiting. Should he stop by? His eyes and heart ached for a sight of Annabelle. But he also desired to attend church.

His mind made up, he started the engine and backed out of the garage. It wouldn't hurt a thing to stop at Sutter's on the way.

He found Annabelle in the yard with Joseph, who was probably the only one in the household who'd gotten a good night's rest. Tom smiled as he parked near the front porch.

Joseph jogged toward him. "Hi, Gompah! I got a new baby."

Tom dropped into a crouch to speak on a level with the boy. "Do you?"

Joseph bumped his fists together. "Sis."

Annabelle gave a soft laugh. "She hasn't been named yet."

Tom smiled at Joseph. "Sis, huh? You're her big brother."

Joseph nodded. "She's too little." His attention drawn by Samson's approach, Joseph took off toward the dog.

Tom rose and looked at Annabelle. Tired eyes gave away her weariness. He wanted to take her in his arms. He smiled instead.

"Are you headed to church?" Her face held a wistfulness he couldn't define.

Did she even realize how much he loved her, needed her? Deep breath, Tom. "I thought I would."

She crossed her arms at her waist. "If I wasn't so tired, I'd join you. I'd probably doze off in the pew."

He touched her arm. "It's all right. I think it's high time I made the effort on my own." He cleared his throat. About last night ... he wanted to tell her, wanted to keep the conversation going. But the timing was off. Maybe later?

He shifted his stance. "Well, I just wanted to stop and say hello." He turned toward the truck. Once inside, he propped his arm in the open window. "Would it be all right if I came back later this afternoon?"

She stepped closer. "More than all right, Tom."

Love shone from her eyes, so thick he could barely get his breath. He started the engine. "Later then."

His throat had gone completely dry. He drove away from Sutter's, his mind in a whirl. He'd always heard it said that God's timing was perfect. Now, he had no doubt.

This morning, he'd make things right.

Chapter Thirty

August 4, 1957

Annabelle hadn't missed a church service since her accident in February. The new baby brought some distraction but slept most of the day. Annabelle and Lillian took turns seeing to her needs when they could steal her away from Alton.

After dinner, everyone else took a nap, but Annabelle sat in the swing on the front porch. She didn't know when Tom would return, but she meant to be awake when that happened. She didn't want another day to pass before she talked to him. Besides, she reckoned it was time to set a date for their nuptials. Connie was right. She'd made him wait long enough.

The mantel clock chimed three times, waking Annabelle. She'd fallen asleep sitting up. She rose from the swing when Tom's truck pulled into the drive. Was he just now home from town?

Before he was out of the truck, she'd descended the steps to greet him. But the look on his face gave her pause. Had something happened?

Tom reached for her hand and pulled her into his arms, not speaking a word. Then he released her and stepped back. "I have something to tell you."

She laid a hand at the base of her throat. Was he breaking up with her? Was he finally weary of her making him wait?

He nodded toward a couple of lawn chairs beneath a large maple tree. After they were seated, he grew quiet.

His brow creased. His lips twitched into sort of a grimace like he was trying to figure something out.

She tried her best to be patient, smoothed her skirt, crossed and re-crossed her ankles. Then she tilted her head to look at him. Should she ask about the service?

He sat forward and rested his elbows on his knees. Then he reached for her hand and held it for a moment, keeping his eyes averted.

Whatever was troubling him, it must be terrible. She'd never seen him like this.

"I grew up in the church, you know that. But last night I … experienced something I have never felt, Annabelle." He drew back to look at her, his eyes questioning. "I'm not sure I was ever truly born again."

She shook her head but held her tongue. She'd let him finish first.

At her silence, he continued, "While you were singing that verse, God touched my heart. In those few seconds, He changed me. It was so real, I couldn't even talk about it. To you, or anyone." He released her hand and sat back. "This morning, I walked the aisle."

The sweetness of this moment nearly stole Annabelle's breath. It may have topped his proposal.

He bowed his head. "I didn't know what you would think. I've been fooling everyone, Annabelle. I tried to live right, do good, help others, but all the time I was—"

Annabelle laid her hand on his arm. "You were always on this path, Tom. There was nothing wrong in the way you lived your life. You were seeking, doing what you knew to do. Who can know God's timetable, other than God himself? He led you here. That's the important thing. You want to know what I think? What you just told me only increases my love for you, Tom."

He gazed at her with such longing in his eyes, it stabbed her like a knife. He looked away again. His voice seemed to come to her from a distance. "I spent quite some time talking with Pastor after the service. He's been my friend, all these years, even knowing I needed to let go of some things." He cleared his throat and clasped the back of his neck. "He never judged me."

Annabelle caught her breath. She lowered her head as sorrow flooded her heart. She had judged him. She'd found him lacking and told him so. "I judged you." She looked up at him. "I judged you."

Maybe her refusal of him had brought Tom back sooner, but it could've gone the other way—driven him farther out. It was the pure goodness of his heart that held him. That, and his love for her. A love she'd almost thrown away.

He touched her chin, brought her eyes to his. "You kept me here, Annabelle. I wanted to do right because of you. It was you who allowed yourself to be used by God when you sang that song with your whole heart." He leaned forward to kiss her, softly.

She wasn't fooled by the softness. He longed for her. "I think we need to talk to Pastor, Tom. Together."

A smile quirked his lips. He nodded. "I think so, too."

Chapter Thirty-One

August 18, 1957
Trenton, Tennessee

During the offering, Annabelle sent a stealthy glance down the pew to where Tom sat next to Riley. Thelma caught her looking and gave her a knowing smile. The more Annabelle tried to pay attention to the service, the more her mind kept skittering about.

Looking pretty in a pale blue dress, Judith sat beside her mother with Preston Weatherby. Lillian was next, with Annabelle between her and Connie. Alton sat on the end.

The pew behind them held the younger Franklins and some of the extended family. Jensen, Marla, and their boys sat in their usual spot on the opposite side of the sanctuary.

Poignant memories of their first days back here after losing Ray and the boys flowed like water in a rain-soaked stream. She and Connie had occupied this same pew with Thelma and her bunch. Folks spoke in low whispers, wondering what Annabelle had done to deserve such a tragedy. But when Annabelle and Connie moved into the old Sterling house, most of the congregation showed up to help get the place livable. They brought used furniture and food. Throughout that long first year, these folks were there for her, praying and helping whenever they could.

Lillian jabbed her in the side. Annabelle forced herself to focus on what Pastor was saying. He'd announced Lily Anne MacKenzie Wade's name to the congregation, in case they hadn't heard. Most had, of course. His next statement brought a rush of heat into Annabelle's cheeks. Though she kept her chin high and tried to appear aloof, she longed to seek shelter beneath the pew.

"As I announced last week, we will celebrate a wedding immediately following this morning's service. Mr. Tom Franklin and Mrs. Annabelle Cross would like to invite you to attend their nuptials, and there will be a reception afterward."

He allowed folks to settle before he spoke again. "As I prepared this morning's sermon, I was reminded of a passage of scripture that seems quite appropriate whenever I think of Annabelle Cross and her family.

It's found in Ruth, chapter one. Verse 16 says, "And Ruth said, Intreat me not to leave thee, or to return from following after thee: for whither thou goest, I will go; and where thou lodgest, I will lodge: thy people shall be my people, and thy God my God."

He made eye contact with Annabelle. "This was, of course, Ruth speaking to her mother-in-law, Naomi. This particular verse is often used in wedding vows or wedding sermons."

He continued, but Annabelle's mind took another turn.

What a morning they'd had. All the bustle and rush of the last few days had finally come to an end, but not without trouble. Everything that could go wrong, had.

Her dress had been delayed when the seamstress fell and sprained her wrist. She had to find someone to help her finish the alterations.

A stray dog had gotten into the hen house and upset all the chickens. One of Alton's prize cows had gotten out and ended up over in Tom's backyard.

The baby fussed so much after breakfast, they feared she might have colic. When Annabelle went to pick her up, Connie shooed her away. "No, Momma, she'll spit up or spew something and your beautiful dress will be ruined."

She was right, but Annabelle's arms ached to hold

Lily Anne. She and Lillian had almost busted their buttons when the kids told them they'd named the baby after both her grandmothers.

Lillian nudged her again.

Pastor Nathan seemed to be closing out. "God woos us. He loves us and doesn't want to leave anyone behind. His love encompasses, surpasses all other loves. We are His and He is ours. He knows the end from the beginning."

She glanced at Tom, who was looking at her, a faint smile on his handsome face. Did he guess her mind was wandering? Had she missed most of the sermon? Apparently so, since Rose Ella was headed to the piano.

When the congregation rose, Tom and Annabelle slipped out with Lillian and Riley.

In a room to themselves, Lillian helped Annabelle with her final preparations. She slapped at Annabelle's hand when Annabelle fooled with her hair. "Your hair is perfection. Don't mess with perfection."

A knock at the door meant it was time. Lillian picked up a nosegay of blush pink rosebuds, which she handed to Annabelle. "You look lovely. Now take a breath."

"I'm fine."

"Sure, you are. That's why your fingers are

trembling like that. Take a breath, Annabelle, slow and easy."

There was no use arguing with Lillian. Annabelle did as she was told. "Thank you, for everything."

Lillian smiled. "It's my honor, dear friend."

When Tom took his place beside Pastor Nathan at the front of the church, he couldn't help remembering how he'd stood in this spot, only a couple of weeks ago. He'd made his confession and declared his intent to live as a new creation in Christ. Most of these folks who waited with him now were there at the time. They were present when Pastor baptized Tom.

On Tom's left, Riley cleared his throat behind a fist and fingered his tie. Tom suppressed a grin. He had only seen the man dressed like that once—at his father's funeral.

At a whispered command from Lillian, Rose Ella began to play. Tom couldn't remember the name of the song. It hardly mattered. Every other thought skittered away when the door opened and Lillian entered, followed by Annabelle in an ivory-colored dress. She carried a bouquet of wild rosebuds. Her eyes shone with love. Or was it nerves?

An ache started in his chest, followed by a lump in his throat. He forced himself to take a breath and slowly ease it out.

She took her place beside him, briefly lifting her eyes to his. Her lips formed a tremulous smile. He envied her composure until he noticed the flowers were quaking. She must be as nervous as he, just better at hiding it.

Pastor began to speak.

Tom didn't want to take his eyes off Annabelle, but good manners won out. He spoke about the sanctity of marriage and how God had planned this from the beginning. At last, he asked Tom and Annabelle to face each other.

Now, Tom could look at his beloved and not be rude to Pastor.

Was she dreaming? It seemed Annabelle blinked her eyes and here she stood, facing Tom in front of their church. She allowed her gaze to take it in. The beautiful sanctuary, the stained-glass windows, the way the sunlight filtered through. Her friends, Tom's friends. And they were all watching her. And Tom, too, of course.

As Rose Ella finished playing *O Perfect Love*, Annabelle's heart sang. Her lips formed the words, "…grant them the vision of the glorious morrow that will reveal eternal love and life."

All was quiet.

Pastor Nathan's voice came to her out of the dream, "Will you, Thomas Allen Franklin, have Annabelle Frances Wade Cross to be your wife? Will you love her, comfort and keep her, and forsaking all others, remain true to her as long as you both shall live?"

His eyes on her, Tom spoke, "I will."

He looked so handsome today, dressed in his finest black suit, white shirt, and blue tie. How she loved him.

Pastor Nathan spoke again, "Will you, Annabelle Frances Wade Cross, have Thomas Allen Franklin to be your husband? Will you love him, comfort and keep him, and forsaking all others, remain true to him as long as you both shall live?"

She blinked away tears, along with a fleeting vision of Ray's face. Tom stood before her, his loving gaze embracing her. He'd promised to always care for her. She took a breath and spoke, "I will."

Tom placed a ring on her finger, repeated the words, "With this ring, I thee wed."

Annabelle placed a ring on his finger. "With this

ring, I thee wed." If this was a dream, it was truly the sweetest one she'd ever had.

Tom squeezed her hand.

Wake up, Annabelle. She blinked her eyes. It was not a dream, or a vision, it was real.

With a smile, Pastor Nathan introduced them as Mr. & Mrs. Thomas Franklin. They were now man and wife.

Holding both her hands in his, Tom leaned forward and kissed her softly, his eyes on her, as though the two of them were the only ones in the room.

With a grand flourish, Rose Ella began to play *Joyful, Joyful, We Adore Thee*.

Annabelle looked heavenward, closed her eyes, and let the melodious sounds wash over her. The journey she had begun three years ago in San Diego had finally led her back to joy.

Epilogue

October 5, 1957

Annabelle finished the dishes and dried her hands. Outside her window, a beautiful moon lit the backyard. She stepped out the door onto the porch where a refreshing, gentle breeze caressed her skin.

Ginger jumped down from her favorite spot on the railing and rubbed against Annabelle's ankles. The cat had adapted well to her new home.

Annabelle scanned the moonlit fields. Her gaze came to rest on the skeleton of a new house rising from the foundation of the one destroyed by the tornado. By spring, she hoped to have a family moved in to care for the place and till the crops. And it was all paid for. The money had come from the estate of Charles Wade, Sr., as a wedding gift to his granddaughter. Jensen felt it was the least they could do, after all that had happened.

Her eyes on the moon again, Annabelle barely

noticed when the screen door opened, and Tom stepped out.

"What are you looking at?"

She breathed out a sigh. "That big moon. This perfect night."

He walked over to stand behind her, his hands on her shoulders. "It is beautiful. Looks almost like a harvest moon." After a moment of silence, he moved away. "Wait right here."

She glanced over her shoulder but knew better than to ask why. He loved surprising her.

He had been gone a few minutes when she heard music playing. Doris Day was singing "By the Light of the Silvery Moon."

Tom came out, a smile on his face. "Do you recognize the song?"

"Of course."

He wrapped his arms around her. "I know you know the song. But do you recognize it?"

She smiled into his eyes. "Hmm. High school. It wasn't Doris Day, of course, but I believe they were playing that song when you first asked me to dance."

He nodded. "You said no. 'I'm a good Baptist girl, I don't dance.'"

"That's right. Pretty much word-for-word."

He nuzzled her cheek. "What about now?"

"Well, I'm still a Baptist."

"That night after the carnival, you said you might dance with me one day."

"I remember saying I might."

His eyes sparkled. "I took that as a yes."

"You would."

He stepped back and held out his hand. "Will you consider dancing with your husband?"

She took a breath, then caught her lip between her teeth, pretending to think about it. "I've never danced in my life. So, you'll have to teach me.

He grinned. "I'll be happy to." He guided her hands, placing one on his upper arm, the other, clasped firmly in his. "We'll try a waltz first. The box step, it's easy. Just follow along. When I step forward, you step back."

After a few minutes of clumsy shuffling about, she started to catch on a little.

The music ended, but he still held her. "Well? What do you think?"

She'd enjoyed it immensely but had no intention of telling him. Not yet. It was too much fun teasing him. "I love you, Tom Franklin."

"I love you, too, Annabelle Franklin."

Another record dropped. She heard Frank Sinatra crooning. Tom lead her through another round of box steps. She could learn to enjoy this.

Acknowledgments

My longtime friends, Patti Thornton Coleman & Linda Hillenbrand (the Herrick sisters), through their heartbreak and adversity, gave me insight into the emotional journey through devastating loss. These two sisters lost their husbands within months of each other. Though painful to watch, their individual journeys inspired me and helped me flesh out Annabelle's emotional passage. I love you both and thank you for your continued friendship and love.

I write best when inspired. It's mainly a solitary pursuit, but after the words are written, I depend upon my stellar team of critiquers to help guide my way. Nike Chillemi, Gail Johnson, and Kristi Robinson Horine added their expertise and insight to my humble scribblings. Thanks, dear friends, for the many hours you contributed to this work. Thank you also, American Christian Fiction Writers (ACFW) for providing us a Scribes Loop, where I connected with these three dear friends.

My publisher, Marji Laine Clubine, continues to encourage and guide me through the process of creating a finished work. She's not just the owner of the company, but she's our champion, pushing her writers beyond their own personal limitations to achieve excellence. Thank you, dear friend. Thank you, Lill Kohler, my editor, who asked the tough questions and helped keep the story consistent.

My patient husband supports me and gives me time to write. He's my biggest fan and often pushes me to stay the course when I'm ready to throw it all away. I love you forever and appreciate your steady faith in me.

I have a wonderful church family who stands with me and prays for me. They are too many to mention here, but they know who they are. Among them, one of my most ardent and faithful fans, Carol Brewer, who moved to her heavenly home just prior to the release of this final book. I will miss you, Carol.

Cherry Brooks and Debbie Northcutt Holston, my partners in all things fun—when I've needed a sounding board, they're always there for me to listen and lift me up in prayer. And of course, Jennifer Hallmark and Gail Johnson, who've gone the extra mile to encourage me in my writing.

Warm memories of my Tennessee family continue to inspire and give substance to my fantasies. I still hear the echo of their voices, imprinted on my soul.

To God, Who drew me to Himself so long ago and continues to guide me daily, thanks for the wonderful gift of life and imagination.

About the Author

Betty Thomason Owens loves being outdoors. Her favorite season is spring when she can work in the yard or take long walks while thinking through a troublesome scene in one of her stories. She considers herself a word-weaver, writing stories that touch the heart. She leads the Louisville Area ACFW group, serves on the board of the Kentucky Christian Writers Conference, and is a co-founder of the multi-author Inspired Prompt blog. Married forty-four years, she's a mother of three, and a grandmother of eight. A part-time bookkeeper at her day job, she writes for *Write Integrity Press* and has eight novels in publication. You can learn more about her at BettyThomasonOwens.com. Connect with her on Facebook, Twitter, Pinterest, Instagram, and at Inspired Prompt.

A Special Note

Once again, I'm saying goodbye to old friends who've occupied my thoughts for so many years as I write their story. I will miss Annabelle, Connie, Lillian, Alton, Tom, and Miss Lucy, but they'll never be far away.

Annabelle Wade Cross was directly inspired by my paternal grandmother, Ada Wade Thomason Griggs, and her sister-in-law, Lona Wade. Connie Cross Wade's character was inspired partly by my precious cousin, Norma Sue Loyd Thweatt. She was the one who was teased in school for her dark complexion. I'd heard that story most of my life, so incorporated it into the first book of this series, *Annabelle's Ruth*. Connie's character was also loosely based on my mother's early life when she followed my southern-roots Daddy from her home in Seattle to his home in west Tennessee. Miss Lucy was inspired by my grandmother's neighbor, a woman who worked in their fields, and went out of her way to take care of Grandma when she was "feelin' poorly."

Though racial tensions rose and fell all around them, neighbors were still neighbors. They worked alongside one another, asked after each other's children, prayed for one another, and saw to each other's needs when illness or death touched their lives. As a young girl, I observed and wondered.

Many of the events of these books were inspired by those times.

Most of the inspiration for *Annabelle's Ruth* came via the biblical story of Ruth, one of my favorite books of the Bible. I wrote the original book as a standalone, but when my publisher asked if I could expand it into a series, I made up something. She liked it, so I wrote Sutter's Landing. The fans of these two stories insisted Annabelle needed closure. They wanted her to find a forever, so I set out to finish the story.

Annabelle's Joy is a spiritual journey. What we believe sometimes colors our lenses and we tend to judge others by our own perceptions of what we think they are. But faith requires more. It's a journey of the heart. Only God knows what a man holds in his heart.

Betty

Also By Betty

The Legacy Series

Three generations of strong women, determined to succeed through the most turbulent of times.

The Kinsman-Redeemer Series

The Biblical saga of Ruth comes alive amid the racial tensions and quiet life of 1950 Tennessee.

Recent Romance Releases

She's the icon of a put-together woman - beautiful, successful, prominent. Until the shadows of her past begin to haunt her, insisting that she face the woman she really is.

Focused on his faith, missionary doctor Brock believes he has also finally found a woman who is his perfect match. Why would God seem to want to take her away from him?

Annalee Chambers changes her entire life with a single word. Believing that she is the one giving the assistance, she is left to wonder what a bunch of downtown kids can teach an uptown, uptight Texas Princess.

**Thank you
for reading our books!**

**Look for other books
published by**

Write Integrity Press
www.WriteIntegrity.com